"Every time we look at each other it's like lightning and I want—"

"I'm married!"

"Dammit, don't you think I know that! If I could find your husband, I'd shoot the son of a bitch where he stands just for leaving you and Katie."

"Oh, I see. If you can't get the land by making love to me, then you'll resort to shooting my husband."

This time it was Ethan who paced away. "You aren't going to listen, are you?"

"No."

"Molly," he said softly, reaching out to her, wishing, praying she'd reach back.

She didn't.

"Leave, Ethan" was all she said.

"Molly…"

Tears glistened in her eyes and clogged her throat. "I am telling you for the last time to get out of here! Get away from me! Stay far away from me!" She swiped at the tears that ran down her cheeks. "Damn you, Ethan Wilder…!"

Dear Reader,

Much of the beauty of romance novels is that most are written by women for women, and feature strong and passionate heroines. We have some stellar authors this month who bring to life those intrepid women we love as they engage in relationships with the men we also love!

We are delighted with the return of award-winning author Susan Amarillas. Dubbed "queen of the frontier romance" by *Affaire de Coeur*, Susan follows suit with her new Western, *Molly's Hero*. Here, Molly Murphy is trying to make ends meet after her husband disappears, leaving her alone with their small daughter and big ranch. Things get complicated when handsome railroad builder Ethan Wilder shows up, determined to talk her into selling her land. Only, Ethan starts falling in love with her instead.... Don't miss this wonderful tale of forbidden love!

In *The Viking's Heart*, a medieval novel by rising talent Jacqueline Navin, a proud noblewoman unexpectedly falls in love with the fierce Viking sent to escort her to her own arranged marriage. Will she choose love or duty? *My Lady's Dare* by Gayle Wilson is a Regency-set tale that will grab you and not let go as the Earl of Dare becomes fascinated by another man's mistress. Nothing is as it seems in this dangerous game of espionage and love!

And don't miss *Bandera's Bride*, in which Mary McBride gives her Southern belle heroine some serious chutzpah when, pregnant and alone, she travels to Texas to propose marriage to her pen pal of six years, a half-breed who's been signing his partner's name....

Enjoy! And come back again next month for four more choices of the best in historical romance.

Sincerely,

Tracy Farrell,
Senior Editor

Molly's Hero

Susan Amarillas

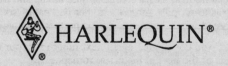

HARLEQUIN®

TORONTO • NEW YORK • LONDON
AMSTERDAM • PARIS • SYDNEY • HAMBURG
STOCKHOLM • ATHENS • TOKYO • MILAN • MADRID
PRAGUE • WARSAW • BUDAPEST • AUCKLAND

ISBN 0-373-29118-3

MOLLY'S HERO

This edition published by arrangement with Harlequin Books S.A.

® and TM are trademarks of the publisher. Trademarks indicated with ® are registered in the United States Patent and Trademark Office, the Canadian Trade Marks Office and in other countries.

Visit us at www.eHarlequin.com

Printed in U.S.A.

Chapter One

The stranger cut the trail at the base of the ridge and rode straight up the hill. The horse's hooves sent rocks flying as the gelding lunged up the steep bank. At the top of the rise, he reined in. For several minutes he merely sat there, staring down at the isolated ranch.

One hundred and twenty acres, according to the records he'd checked at the land office in Cheyenne—mostly dirt, spotted with buffalo grass. That was enough to graze, oh, four steers. Yeah, not much of a ranch by Wyoming standards or anyone else's, for that matter.

From his vantage point, he could make out a log cabin with a tin roof and a cottonwood log corral that looked as though it had been built by a drunk, it was so crooked. There was overturned earth beside the cabin, which he figured was a garden of sorts. But was that supposed to be a barn over there? Hell, he'd seen kids' tree houses built better. There wasn't a drop of paint anywhere and he knew, sure as sunrise, that by August that siding would be dried and curling like smoke. Not that he cared. They'd be gone long before August. Yeah, long before. That's what he'd come for.

He snatched off his tan hat, the crown stained dark from sweat, the brim bent in the front and back from too many rainstorms. He plunked it down on the saddle horn and wiped his face with the curve of his elbow. Perspiration turned the faded blue of his shirt a navy. There were thunderheads building over the mountains to the west. Maybe there'd be rain.

The gray gelding bobbed his head, making the reins tug and slip in his work-hardened fingers. "Easy," he said, and soothed the animal with a pat. "Easy." The creak of leather and the startled call of a meadowlark punctuated his words. Overhead, the sky was slowly fading from blue to gray.

Touching his spurs lightly to the horse's side, he rode the ridgeline in a lope, moving easily with the rhythm of the horse. Four years in the Union cavalry had taught him two things—how to ride and how to kill.

He surveyed the land with a trained eye, taking in the way the flat prairie rushed to meet what was really only the foothills of the Laramie Mountains. There was one and only one opening through those hills for a hundred miles.

And it was right down there. Right through the middle of that ranch.

Rage mixed with frustration. Goddamn, this should never have happened. He had scouted this area a year ago and it was all open range. Even six months ago there hadn't been a thing but jackrabbits and now this. Billy had botched things but good.

He'd sent a couple of thick-necked types to handle negotiations. Myers and Oberman had wired that some hardheaded woman had run them off the place with a rifle. Now that he would have liked to have seen.

A smile tugged up one corner of his mouth—but it was gone in an instant. This was serious business. Woman or no woman, he was going to get what he'd come for.

He reined up again and reached for the canteen hooked over the saddle horn. Just as he raised it to his lips, something moved and caught his eye.

A little girl dressed in bright-yellow calico darted out of the cabin and raced toward the corral. Behind her came a woman, dressed in a black skirt and a white blouse. Sunlight glinted on her auburn hair making it the color of flame. So that was her, he thought.

His adversary.

Putting up the canteen, he settled his hat more firmly on his head and started down the hill.

Lady, you're about to meet your match.

Sunlight appeared from behind a cloud and sliced knife sharp into Molly's eyes. A sudden flood of tears blurred her vision. Her steps faltered. She blinked hard and turned her back to the sun long enough to swipe at her eyes. Jaw clenched, she turned around again and headed straight for the corral. She didn't have a minute to spare.

She was sick—throat-aching, head-pounding sick, had been since around midnight, close as she could figure. That was when her fever had started or at least when she'd first noticed.

Now she had the chills so bad that even on this hellfire hot morning, it was all she could do to keep her teeth from chattering she was so cold. This wasn't good.

"Katie, honey," she called to the little girl who'd already climbed between the rails. "Be careful around the horses." Molly slid the cottonwood log from the corral fence and let it slam to the ground with a bouncing thud that sent a small puff of dust to coat the front of her skirt.

"I will," Katie shouted back in the way of five-year-olds who aren't really listening at all.

Molly was having trouble getting her eyes to focus and it was taking a conscious effort to get her legs and brain to work in unison. Two steps and the breeze—there was always a breeze in Wyoming—came whipping between the barn and the house lifting the hem of her skirt, chilling her bare legs beneath. "Stop it," she ordered as she shoved the hem back in place. The skirt hung on her like her grandmother's nightgown. She wasn't wearing petticoats or stockings—only the minimum amount of underwear. She was lucky she'd managed to get dressed at all the way her head kept spinning.

With three unsteady strides, she circled around the two draft horses munching on the last of the hay in the feed trough. Her destination was blessedly in sight—the harness shed. Okay, it wasn't actually a shed, in fact it was nothing more than a couple of pegs on the shady side of the barn wall with a little roof-type covering jutting out. Jack had promised to make an enclosure. Jack had made a lot of promises. This shed was the least of 'em. She and Jack... Well, that was another story, a long and exasperating story that made her sad as much as anything. Poor Jack. He'd tried, she supposed, it was just that his goals and hers—

"Mama, watch me!" Katie called as she slid down the haystack just inside the barn door opening and landed with a thump on the hard ground. Immediately she was up and climbing again.

"Be careful," Molly cautioned with a painful rasp in her voice. The child knew no fear. For that matter, most of the time neither did Molly, at least she'd never admit to any.

Lifting on her toes, she strained up to unhook the harness. Muscles in her back ached for the effort. Her fever was building—fast. Her throat was on fire and she was seriously thinking of taking up spitting because it hurt so much to swallow. At this rate, she'd never make it into town.

"Mama, can we get licorice at the mercantile?" Katie asked. Molly liked the way the child had taken to calling her mama even if she was really only her aunt.

"No. Oh, maybe." She was distracted by something else, something called survival. She had to survive, if not for herself, for Katie. No way was she going to die. No way would she leave this child an orphan—not again.

"Watch me this time," Katie called, and Molly did. Sick as she was she couldn't help feeling proud looking at the child who was a joy, *her* joy now, she thought sadly, remembering the pain of her sister's death less than a year ago in that miserable excuse for a tent in an even more miserable gold camp. The child's father and Molly's own father had died only a few months later in a mining accident. To lose so many so fast had been almost more than Molly could bear, like tearing the heart right out of her. But then there'd been Jack, full of charm and smiles and promises of forever after. While she didn't exactly love Jack, she liked him and he treated her and Katie kindly enough. What else could a woman expect? So they'd married. As winter had closed in, life in the camp had gotten miserable, wet, muddy and well-bottom cold. Then, lo and behold, Jack announced that he had the deed to this piece of property he'd taken in payment of some gambling debt. He'd never seen it but...

Molly didn't care. Land. Their land, not the muck and mire they'd been used to at the camp. As far as she was concerned there was nothing to discuss. She packed faster than a person could say, "So long."

Snow was falling as they pulled out of camp headed for their new home. Her first and only home—finally.

Home. The word fairly rang in her head. Her home. Katie's home. Their home. The first time she'd seen it she'd fallen in love. It was as if this spot had been made just for her: big green trees, a brook running year-round, even some structures. A cabin and a barn, at least. It was a start. It was heaven.

"Mama? Are you watching?" Katie's voice cut Molly's thoughts short.

"Good, Katie." Molly waved then swallowed hard.

Grinning, Katie went right back to climbing and Molly went back to working on getting that darned harness down. It hadn't seemed so tough when she'd put it up here last week.

With a final effort, she managed to release the heavy leather straps that came falling toward her and nearly sent her sprawling. Feet braced, she steadied herself. She was going to do this. Molly was nothing if not stubborn. That was the Irish in her, she supposed.

She straightened, positioned the harness over her left shoulder and started for those horses.

"Mama, can I play with Timmy when we're in town?" Katie stood breathless in the opening that should have had doors, but didn't because Jack hadn't... Oh, the devil with it.

"Sure," Molly replied, wincing at the tear in her throat the answer cost her. Young Timmy was the son of Mr. Brinsfield, who owned the local mercantile. He and Katie had hit it right off. Unfortunately, he'd been sick the last time they'd been in town, even Mr. Brinsfield had been sneezing and wheezing. Is that where she could have gotten this...whatever this was?

She was hoping a few doses of Dr. Campbell's Patent Remedy would fix her up.

Molly went back to work. Sunshine heated her

shoulders. A couple of blackbirds fluttered down to peck at the grain near the feed trough.

Molly half dragged, half carried the heavy leather in the direction of the horses. Her loose hair kept blowing in her eyes and annoying the hell out of her. She made a quick motion with her head to get it clear. Big mistake. That motion sent a blinding wave of dizziness washing over her. Her eyes slammed shut. Hand out, she came up short. Her knees threatened to buckle but she refused to give in. She was going to be all right.

A few deep breaths and she felt better, steadier anyway. What was wrong with her? Words like *typhoid, diphtheria, pneumonia* ran through her mind.

No. She wouldn't think that way!

"Katie?" she called out the way a mother does, not looking, just needing a confirmation that her child was okay.

"Yes?" came the answer from somewhere deep in the darkness of the barn.

Satisfied, Molly made her way toward Elmo, the brown draft horse who'd already seen her and was turning away with one of those, if I don't look at her, she won't make me do this looks that animals and small children seem to master early on.

"Don't you walk away," Molly admonished, speaking to the horse's hind end and getting only a swoosh of tail for a reply. She grabbed Elmo by the halter. A big black horsefly buzzed her head and she swatted the creature away. "Come on, Elmo," she said to the horse, "we're going into town whether—"

As she turned, she spotted the man. A lone rider

about three or four hundred yards south and coming in slow. She stilled and released Elmo long enough to shade her eyes. Was it Jack? After six months, she'd hoped he'd return.... The rider got closer. Her momentary relief dissolved faster than butter in a skillet. It wasn't him.

But if he wasn't Jack, then who?

Cautiously, she watched. Molly liked people generally, liked parties and friends. She had darned few of those being new here. But these days strangers made her nervous. For a woman alone, a strange man could be dangerous. That thought sent a whole new sort of shiver prickling down her spine.

Why the devil hadn't she grabbed that Henry rifle she had loaded and propped inside the door of the cabin for this kind of occasion? But, of course, she'd forgotten. Now she was sick and weary and weighted down with the harness and she couldn't run to the cabin if her life depended on it. She hoped it didn't.

He wasn't more than a hundred yards away. She figured she'd bluff it through. After all, odds were he was some cowboy riding the chuck line, wanting water for his horse, maybe a hot meal for himself.

Pretending not to be wary, Molly led Elmo to the wagon and backed him into his place. She let the harness slide off her shoulder and it hit the ground with a thud and clink of metal buckles. Her white shirtwaist was streaked with dirt. Her skirt was just as bad. "Good, Molly. Always wear white when you have to harness the horses." It was habit more than concern that made her brush at the stains.

The steady clip-clop of the horse's hooves told her he was close. She kept on working.

"Morning," he said in a deep, rich voice. She turned to see that he was still seated on his horse. "Mind if I step down?"

"Suit yourself," she told him, relaxing at his polite tone. Murderers hardly bothered with pleasantries.

She reached for the harness.

"Here, let me help you with that," he said, that deep voice of his easy on her ears yet stirring some strange feeling low in her stomach.

Must be the fever. "No, thanks." She gave him a quick once-over, just enough to notice that he was tall and broad shouldered and wearing a Navy Colt on his right hip in the comfortable way of a man who knows how to use one. His dark clothes were trail stained with dust. His hat shadowed most of his face, except for his mustache, which was black, streaked with gray and curved down almost to his jawline. He looked strong and rugged and imposing. He looked one more thing—dangerous—but in ways that had nothing to do with her personal safety.... Or did they?

"Name's Wilder. Ethan Wilder," he finally offered up. Not that she'd asked, but he figured he'd try the polite approach first. She was obviously having trouble with the harness so, ignoring her earlier refusal of help, he tossed down the reins and took a half step in her direction. "I'll *do* that," he told her, trying to take the leather out of her hands.

"I said no!" Molly lashed out at him, her temper riled by fever and fear and what she knew to be unreasonable independence. "Who'd you think does this for me when you're not here!"

"Well, you're welcome," he came back, his voice dripping with sarcasm. "You don't have to take my head off. I was only trying to—"

"Don't try."

"Now, look, lady, I—"

"If you want water for your horse, the trough is over there." Molly motioned with her head and got another wave of dizziness for her trouble.

"I don't want water," Ethan snapped back, his temper rising to match hers. Here he was trying to be polite and she was acting as if he'd asked her for the family silver. Well, he'd set her straight right now. "What I want—"

"I'm not hiring." She kept working, pushing those straps along the horse's sweat-streaked back, doing up the buckles with shaky fingers, but doing them just the same.

This was crazy, Ethan thought as he watched her work. The woman was a royal pain in the posterior and that was a rare thing for Ethan to think. Ethan liked women. Until about ten minutes ago, he'd have sworn that women liked him. So much for male pride. That nudged his temper up another peg.

"Woman, did anyone ever tell you that there's such a thing as good manners?"

"If they did, it's none of your business. Now get your water or get moving."

Just like that she walked away. The damned woman turned her back on him and walked away as if he were some ignorant ranch hand being dismissed for forgetting to tip his hat to the lady of the

manor. Ha! This place was no manor and she was...
Well, the *lady* part was up for discussion.

He tried to remember the saying about catching
more flies with honey than vinegar. He tried not to
lose his temper. Why he even said the first three
psalms to himself in an effort to rein in his ire.

He failed.

He stalked after her, grabbed her by the shoulder
and turned her toward him. "I don't want water and
I won't help you with the damned harness if it's so
all important to you. I'm here on business, and if
you'd stop being so damned cussed ornery—"

It was then that he got a really good look at her
face. She was white as winter, except for her cheeks,
which were flushed like summer roses. He had the
sudden feeling that the sweat beading on her forehead had nothing to do with the temperature outside.
With his hand still gripping her shoulder, he felt her
shake, tremble, and he didn't think it was from him
this time.

Instinct made him take her other shoulder in his
hand, as though sensing she needed holding up. His
temper eased off. "Lady, you don't look too good.
Are you all right?"

She hesitated a fraction of a second, her gaze
locked with his in a look that directly contradicted
the words she spoke. "I'm fine." She easily twisted
free and started to lead the second horse back to the
wagon.

"You should go inside and rest."

"You should mind your own business."

Ethan caught up to her. "Hey, I know sick when
I see it."

"You a doctor?" she snapped as she backed the horse into his place, his coat warm and damp with sweat against her hand.

"No, I'm not a doctor. But it doesn't take one to see you're close to keeling over."

"Oh, really." Molly had taken care of herself for a long time now and done a pretty fair job of it, too. She did not need him or Jack or anyone else telling her what to do, how to do it or when. With a toss of her hair she said as firmly as she could with a throat that was on fire, "Then we have nothing to say. Get out of my way and let me finish."

"Gladly," Ethan said, his temper moved into the dangerous part of the scale. Now he could have ridden off and any other time he would have done just that, but two things kept him here. One, she was obviously sick, real sick and two, he needed to talk to her about their business.

But he was done arguing. He could see she'd have to run her course. Which shouldn't take long. Hell, he could see she was shaking harder than an aspen in the fall. Fever would be his guess, maybe sore throat, who knew what else?

So he led his horse over to the corral fence and leaned against the post, arms crossed lightly over his chest. Twenty minutes, he told himself. No, ten. That's how long he figured he'd have to wait until she gave up and asked for help.

She kept working. He kept watching. She was tall, he noted absently, not one of those tiny little things that looked like some oversize doll. But she was thin. He usually liked his women with a little meat on their bones, a little roundness in the hips, a fullness in the breasts. Of course, in the clothes she was wearing it was tough to tell much.

Her skirt sagged on her frame and her blouse was large enough to conceal any womanly attribute that might—he emphasized the word *might* in his mind—be there. Her face was dotted lightly with freckles, mostly across her cheekbones. Her eyes were dark blue like the Pacific Ocean he'd seen once on a trip to San Francisco. Other than that, there was nothing really unusual about her. Well, there was one thing. Her hair. The most beautiful shade of red he'd ever seen.

It was loose, hanging nearly to her waist. Occasionally, the breeze would lift a few strands to drift across her face or rise in the air like a halo. All the while, the sunlight glinted and sparkled on her hair, making it the color of liquid fire. Yes, liquid fire. Those were the only words he could think of to describe it. And he wondered, just briefly, what it would be like to hold liquid fire in his callused hand.

The first faint stirrings of lust made themselves known. He shifted awkwardly, surprised at the sudden reaction of his body to this otherwise thoroughly disagreeable, dislikable, and now disturbing woman.

Molly was busy finishing up the harness, hooking the chains to the wagon tongue. If he wanted to stand there, then let him. He could stand there until hell froze over for all she cared.

Trouble was, this harnessing business was getting tougher by the minute. Every time she bent down, her head whirled and spun like a carousel.

Suddenly, his watching made her annoyed. "For pity's sake, Mr...."

"Wilder," he told her for the second time.

"Mr. Wilder. I'm not hiring. If you don't want to water your horse, then mount up and move on." Lord, her head hurt and her throat and just about every part of her body, from joints to skin.

The man straightened away from the post he'd been leaning on and came toward her, his stride long and easy. "I could argue the point with you. Judging by the look of that barn and the fence, I'd say you need help all right or you need to move on perhaps. Move on to some place more…finished."

Molly didn't have to think twice to know he was right. But her knowing was one thing and him knowing or, more importantly, him being audacious enough to point it out to her, that was another thing entirely.

"Look. I'm not hiring. There's no sense you waiting because you aren't talking me into anything." She had no money, at least not enough to go hiring hands.

He closed in on her, slowly, intently, sort of like her life these days. She kept fumbling with the buckles on the straps. Just a couple of more and…

"Mama, come see me slide down the haystack again," Katie's high voice called.

"In a minute, honey," Molly answered back over her shoulder. A fit of coughing seized her and she hugged her ribs against the sudden spasm, her forehead resting on the sweaty flank of the horse.

Next thing she knew the stranger's hand was on her back, rubbing. "Take a slow, deep breath," he encouraged.

This time Molly complied, appreciating the soothing motion of his fingers gliding up and down her spine. Yet, she couldn't seem to stop coughing.

"Come on," she heard him say, his hands curling over her shoulder. "Let's get you inside."

Molly balked and straightened away from the horse. "I don't…need…" She waved him away. He didn't go. Instead, he stood by, one hand resting ever so lightly on her shoulder in a way that was strangely reassuring.

A breeze swirled the hem of her skirt and, she noted, ruffled the full sleeves of his blue shirt. The sun beat down from around white puffy clouds and she held on to the harness with one hand.

"Come on. You're sick," he said, his voice taking on a firm tone. "I'll help you into the house and we—"

"Mama. Mama!" came a child's voice again, and Ethan turned in time to see the little girl he'd seen earlier skid to a halt beside them, her calico dress smudged with dirt like her face. "Mama?" she said suspiciously, then glared at Ethan. "What did ya do to my mama?" she demanded, her hands balled into tight fists which she held in front of her.

"Me?" Ethan countered incredulous. He'd never been much good with kids, probably because he'd never spent time with any.

"Yes, you!" she returned, her little jaw squared, her blue eyes sparked with anger, those small fists turned white at the knuckles.

He tugged down on the brim of his hat. "Look, kid, I was only—"

The darned kid hauled off and hit him. Okay, it was in the thigh and it didn't hurt, but when she reared back and hit him again, he figured he'd better take a little defensive action.

"Hey, wait a minute!" he shouted, and grabbed the pint-size pugilist around the waist and hoisted her into the air for safekeeping until he could get the facts straight. "Now look, kid, I didn't—"

Gasping for breath, Molly said, "Don't touch her!"

"What?" Ethan's gaze flicked from mother to daughter and back again. *He* was the injured party here, but she had that mother bear protecting her cub look in her eyes. A smarter man probably would've backed away. Yeah...a smarter man. Trouble was Ethan wasn't feeling smart, he was feeling angry. He'd been abused by the woman and now the kid. Enough was enough. "I'm not the one doing the hitting around here. If you can't control your kid, then—"

"Put her down or else." Molly's expression was fierce, her mouth drawn down into a thin line. The horse shied, flicked his tail and Molly lost her grip on the leather straps.

"Or else what?" Ethan challenged, holding the kid suspended in midair, his hands clamped firmly around her waist.

"Let me go!" the kid screamed and flailed, her feet coming dangerously close to his chin. This was getting serious. What the hell had he gotten into here?

"Or else this!" This time it was the darned woman who swung on him. Oh, she missed him by a mile and succeeded in spinning herself around like a wooden top.

Ethan shook his head in disgust. ''You're crazy. You know that?''

But when she stopped turning, he saw her reach out for something and get only a handful of air. Her eyes slammed shut, then popped open again. ''Oh, no...I think I'm...''

Ethan knew she was in trouble. In one quick motion, he plunked the kid on the ground and made a grab for the woman. Somehow he managed to catch her just before her head hit the hard-packed earth. He didn't have a clue how he pulled that off.

Down on one knee, his grip tightened around her trembling shoulders. Her face was cloud white and her cheeks brighter than sunset. A quick touch to her forehead confirmed that the lady was running one hell of a fever. Her body was limp in his arms. ''Woman. Dammit don't you die on me,'' he ordered, as if that was all it took. What did he know about fevers and such? Nothing. A broken bone or a bullet wound fine, those were things he knew about, could handle.

The horses pawed the ground and shivered, making the wagon move slightly forward. Ethan glanced up at the cabin about twenty-five or thirty feet away. He wanted to get her inside out of the sun but she was so still he wasn't sure he should move her. He shielded her face from the sun with his body.

Just then she moaned. He hadn't been so relieved since '65.

''Lady? Can you hear me?'' He lifted her a bit more upright, his arm curving protectively around her shoulders. ''Lady?''

The little girl, who moments ago was set to fight,

was down on her knees beside him, the hem of her dress dragging in the dirt. All worry-faced, she pushed at his shoulder. "What's the matter?"

Ethan was too busy to answer. The scent of dust filled the air as the breeze stirred the ground. With one hand he brushed the damp hair back from the woman's face. So fire felt like silk, he thought absently.

"Mama? Wake up, Mama!" The child reached around him to shake the woman's forearm. When she didn't respond the kid looked up at him, and in a voice barely audible, she said, "She's dead isn't she?"

"Dead? No," Ethan corrected, surprised by the child's pronouncement. Why would a child so young know about death and dying? "She's fine. Honest." They both knew that wasn't true but at this point he wasn't real sure what to say. This was called a delaying maneuver.

Think, Wilder.

Okay, she was alive and they couldn't stay here in the dirt. So he had to take action. His only plan was to get her inside. One thing at a time. Scooping her up took no effort at all. Hell, he thought his saddle weighed more.

She roused and, true to form, she said, "Put me down." He laughed. She was sick as a dog but still stubborn, still fighting. Well, she had spirit, he'd give her that much, this Wyoming flame.

"I'll put you down—" the cabin was only a few steps away *"—inside."*

This time she didn't argue—another first. Instead she rested her head against his shoulder in a way that was totally unfamiliar yet nice—no, something more, much more. His body stirred. His grip tightened on her, feeling the shape of her thigh and the curve of her breast against his body.

Wilder, you're too long without a woman.

Ducking his head to clear the doorway, he spotted the two beds.

"That one," the kid said, pointing to the larger of the two.

"Thanks." He put her there. A quick glance around the single room showed no sign of a pump, so he retrieved the canteen from his saddle and, using his bandanna, he wet it and dabbed her face.

Seated on the side of the bed, he kept at his task while the little girl had wedged herself between the bed and the wall on the other side. She held her mother's hand, patting the back lightly.

"That's good," he told the child, but she never looked away from her mother's face.

Ethan wet his neckerchief again, squeezed some of the excess water onto the wooden floor and began again to wipe her face and neck and hands. He found himself suddenly fascinated by the slender arch of her neck as it rose from shoulder to jaw. Slowly, he caressed her face with the cool neckerchief, noting for the first time, her high cheekbones. He liked that…high cheekbones. There were always certain parts of the anatomy that attracted him to a woman: high cheekbones, big eyes and long legs…preferably in black silk stockings. His mouth crooked up in a smile at that thought.

Business, Wilder. Get your mind on business.

Sitting a bit straighter, he touched her forehead

again. Hot. Really hot. "Lady, you're burning up," he said as much to himself as to her.

She mumbled something he couldn't understand so he turned to the child as if he were still a major giving orders. "How long has your mother been sick?" If she'd just come down with this it might not be so bad. If she'd been sick for a week, well, the outlook wasn't as optimistic.

What he got back from the kid was a look of panic, a quivering chin and the unmistakable glistening of tears in a pair of pale-blue eyes. Terrific. One sick and now one was going to cry. Just what the hell he needed.

"Don't you dare cry," he ordered the little girl.

She stared at him, blinked a couple of times, sniffed once and said, "Okay."

Finally something was going his way. He snatched off his hat and plunked it down on the foot of the bed near the woman's shoes.

Sloshing more water on his neckerchief, he wiped her burning cheeks again. She roused and made a small helpless kind of sound in the back of her throat. He shoved the hair back from the woman's forehead and she blinked and opened her eyes. "What hap—"

"You fainted."

"Never."

He made a sort of chuckle in the back of his throat. "I know fainting when I see it. Why the hell do you think I carried you in here?"

"I…" She made as if to sit up.

Ethan pushed her gently down. "You're sick. Lie still and maybe you won't *faint* again."

He wiped her face and neck and hands. But when he undid the top two buttons of her shirtwaist, Molly grabbed his hand surprisingly hard, stopping him dead in his tracks. Her eyes met his in an unmistakable challenge. He answered her challenge with the gentlest of words, "Either you trust me or you don't."

Anyone who knew Molly Murphy knew she was not a woman given to flights of fancy, but something came over her, something that made her hesitate, for a heartbeat, no more. It was enough. She wasn't afraid anymore. Instead she felt safe, safer than she had felt with anyone in a long time. And she knew that she'd remember this moment, the look in his eyes, for all her life. Then he blinked or she blinked but the strange lightness was gone, the way a lightning bolt disappears from the stormy sky. She was breathless and a bit excited at the same time, by the man, by his nearness.

She swallowed hard and released his hand. This was silly. *She* was being silly. It was the fever making her mind go off in strange directions. Whatever it was, it took her a few seconds to regain her composure—enough time to take him in more fully.

Her vision was blurred, but she could see that his hair was black as midnight and curled around his ears and down along his collar.

He wiped her face again. The water felt good even as it sent gooseflesh skimming down her body. She blinked again. His face was square, she could see, now that he'd taken his hat off. Dark, winged brows, chiseled cheekbones and a chin that had a stubborn tilt to it. There was a scar, a couple of inches or so long, over his right eye near his hairline and she wondered how he'd gotten it. She wondered why she cared?

His mouth was framed by a thick black mustache, which she'd noticed earlier. The lines in his face indicated he was a man who smiled a lot, though she'd yet to see that side of him.

Her gaze drifted up the length of him, taking in the way his well-worn denim trousers were molded to his lean legs as if they'd been put on wet and shrunk to fit.

He turned and splashed more water on his neckerchief, then repeated his earlier procedure. Her pulse did a darned double kick again then settled down.

All in all, the man was rugged, reasonably good-looking, but mostly he had an air about him, a presence, that would a make a woman remember him.

Fortunately for her, she remembered one other important fact. She was married. At least that's what the preacher had mumbled faster than a rock rolling downhill.

Chapter Two

"**M**ama, are you all right?" Katie's voice cut into Molly's momentary musings.

"Yes, honey." Molly reassured her daughter, grateful for the diversion. Yeah, really grateful.

But she quickly learned it was tough to get her mind off someone when that someone was plunked down on the side of her bed, so close his gun handle pressed against her hip.

She also reminded herself that he was a stranger for all his help, and she had no idea what *exactly* he was after. Just what did he want?

Katie's incessant tugging on her sleeve got Molly's attention.

"What, sweetie?"

"I thought you were dead like—" Her face puckered up as though she'd eaten a lemon.

"Oh, no, sweetie, I'm not dead. See? I'm just fine. A little sick but fine." Molly coughed and rubbed her throat.

A grin slashed across Katie's sun-browned face and she climbed up on the bed. Her sharp knees dug into Molly's legs as the child scrambled to the opposite side of the bed to lean her back against the wall. Her legs looped over Molly's.

"See," Molly said again, "I'm perfectly—" Another cough made her hunch over and cover her mouth. Pain bounced off her ribs and down the center of her chest. All she could do was pray for the coughing to end.

When she looked up Katie's smile was gone, as was the one on the stranger still seated on her bed. So she did what any mother would do, she forced a smile she didn't feel and reached out to give her daughter a hug—just a little hug. She didn't want Katie getting this thing. Katie was her joy, her life and the spitting image of Molly's sister.

The cough came again and she slammed her eyes shut while she tried not to breathe, not to move, so the cough would leave as suddenly as it had arrived.

"Come on, there," she heard the man's voice say, and she opened her eyes a slit to see him reach over her. "Let me hoist you outta there, kid, so your mother can get some sleep."

Katie hesitated a fraction of a second, then let him swing her high into the air before settling her on the floor. That grin was back. That was Molly's grin. The one reserved for her alone and Katie was sharing it with some stranger!

"Do it again," she demanded, arms outstretched.

"Uh, how about later, after we get your mother settled in?"

"You won't forget?"

"I won't forget."

Katie had suddenly gone from hitting the man to

hugging him. Right now she was sidled up against him as though he just invented candy.

Molly's temper started up the scale. Yes, she knew she should be grateful. She *was* grateful but he was getting too...too. Well, just *too*.

When she caught her breath, the stranger was perched on the edge of her table, his long legs stretched straight out in front of him, his boots crossed at the ankles. His hand gripped the edge of the handmade table.

The white china shade on the lamp rattled dangerously as he moved slightly. ''Sorry,'' he muttered, reaching back to steady the lamp with his hand. He stood and studied the table legs. ''Floor's crooked—or the legs are.''

''I know, thank you very much.''

His head came up sharply. ''Hey, I didn't mean anything by it, I was just making a comment.''

''Well, I don't need your comments.''

Her cough erupted again and she rolled onto her side, hands covering her mouth, knees drawn up. It hurt. She wanted to cry she hurt so much.

Just as before, he was there, on the edge of the bed, rubbing her back in a gentle soothing way that warmed her deep inside. ''Try to breathe slowly,'' he said, his voice rich and calming.

And so she did. After what seemed an eternity but was probably only a couple of minutes, the coughing had passed, the pain in her chest had eased.

Shoving her hair back, she looked up as he stood. ''Mr. Wilder...''

He arched one black brow.

"Thank you." She owed him, and she always paid her debts.

"My pleasure." He smiled, a slow, sort of easy smile that appeared from behind his mustache, making those lines in his cheeks deeper. He was transformed, from dark to light, from winter to spring. She was held in his gaze and felt all funny inside, as though she'd been caught in some mischief. This time the shiver that skimmed up her spine had nothing to do with her fever. The woman in her knew it even if her mind denied the feeling. She was a married woman—a happily married woman, dammit.

Being close to him was doing something unfamiliar to her, something she didn't trust. She tore her gaze away and focused on Katie, poor frightened Katie. Yes, that was it. Think about Katie or town—or anything but his tantalizing smile.

A slice of sunlight, the color of fresh butter, slipped in around the blue calico curtains she'd made last month. It flowed over the edge of the handmade pine table and across the rough-hewn floor. Dust motes floated on the air. The man, Wilder, moved, to perch on the edge of the table again. He crossed his feet at the ankles as he had before. That same sunlight glinted sharply on the rowel of one spur, making Molly blink, making her take notice of him—which she was trying not to do, not in that way a woman usually notices a man, at least.

Poor Jack might not be the best husband in the world but he wasn't the worst, either. He'd always pretty much left her alone, except on Saturday nights. She didn't like to think about that. The truth was, a woman needed a husband. Or so she'd been taught. But now there were times she wondered, especially since he wasn't even here. That had her worried.

Before she realized what Wilder was up to, he came over to the bed. Her gaze went instantly to his face, to his dark, dark-brown eyes. Eyes as soft as velvet. Something was happening here. She wasn't quite sure what, but she knew it wasn't good. No sir, it wasn't good at all.

Just then she felt his hand on her forehead. She hadn't even realized what he was about she'd been so lost in thought.

Get a grip, Molly. Now!

"Lady, in case you haven't already figured it out...you're sick. Really sick by the feel of you."

It was anger at herself that made her jerk her head away. *Wedding vows, remember?*

"Gee, I thought I was coughing for no reason at all." She tossed her hair back over her shoulder and swiveled on the bed, effectively making him step back. That was good.

"Hey, don't go getting sarcastic with me. I carried you in here, remember. If it wasn't for me you'd be lying out there in the dirt." He gestured toward the doorway with his thumb.

Okay, she thought, this was good. He was angry. She was angry...well sorta. Anger was a good emotion, a safe emotion that she understood.

He stalked away, stopping near the kitchen sink. He leaned one hip against the wooden counter, arms crossed over his chest.

"I know very well my condition and I've already

said thank you for helping me. What were you expecting? A medal?''

''No, I wasn't expecting a damned medal. I've got more than I ever wanted.''

She was about to ask him what that meant when he stalked back to the table. Hands braced on the table, he leaned toward her.

''What I'd like to know,'' he began before she could say a word, ''if it's not too much of an imposition is—''

''What?'' she snapped. Maybe he'd leave and take that soft lazy smile with him.

''If you knew you're sick then what the *hell* were you doing out there harnessing the horses?'' He motioned toward the door with his hand, his gun hand, she noted.

''This is my house and I'll come and go as I please. I appreciate what you did but I can handle things from here on.'' Her gaze met his square on. Help or no help, sick or well, she wanted things back the way they were.

''Fine.'' He closed on her, his spurs jingling as he did. ''If you want to be so hardheaded, go ahead. Just remember that if you drop dead somewhere out there then—''

''Mr. Wilder!'' Molly's wild gaze flicked to Katie, who was quietly seated on the foot of the bed taking in every word as if she were front row center at the theater.

One look and Ethan came up short. He'd totally forgotten about the kid. Her round face was all drawn up and her chin had that threatening quiver again. Dammit! He hadn't meant to scare the kid, it was just that the woman got him so riled. Besides, there'd been a moment back there when she'd looked at him and said "Thank you" that he'd felt as though something had happened between them. Something… Aw, hell. He didn't know what he was thinking. He was an idiot.

Just take care of business and get on with it.

Yeah. Yeah. But he couldn't walk outta here until he set things right. After all, he wasn't an ogre. With a deep sigh, he hunkered down in front of the child, one hand resting on the square top of the bed leg. "Look, ah, what… Ah, Katie, isn't it?" He touched her hand lightly in what he hoped was a reassuring gesture.

Her sun-bleached hair fell across her face. But her chin still quivered dangerously. Okay. It wasn't the end of the world if the girl broke out in tears. Kids cried all the time. It was just that for reasons he couldn't explain, he didn't want to be the cause of it. "I was only fooling when I said that about your mother dying. Like when you asked me before. You can see she's fine the same way I told you then." She watched him closely, like a cat watching a fish in a bowl. He felt about as cornered. "You're fine," he angled around and asked Molly, "aren't you?" It was an order, not a request.

"Sure," Molly confirmed, her expression dark with restrained rage.

The kid looked at him with all the skepticism of a schoolmarm listening to an excuse about incomplete homework. Fortunately for him, this time it was the woman who did the rescuing.

"Mr. Wilder here was *wrong*."

There was a certain smug edge to her tone that riled him, but he held his temper. "I can see now that I...misspoke," he corrected. As far as he was concerned he was right and this charade was for the kid's benefit.

"Are you sure?" Katie pressed, her free hand twisting the hem of her skirt into a knot.

He gave the kid his best smile, the one that usually got him out of trouble with females from nuns to whores. Evidently, it still worked because, lo and behold, he got a smile right back complete with dimples, one dimple anyway, deep in the left cheek.

"Sure," he confirmed with another pat of her hand.

Katie gave a deep sigh and fussed with straightening her yellow skirt, her head down as though thinking it over. Suddenly her head came up and there was a smile, complete with a missing front tooth. "Okay."

Just like that it was over. Molly breathed her own sigh of relief. Ethan stood, his smile still in place.

"Katie, honey." Molly held out her arms and couldn't resist giving her child a small hug, contagion be damned. Putting her at arm's length, she said, "How about you go on out to the barn and check on Boots and the kittens?" Now that that crisis was past Molly had a few things to say to *Mr. Wilder.* A distraction was necessary and a basket full of week-old kittens seemed the perfect solution.

Katie's eyes went wide at the mention of the cats. "Can I pick 'em up?"

Molly nodded. "Watch out for the mama. She gets kinda protective."

That was all it took. Katie turned on the heel of her scarred black shoes and ran for the door, her fears evidently forgotten.

But Molly hadn't forgotten or forgiven, and as soon as Katie banged the door shut, Molly turned her fury on the man standing a couple of feet away.

"Who the devil do you think you are coming in here and telling me what to do?" She surged to her feet, her skirt twisting around her legs as she did. She grabbed the cotton and pulled it free. Her throat hurt like blazes. "And what's the meaning of scaring my child? How dare you?" Her throat felt like raw meat and she was cold, so cold.

"Me?" He paced away then turned back. "Why the hell is this my fault? I'm not the one who's stupid enough to be outside harnessing horses when I'm sicker than a saloon dog on Sunday morning. I'm not the one who—"

Molly was seized by the worst fit of coughing yet. Her chest ached as if she'd been mule kicked as did her ribs and her gut and just about every other part of her body. She sank down on the bed, lying on her side. Hands clamped over her mouth, she coughed until she was sure there was no breath left in her.

When she finally managed to sit up, he was seated on the edge of her table, *her* table, with one of those I-told-you-so expressions that men are so great with.

Hooking her hair behind her ears, she shot him a look that dared him to say it. Wisely, he didn't say a word.

Molly gulped in a couple of lungfuls of air and

rubbed her throat, trying in vain to ease the ache there.

"Well," she said after a moment.

"Well what? You want me to apologize for helping you? Okay. Fine." He paced away again, boot heels thudding on the bare floor. "I'm sorry I helped you instead of leaving you passed out in the dirt."

Ethan knew the look he got. She was glaring at him, lips tight, eyes hard, jaw clenched. It was one of those you'll-be-sorry-for-that looks that women use on small children and men of all ages. He hated what he thought of as "the look," didn't know a man who didn't. This particular woman was all temper and determination and not a lick of sense.

She's also sick and trying to take care of herself and a child all alone.

Okay. For that he felt sorry for her. But only for that. So he decided not to say "I told you so" since *he* knew that she knew that was exactly what he was thinking. There was a certain joy of victory, even if it was a very small one. Kinda made up for having to endure the dreaded "look." A smile threatened, just a tad, a sort of twitch in one corner of his mouth hidden behind his mustache.

Of course, there was nothing really to smile at. Looking at her with her face all flushed, her hair in disarray, her breathing shallow and fast. She looked riled and wild, and any other time he'd have thought she'd just been made love to. That thought stirred him a bit.

He tamped down the feeling. Hell, she was sick, not being seductive. Too bad, was his fleeting thought. Enough of that. What he wanted from her had absolutely nothing to do with sex. He had business on the mind, nothing more.

Unfortunately his business was going to have to wait because he'd showed up at exactly the wrong time and he and the woman, well, they weren't exactly best friends...yet.

Still, he figured he'd try the sensible approach. Slapping his hat on the table behind him, he dragged out a chair and sat down. "You need a doctor."

"Maybe." She eyed him suspiciously.

"Maybe?" His tone was exaggerated. "More than maybe."

She swung her legs over the side and faced him directly. "Now, look, Wilder, I—"

He stopped her with an upheld hand. "I'll go into town and bring the doctor back. I'll even pay if that's what's worrying you."

Twisting in the chair, he grabbed his hat and made to stand.

"First of all, I don't take charity and second, there's no doctor in town."

That brought him up short. "No doctor?" His brows came together. "What do you mean there's no doctor? There has to be a doctor."

She coughed slightly. "Sorry to disappoint you but there's no doctor."

"Well, where *is* the nearest doctor?"

She shrugged.

"No doctor." Great. Just great. He dropped down in the chair again, the wood creaked under his sudden weight.

She shook her head. The beautiful red hair of hers spilled over one shoulder as she moved. Another cough. The sound was deep and painful to listen to. Suddenly he was very anxious to do something…anything.

"A friend, then? Someone who could help out while you—"

She shook her head again. "We haven't been here that long. I don't know anyone as much more than a passing acquaintance."

No doctor. No friends. Her sick. All alone. Little kid. This was a hell of a fix. He fell back in the chair, raking one hand through his hair in an agitated gesture. Now what?

He didn't have time to make that decision. Next thing he knew, she was up, wobbling a bit, but up and moving for the damned door again.

"Where do you think you're going?" He slapped his hat on his head and caught up.

"I think I'm going to town." She kept walking, and he mirrored her stride.

"What's the point if there's no doctor?" he repeated. "This is a waste of time and energy—and by the look of you, you don't have much of either to spare."

"You've so kindly pointed that out before, Mr. Wilder." She never slowed. Outside she headed for the wagon, Ethan right in step, though he chose to walk backward so he could look at her better. He didn't like what he saw. She was still trembling and pale and coughing and struggling to talk. It could be a bad cold. It could be something a lot worse.

"I'm against this," he announced. "Don't be stupid."

"Thank you for the insult."

They ended up at the wagon in a dead heat. The horses pawed the ground nervously as though sensing the tension going on. A couple of big horseflies buzzed around making the horses swoosh their tails. Sweat already glistened on their backs.

Katie came running full steam ahead across the yard from the barn. She skidded to a halt beside Molly and tugged on her skirt. "Look at this one." She had a strangle-tight grip on an orange-striped kitten and thrust the mewing cat in Molly's direction.

"Nice," Molly replied absently and punctuated her statement with a little pat on Katie's head. She wasn't interested in kittens; she was interested in getting rid of this man, going into town and getting some medicine to make her head stop feeling as though it were going to explode. What she would give to curl up in a nice dark corner somewhere and wait this thing out. But that wasn't going to happen. Having to converse with this cowboy was only making her feel worse.

"No one's keeping you here, Mr. Wilder." She shaded her eyes with her hand as she looked up at him, his face lost in shadow. "In fact, I'm telling you to ride—"

Katie's high-pitched voice cut across her words. "Mama, can I take him with me?"

"What?" Molly looked down. It was as if she were seeing Katie and the cat for the first time, she'd been so distracted by this man who kept bossing her around. More annoyed at the man than the child, she snapped, "No!"

It was hard to think. It was impossible to carry

on two conversations at once. She decided she didn't want to carry on any. So, teeth gritted in determination, she shouldered past the man, hitched up her skirt, and managed to hook one foot on the wheel hub. But the world spun dangerously again and before she knew what was happening he had her around the waist and wordlessly lifted her onto the seat.

She muttered a quiet ''thanks,'' then settled on the seat, adjusting her skirt down around her ankles. The breeze made her shiver. The sunlight made her eyes water. The man made her temper boil. If he wouldn't leave then she would. It was as simple as that.

''But I wanna take the kitten,'' Katie piped up, wagging the week-old cat in Molly's general direction, the poor cat's feet flailing in the air while it made a pitiful meowing sound.

Molly looked hard at Katie, blinking to make her eyes focus, to make the scene sink in. There was Katie and the kitten that was too young to be away from its mother, and there was the cowboy. Oh, yes, by all means let's not forget the cowboy. Mustering all the calm and control she had she said, in what she thought was a firm but kindly voice, ''No kitten.''

That got her a pout that would have made Lotta Crabtree envious.

''But, Mama—''

So much for calm and control. ''Katherine Louise, put the cat back!'' That cost her throat dearly, and she rubbed from the outside as though it would help, which of course it wouldn't. Nothing would.

She'd be sick for the rest of her life, she knew it. If only Jack were here. If only she had some help. If only…

A steady look proved that Katie hadn't budged an inch. She still had the kitten cradled in her arms like a baby, rubbing its little tummy.

Contrite, Molly said, "Put the kitten away and come climb up here with me. We have to go." She patted the spot on the seat beside her, the wood split and rough from the weather.

Katie was shaking her head. "Why *can't* I bring the kitten?"

Exhausted, Molly relied on the old standby that her mother had used so many times on her. "Because, I said so."

Katie's chin got all stubborn and she made a show of digging the toe of her black leather shoe into the hard-packed earth. She clutched the kitten and she wasn't moving. Sunlight caught in the fine blond strands of her hair making it seem nearly white. Ten yards away, a dust devil lifted in the dirt near the barn door hurling pieces of hay into the air before it dashed across the corral and disappeared like a magician's trick.

In the meantime, the Wilder man had grabbed the horses' halters. He stood there taking in her predicament as though he were waiting to see who'd win this tug of wills. Well, he was dead wrong if he thought Katie was going to win—or him, for that matter.

"Put the kitten back," Molly ordered one more time. "Do it!"

"Oh, okay," Katie muttered in one of those tones

that bordered dangerously on disrespect. Head
down, like a prisoner on her way to the gallows, she
walked back to the barn.

Molly's gaze was fixed on Katie when she heard
Wilder's whiskey-rich voice close up. When she
turned he was standing right beside her seat, one
hand curled over the iron trim. "Look lady—"

"Stop calling me 'lady.' I'm Molly Murphy."
The breeze shoved her hair across her face and she
snatched it aside. "*Mrs.* Molly Murphy to you," she
repeated with a strong emphasis on the missus part.

"I never—"

"Just stop. Mostly, I want you to stop telling me
what to do." She blinked hard against the ache behind her eyes. "When I want your advice, Mr. Wilder, I'll ask for it."

Son of a bitch was the first and only thought in
his mind at that precise moment. Here he was trying
to help her—had helped her by God—and this was
the thanks he got? Head down so he didn't have to
see her, he gave the brim of his hat a hard tug as
the only visible show of temper because he was trying like hell to remember that she was sick.

"All right, Mrs. Murphy, then—"

"Katie, hurry up!" her voice cut him off. The
woman was more stubborn than a big yellow dog
he'd had once. Every time he'd said "Sit" the
damned thing would stand.

Yellow dogs and flame-haired women who
wouldn't do what was good for them if they heard
it, and she had heard it, definitely tested his sanity.
He wondered, not for the first time, what he was
still doing here. Why the hell hadn't he ridden out

when he'd seen she was sick? Why didn't he ride out now? He actually turned away and took a step.

But then he glanced back over his shoulder at her perched up there on the wagon seat, all alone. Aw, hell, was he really gonna ride off and leave her out here, with a kid to look after? He sighed, one of those sighs that's more resignation than willingness.

Moving up to the wagon again, he rested his hand on the wheel. "Mind telling me how far is it into town?" He was pleased his voice sounded so...controlled.

"Twelve miles, give or take." She twisted away from him and faced the barn more fully. "Katie!"

The little girl appeared in the doorway and inched her way toward the wagon, still pouting.

"Twelve miles," he said, tugging on the harness straps as he checked them for tightness. She had done a good job. He'd give her that much. "That's quite a distance. You make the trip often?"

"No."

Well, that was blunt. Looked as though the conversation was dwindling. About that time, Katie finally made it to the wagon. He didn't wait for instructions, just grabbed the little actress around the waist and plunked her down on the seat beside her mother. "There you go."

"Thank you." Katie beamed. "You're strong."

Ethan chuckled. Why was it kids had a way of getting around people, especially when they didn't want to be gotten around?

There he stood looking at the two of them silhouetted against the ever darkening afternoon sky. Any idiot could see that they were never going to make it into town—not without help.

Common sense told him that she didn't want his help, that this was not the time to talk about business. And, to be blunt, he didn't owe them a thing. Nope, not a thing.

So why the devil was he climbing up on the wagon seat? The metal springs creaked with his added weight. A sliver of sunlight glittered in his eyes, forcing him to squint.

He reached for the reins just as Molly did. Their hands touched for the briefest second and he looked at her over the top of Kate's head.

"What are you doing?" Molly released the reins and slid her hand free of his.

"I'm taking you to town."

"I didn't ask you."

"I know. I have the feeling you don't ask for much of anything, do you?" Before she could answer, Ethan shifted the reins to his right hand and, tucking the thumb and forefinger of his left hand in the corners of his mouth, he whistled, a sharp, shrill sound that made Molly wince.

His gelding trotted up alongside the wagon, ears up. "Let's go, boy." He slapped the reins hard on the team's rumps and the wagon lurched off.

The trip was slow going. All she could do was keep her head down, hug her ribs and will herself not to shake, not to cough and not to be sick. It wasn't working.

The team plodded along at a turtle's pace, churning up choking dust with their heavy steps. The sky was gray, dotted with white clouds. She was praying it didn't rain before they got to town. Why was it trouble always came in bunches? First Katie had had the sniffles last week and now Molly felt like death warmed over. She'd never felt like this before. Nothing even close. It scared her—she'd seen people die of fevers in the mining camps. Her own mother.

Was it something fatal, something contagious, something she'd already given to Katie?

Thoughts turned to fear and then panic. What if the medicine didn't work? What if she couldn't drive home? What if she drove home and then got worse? *Oh, Jack, why aren't you here? I need you.* Jack had been so good when her father died.

The wagon rumbled on. She didn't know what hurt more, the occasional splash of sunlight or the jolting and jarring.

"Watch out for the ruts," she snapped, taking her misery and frustration out on the man seated close to her. In truth, a very secret truth, she was glad he was here, gladder still he was driving. She wasn't telling him that, but she was.

The wagon creaked and groaned like an arthritic old man and made her grab on to the side of the seat, the weathered wood rough and splintery against her fingertips.

Overhead a pair of red-tailed hawks circled, gliding on the wind currents and in the distance she could see the green ribbon strip of cottonwood trees that snaked down the side of the mountain along the creek that eventually made its way to her cabin.

The harness jingled with every movement, the horses' tails swooshed back and forth against the constant buzz of flies. Molly tried to think of something pleasant, something good. She consoled herself with promises that she'd be fine in a few days, a week at most. She had her garden to tend, chores to do.

Suddenly, there was a loud creak. A shudder moved through the wagon. A louder snap and the wagon tilted precariously to the right. The horses stopped dead in their tracks. Katie banged into Molly's side and she grabbed the child and held her against her shoulder.

"What happened?" she asked.

Ethan was already swinging down off the wagon seat and heading for the back of the wagon. Of course, he didn't have to look. He knew the answer. "Wheel's broken," he called out.

The breeze fluttered his sleeves and the bandanna at his neck and he turned more into the wind. About that time he saw her pivot in the seat, saw that same breeze lift the hem of her skirt, revealing bare legs from the tops of her black leather shoes to the ruffle on her pantalets. Nice legs, he thought. He was a man, after all.

She pushed the skirt back in place and said, "The wheel can't be broken."

"Yes it can, and it is. The rim has come off and three of the spokes have split."

"That's impossible."

"Evidently not. Didn't your husband take care of the tires?"

Though Jack had tried, his heart wasn't in ranching. "I couldn't say," was all she answered.

"Didn't you soak the wheels?" he chided.

"Oh, sure, every day." Her fever and her fear

fueled her temper. "I jacked up the wagon and took off all four wheels."

"Look, lady, this isn't my fault, you know. It's your wagon," Ethan muttered. Mother and daughter stared at him as if they expected him to say, "I'll have it fixed in a minute," which he couldn't, not here and now, anyway. Back at her place, with some tools, sure, he could fix it, at least enough to get them to town and a replacement.

With a sigh, he walked up to them, to her—the stubborn redhead. "Well," he said, "so much for going into town."

Molly grabbed up her skirt and before he knew it she climbed out of the wagon. He helped her because he thought she'd fall flat if he didn't. Ignoring him, she went back to inspect the wheel as though looking at it would somehow make it not broken.

He helped Katie down. "Come on, kid," he said, and the little girl leapt into his arms, her small feet banging lightly against his ribs. He settled her on the ground, and next thing he knew, she'd shoved her hand into his. It was kinda nice, he thought as they went to join the stubborn Mrs. Murphy.

Molly stood there staring at the shattered wheel. It had fallen apart as suddenly as her life these past few months. She was alone and trapped once more. The panic rose in her, making sore muscles tense. Now what? It was too far to walk to town in her condition—she'd never make it and there was Katie to consider.

A cough erupted and she had to steady herself on the wheel until the spell passed.

"I'm taking you back to your cabin."

Molly shook her head in adamant refusal.

As soon as the coughing stopped she said, ''We'll ride the…horses.''

He stared at her a moment, then, without a word, he lifted Katie and plunked her down on the saddle of his gray gelding. Thank goodness. Finally, the man was going to do what she asked. She didn't know what she'd done or said but she was grateful, very grateful.

Katie was busy being Katie. ''What's your horse's name, Mr.…''

''Ethan. Call me Ethan. My horse's name is Four.''

''Four? You mean like the number?'' She patted the horse's neck and giggled as the animal twitched in response.

''Yes.''

''Just Four? How come?''

''After the first three were shot out from under me I gave up naming them.'' Turning to Molly, he said, ''I'll help you up…that is if you agree.''

Molly eyed the stirrup and the horse. ''I can manage.''

Well, she did manage to get her foot in the stirrup and bounced a couple of times trying to get some momentum going to propel herself onto the horse. Nothing. She was as weak as that kitten Katie had been holding earlier.

Suddenly, he was there looking all smug. ''Help?''

She answered with one sharp nod. Instead of giving her a leg up, he scooped her up in his arms and deposited her on the horse. This was getting to be a habit, this being in his arms. Trouble was, she was beginning to like it.

No. That was wrong. She did not like it.

He was looking up at her in an odd way, sort of quizzically, his hands resting on the saddle very near her thigh. This time she refused to thank him so she busied herself with adjustments, blouse, hair, skirt— anything that kept her from looking at this man who was making her feel things more than just anger.

"I'll get the team," he finally said, and walked away.

She was relieved.

A minute to unhitch the team, and he led them back to where his own horse waited with Molly and Katie on board. Without a word, he grabbed up his horse's reins and, leading all three animals he started walking—south!

Molly couldn't believe it. "Wait. You're going the wrong way! I don't want to go back to the cabin. I want—"

"To go to town." He never even turned to look at her. It was as if he were speaking to some empty space on the road. "You've made that abundantly clear, but War Bonnet is too far and I'm not walking ten miles in this heat."

This couldn't be happening. It couldn't. Molly needed some medicine, needed to get into town on the off chance that she got worse. She couldn't leave Katie alone at the ranch.

Desperate, determined, Molly reached around Katie and grabbed a handful of the horse's mane, intent on countermanding his intentions. "Now look, Wilder, I'm going to town and that's the end of it."

The horse shied and bobbed its head.

"I wouldn't do that," Ethan told her, "not unless you want to get bucked off." She released her hold. He kept walking.

"Stop this horse!" she ordered. "I'll walk to town." It was ridiculous, but at that moment she was frightened enough to try.

"No. End of discussion."

"Why you son of a—"

"You shouldn't cuss in front of the kid." Ethan kept walking. He never looked back, mostly because he was kinda enjoying this victory of his.

Oh sure, he could have ridden into town, or let them ride Four. But it was ten damned more miles…on horseback. Judging by Mrs. Murphy's condition, they didn't stand a snowball's chance in hell of making it. They'd get another couple of miles and she'd pass out—then he'd really have trouble on his hands. Nope, this was the best way, the only way, as far as he was concerned.

"Don't you see?" she called to him. He kept walking. "I can't take care of Katie. I have to go to town."

"Yes, I know. You want to go to town and hope some stranger will take pity on you." He spoke over his shoulder.

"Not pity. Help. I *need* help."

Ethan glanced back at her, the sunlight glinting red-gold in her hair, her delicate face ashen and drawn. Finally they agreed on something. She did need help, which was probably why he'd hung around for so long—that and the fact that she was so stubborn, so determined and so damned helpless.

It was the helpless part that tugged at his gut. He knew what it was to be alone and scared. Before he had time to think on it more he said simply, "Then you've got it."

"Who?"

"Me."

Chapter Three

Fortunately they weren't all that far from the cabin, about two miles or so Ethan figured, judging by the way his new boots were making themselves known. Boots were never made for walking no matter how worn in they were.

The woman, the one causing him so much trouble, had been quiet. He'd kept looking back to make sure she was there, upright. She was. Arms wrapped around the little girl, they were both quiet. Occasionally he'd hear her say something to the child, but it was too soft, meant for the child alone to hear. Probably reassuring her, he thought.

He wished like hell someone would reassure him. What the devil had he gotten into?

Ethan Wilder was a man who looked out for himself, for his friends, of which there were damned few except Billy, who was like a kid brother, and a couple of others.

He heard her cough and he turned. She was still in the saddle but for how much longer he wasn't sure. "Stubborn redhead," he muttered under his breath and yet, in a funny way they were alike, he and the woman. Both alone, both making it on their own, both too stubborn to admit what they were up against.

Hell of a thing she was trying to do, living out here by herself. Which reminded him, where the hell was her husband? The land was registered to Jack Murphy, but by the look of the place he hadn't been around for a while. What kind of man goes off and leaves a woman and child to fend for themselves?

Could he be in jail or maybe dead? That was something Ethan hadn't thought about until this second. In any case, he was here and maybe a little Good Samaritan help might be rewarded when he got down to talking business.

The kid's voice caught his ear. "Mr. Ethan?"

"Uh-huh." He spotted the cabin up ahead to the right.

"Can your horse go fast?"

"Sure." He angled across the grassland, saving a few steps, his spurs jingling. Sage brushed against his denim trousers. The three horses followed his lead, the leather reins hard and stiff in his fingers.

"Can he go fast now?"

"No, not now." The three horses' hooves clip-clopped in an uneven rhythm on the hard-packed earth.

"When?"

"Later."

"Can I ride him when you make him go fast?"

"Sure."

Did kids always ask so many questions?

Ethan stopped by the corral. He helped Katie

down first, letting the kid hold Four's reins, not that they needed holding. Four was battle-trained like his master and didn't bolt easily. Maybe that was why Ethan was here, force of habit, no retreat in the face of trouble. But trouble had taken on a whole new meaning when he'd met Molly Murphy.

Silently, he reached up for the woman, the one looking at him so intently. She hesitated then leaned toward him. He fitted his hands easily around her narrow waist.

Their gazes locked and held.

With her hands resting on his shoulders, he kept her there, suspended above him for an instant, the length of time it takes the heart to beat one slow, steady beat.

Married, Wilder. She's married.

Reluctantly, he lowered her to the ground. "All right?"

She looked up into his down-turned face, hers so close he could see into the depths of her eyes, soft eyes that seemed to question, to search his face for the answer to some question known only to her.

Abruptly, she stepped away from him.

Strangely, Ethan regretted the loss, and that surprised him even more. He cleared his throat. "Come on, let's get you into the cabin."

She stopped him with a touch to his sleeve. "Why?"

His brows drew down in question. "Why get you into the cabin? Because—"

"Why are you doing this?"

The breeze lifted fine strands of her hair to fly about her face. He had the sudden urge to brush them back, to feel the softness, to... This time it was Ethan who took a half step back, needing distance. "I—"

"You don't have to worry about me. I'll be—" Another spell of coughing.

"You need help, and since I'm the only one you've got—" he made a show of looking around "—I think you're stuck with me...unless you *really* want me to go."

Her cough eased off. "Are you from around here?" She cocked her head to one side, her fingers still lightly covering her lips.

"I'm not from around here." There was no sense telling her more now.

"I don't even know you, Mr. Wilder," Molly asserted as good judgment warred with harsh reality. She needed help. She was trapped without the wagon and even if she climbed up on one of those draft horses she wasn't sure she could stay there, her head was spinning so badly. The man was right. There was nothing and no one in town to help her. He, on the other hand, had been arrogant and bossy and, she hated to admit it, helpful.

"Look, Mrs. Murphy, like it or not you need me, and you know it. But it's your call." He gave a sorta one-shoulder shrug.

She appreciated that he was giving her a chance to send him away, to end their...relationship. She didn't. "I already told you that I have no money for hiring hands, Mr. Wilder, if that's what you're thinking." She wasn't used to people around here going out of their way for her.

"I'm not looking for work. I'm offering to help

you out for a day, maybe two, then I'm headed out. I have my own business to take care of."

"I have no bunkhouse."

"I can use the loft in the barn."

He seemed to have an answer for everything.

This isn't a good idea, she thought.

Sick or not, how would it look, a stranger living out here with her? Besides, what if he was some kind of escaped criminal or worse? No, no, absolutely not.

"I'm—" She coughed again as though to remind herself of her worsening condition. A couple of days was all she needed. No one would know.

She had no choice but to trust him. It was as simple as that...and as complicated.

Her decision made, she said, "All right, Mr. Wilder, I accept your offer." She started for the house. "Come on, Katie."

It took Ethan a full five seconds to realize what she'd said. The woman was actually agreeing with him. "I'll be damned. Hey, wait a minute." He raised one hand like a signal while he strode to catch up. "If I'm staying—"

"You are," she confirmed.

"Then don't be so damned hardheaded." His mouth was pulled down in a determined frown. "Let me help."

He offered her his arm and she accepted. A simple act. A common act of courtesy and yet something passed between them, something electric, something definitely unexpected.

Their gazes sought each other's and found confirmation that each felt what the other had.

Fortunately, Katie broke the spell. "I'll help, too," the child's high voice piped in. She rushed around them to put her hand in Molly's and Molly held it extra tight, like a lifeline, which was silly, she knew, but reassuring all the same.

Once inside, Molly let him help her to settle on the edge of the bed, rumpled from where she'd lain on it earlier. Lord, she was tired. Every muscle in her body hurt. Hell, even her hair hurt to touch.

She knew then that she'd done the right thing accepting his offer—the only thing. Katie crawled up next to Molly and insisted on holding her mother's hand.

Molly looked up at him, perched on the edge of the table and couldn't think of a blessed thing to say, not one thing. He seemed so tall, so powerful, so...*dangerous* was the word that popped into her head. She didn't fear him, though, quite the opposite. None of this was making sense. She rubbed her temples and swallowed against the raw ache in her throat that wasn't getting any better. If anything, it was getting worse.

And he just stood there, looking down at her.

"I was—" she began but he cut her off.

"Do you want me to help you take your clothes off?" His voice was deep and smooth as fine whiskey. That gooseflesh skittered up her spine again— the ones that had nothing to do with her illness and everything to do with the man.

His request penetrated her mind and her body at almost the same second. "Take my clothes off!" Self-defense surged to the fore and she leapt to her feet, managing to ignore the pain behind her eyes.

"You know, Mr. Wilder, I've changed my mind."
She glanced discreetly toward that rifle propped by
the door, calculating distance and time and speed at
which she could run. He followed her line of vision,
then looked back at her.

"Lady." He shook his head and made a sound in
the back of his throat that could have been a
chuckle. "I'm not interested in *anything* but getting
you into bed."

Her head came up sharply. That rifle wasn't close,
but if she made a quick rush she might outrun him.

Instead, he laughed out loud. A smooth, easy
sound that had no hint of a threat. *"I mean,"* he
emphasized the words, *"you're sick and sick people
belong in bed.* You were planning on going to bed
to rest, weren't you?" He slapped his hat on the
table making the lamp rattle lightly, then he raked
both hands back through his ink-black hair.

She looked down and behind her at the bed as
though it were some foreign object that she'd never
seen before.

"Bed," she repeated out loud.

"Yeah, that was your general plan, wasn't it? You
spend some time resting while I take care of
things."

Resting. Bed. Actually, she hadn't thought that far
ahead. She hadn't thought beyond the part about not
being alone and sick, maybe real sick, and Katie.
But this getting into bed business, with him in the
house, was a whole other matter.

He moved from his perch on the edge of the table
to one of the four chairs. "If you want to sit up for
the next couple of days, okay. I just think it's going

to get damned uncomfortable." He draped his arms casually across his chest and waited. "I intend to sleep in the nice soft haystack the kid here was climbing in earlier."

Molly glanced quickly at the rifle, then back at him.

He didn't move. "Go get it if it'll make you feel any better. Unless you plan on shooting me for feeding livestock or cooking dinner, I think I'm safe. You want me to bring it to you?"

The fact that he was willing to let her get the rifle made her know she didn't need it. Aw, hellfire, she'd known almost from the first that he wasn't a threat, not a physical one anyway, or she'd never have agreed to let him stay, sick or not.

A ghost of a smile brushed across her lips. "I don't think that'll be necessary."

"Thank you, ma'am," he said with a sweep of his hand and a partial bow.

That made her smile in earnest. There was something about the man...

Another fit of coughing. "Tarnation," she muttered as she dropped down on the bed.

Katie rushed to hug her. "You'll be okay, Mama."

Molly nodded. "Thanks," she managed to choke out as she gulped for air and wished like crazy this misery would stop.

He merely arched one black brow in sort of a question—a repeat of his earlier instructions, she knew.

That pillow on her bed looked awfully inviting.

All she wanted to do was put her head down and sleep.

Molly glanced at Katie uncertainly.

"I think I can manage," Ethan said in answer to her unspoken question about child care.

Molly decided a compromise was in order. Rest was the best cure for what ails a body. So maybe a few hours' sleep and she'd feel better.

Still, there was no way she was getting undressed with this man standing here. So she simply stretched out fully clothed. She didn't even remove her shoes. "Katie, hand me a blanket."

Ethan shook his head and made a derisive sound in the back of his throat. "This is it? You're gonna stay dressed all night?"

"Maybe." Molly rolled onto her side to face him.

Ethan sighed, one of those deep frustrated sighs. "This is ridiculous."

Katie returned with a faded pink blanket she'd gotten from a trunk under the window.

"Give me that," he said more sharply than he meant. "Woman, either you trust me or you don't. Make up your mind now."

He didn't wait for an answer. Blanket draped over his arm, he headed for the door.

"Katie, get your mother's nightdress and give it to her," he ordered over his shoulder as he ducked outside.

Molly watched him through watery eyes.

Less than a minute later he was back, this time with a rope. He went to work tying the rope to a clothes-peg near the window. He hooked the other end over a nail sticking out of the back wall that had once held a mirror long since broken.

"What are you doing?" Molly rose up on one elbow, muscles in her shoulders ached at the strain. The bed creaked.

He ignored her. "Katie, where's that nightdress?"

He was barking orders like a general and Katie was obeying as fast as any recruit.

Katie plopped the blue flannel nightdress in front of Molly and turned to Ethan. "What now?"

"Get more blankets."

She hurried to obey, her little leather shoes half scuffing, half stamping, across the bare, planked floor.

Molly put the nightdress aside and stood, nearly catching her face on the rope he'd strung up.

"What the devil are you doing?"

Katie appeared with another blanket, this one blue, the bottom half dragging on the floor.

Without a word he tossed the pink blanket over the rope and spread it out, then took the one from Katie and repeated the procedure, essentially making a barricade between them.

"There. Are you satisfied now?"

Molly frowned. She flipped one end of the blanket upward as he peered over the top at her. "What's this supposed to be?"

"Well," he said, "it's supposed to be a privacy screen and a sunshade. I noticed the sunlight made your eyes water."

That stopped her. He was bossy and pushy and he was right—again. Damn the man. Overwhelmed, she dropped down on the bed and rubbed at her temples. It felt as though the top of her head was spinning—as though the whole room was spinning.

"So now you can have some privacy while you sleep, or dress or undress." There was a trace of amusement in his voice. "Right now I think undressing is the order of the day."

"You just love giving orders, don't you?" She grabbed up her nightdress.

"Old habit," he muttered. "I'll go out and check on the horses while you take care of…things. I'll be back in twenty minutes. You better be changed and in bed."

"Fine," she snarled. Lord, her head hurt and this man wasn't helping any. Why the devil did he have to be so all-fired right all the time?

She thought she heard him chuckle but she wasn't sure. She did hear him close the door as he went outside.

Ethan strode for the corral. He took about four steps before reality hit him.

What the hell have you gotten yourself into here, Wilder?

Damned if he knew. Business was going to have to wait. The day felt close. The air alive with electricity. Near the creek the new leaves of the cottonwood trees swished back and forth in the wind. He glanced over his right shoulder at the pitiful excuse for a cabin. *Pitiful* was being generous. Why, they didn't even have running water—and with a creek so close there was no excuse. Then there was the corral fence that was falling down, the barn that was a mess, the garden in the back that needed tending—

not to mention a sick woman and a little kid to look after.

Yeah, what had he gotten himself into here was a very good question. But whatever it was he was in it now and he'd keep his word. What difference could a couple of days make?

He grabbed up the wooden bucket by the corral fence and headed for the stream to fill the water trough. This was going to take a few trips. As he went back and forth, splashing water in the raw wood of the trough, somewhere in the back of his mind an old remedy for colds and such circled. There was steam with a little eucalyptus oil for cough. There was hot tea and honey for sore throat. There was sage tea, but was that for colds or upset stomach? He frowned. She might have to drink some, just in case.

Okay, he thought as he dumped the last bucketful. At least there was something he could do. That made him feel better, more in control. Ethan was a man who liked feeling in control.

He tossed out a couple of forks of hay for the team and Four to chew on. He hadn't taken the harness off the team, thinking that he was going to have to go back and get that blasted wagon. He couldn't leave it on the road. Since he planned to leave tomorrow, he'd better take care of it this afternoon.

As he slammed the top rail home, the whole fence did a wave like a field of wheat in the wind. He grabbed hold of the closest post and gave it a shake.

"The damned log isn't down there more than a foot," he said out loud. "Who the hell built this place?"

Obviously, someone who didn't know or didn't care. In either case, maybe that was a good sign. These folks weren't cut out to be ranchers or farmers or whatever it was they thought they were doing here. Maybe they'd be of a mind to sell when the time was right. Maybe with the woman sick, a kid to take care of and no husband anywhere around, now just might be the right time.

He retrieved his gear from his saddle and took both into the barn. The ladder to the loft didn't look any too strong, which made him skeptical about the loft itself.

He decided to make a spot for himself over near the east wall. Putting his saddle down, he pitched a couple of forks of hay, fluffed it a little, then spread out his bedroll.

"That should work," he said to no one.

He looked around the barn, killing time, giving her a chance to change her clothes, giving her a chance to get used to the idea of him taking care of her.

Hell, he needed a chance to get used to that idea himself. He threw some dried corn he found to the half-dozen chickens that were pecking the ground near the barn door. Then he wandered outside, to what looked to be a garden behind the cabin. At least the soil was turned over, sorta. There was a row of stakes he assumed were for beans and the barest beginnings of something green that might be cabbage. There were even five stalks of corn, less than a foot tall, but corn nevertheless. Not bad.

Hunkering down, Ethan grabbed up a handful of dirt. Dry, and not more than six inches had been dug down. "Hell, this shouldn't work." He was talking to himself again. This was Wyoming soil, hard as clay, not fit for anything but buffalo and cattle and now sheep. Why the devil hadn't her husband plowed deeper?

He looked over the small square patch again and realized that this wasn't done with a plow. This was done with a shovel. He could see the marks in the earth.

Standing, he released the dirt he'd been holding. The breeze carried the dry soil away. He'd bet dollars to doughnuts that the woman had done this. That's why it wasn't turned deeper. He could almost imagine her out here, alone, back bent over a shovel, trying to force the blade into the earth. Tough work. Tough woman, he amended with a touch of admiration.

Truth be told, the place was well situated. There was a stream nearby, and if some of that horse manure that was piled up behind the barn was mulched into the ground…

Wilder, what are you doing? You're not here to fix up. You're here to tear down.

He tugged on the brim of his hat. That was true. He was here to tear down, tear down all her work, her home, not that she knew it. No, she was trusting him to help her.

Maybe it was growing up in an orphanage, never having a home of his own that had him feeling like a low-life cur dog.

Hey, wait a minute, he told himself, *this is business, not thievery, and he wasn't going to feel guilty or ashamed. Business, pure and simple.*

Ethan straightened and started back toward the cabin. She must be done changing by now. He'd make some food. See if he could rustle up some cold remedies. Tomorrow he'd tell her his business and be on his way.

Yup, that sounded fine.

He was cutting a tight corner on the shady side of the cabin when something snagged his trousers. "Ouch," he muttered, rubbing his leg through the denim as he looked to see what had stuck him.

It was a plant in a tin washtub, hardly noticeable in the shadows. He looked more closely.

It was a rosebush.

Who the hell had roses out here? No one. They couldn't take the summers or the winters and yet here one was, looking pretty pitiful but hanging on. A few leaves and the barest start of a red bud.

He touched it, careful not to get snagged on those thorns again.

"A rosebush," he said aloud, his thoughts going instantly to the woman. A smile threatened. Roses and Molly Murphy. A perfect combination of thorns and silken beauty.

Wilder, are you getting poetic on me?

He chuckled. Could be.

Without giving it much thought, he lugged a bucket of water from the creek and poured it on the rosebush feeling strangely as though he was more than helping, that he was part of her life.

He looked at the empty bucket and in the general direction of her garden. Next thing he knew he was hauling more water, soaking the beans and cabbage and corn. The more water he hauled the more he smiled.

Crazy, Wilder. Pure and simple crazy.

Yeah, but what else could he do? He'd said he'd help her and that was what he was doing.

Putting the bucket down by the side of the house, he headed for the cabin door.

Molly was sitting on the side of the bed trying to understand what she'd done.

It was crazy.

It was necessary.

The voice of caution drew her attention to the rifle that was propped by the doorway. Thinking good sense was the better part of valor, she did retrieve it for all her telling him she didn't need it. A few steps there and back and she slid the Henry under the bed—for safekeeping.

"Aren't you gonna change?" Katie stood by the head of the bed like a lady-in-waiting as Molly settled on the rope-strung bed again.

She reached for the nightgown. The thought of lying down was getting more and more appealing.

"Honey, go look out the window and see if you can see Mr. Wilder out there." She was already undoing the dozen or so buttons down the front of her blouse.

Katie scampered away, and the blanket flap settled quickly to the floor in her wake so that when Katie pulled the door open Molly wasn't blinded by the light. She stared at the blankets, her hand gliding lightly down the worn wool. It was a nice thing for him to do. A thoughtful thing. She appreciated it…and him.

"No, I don't. Maybe he's in the barn. You want I should get him?" Katie asked.

"No!"

Katie hurried back to Molly, giggling as she ducked under the blanket again. "This is fun," she told Molly. "Like playing Indian."

"I'm glad you're having a good time." Molly pulled the nightgown over her head and then undressed inside it like a tent, feeling less...exposed. "Now, I'm gonna rest for a little while and you play and be a good girl for Mr. Wilder. He's gonna take care of you while I'm sleeping. Okay?"

"Are you gonna be sick for long, Mama?" she asked, tossing the hair back from her face.

"No, not long," Molly said as much for herself as the child.

Please, Lord, let it be so.

She heard a knock on the door an instant before it opened.

"Okay to come in?" Ethan spoke to the blanket wall.

She couldn't see his face, which meant he couldn't see her, either. "Yes," she answered. She slid under the covers, the coarse muslin sheet cold and rough against her overly sensitive skin.

"Is the kid, ah, Katie, still there with you?"

Katie's head came out between the blankets. "I'm here, Mr. Ethan."

He smiled. He'd never spent much time with kids but he was getting to like this one. "Well, why don't you come on out of there and show me around the kitchen?" He hooked his hat on one of the chairs, and walked the five steps to the cupboard area. Katie scrambled up behind him.

"Whatcha gonna make?" she asked eagerly.

He spoke loudly so that the woman, Molly, could hear him. "Well, I don't know." He started opening and closing doors. The cupboards were pitifully bare. There was half a sack of flour and about the same amount of coffee and lard. There was cornmeal mush, a large piece of salted ham covered by a towel, a white sack of beans, two jars of tomatoes, a can of Coleman's mustard, some dried apples, salt, pepper and green tea.

"You got any honey?" he called to her.

"No," Katie and Molly answered almost in unison.

More softly to the child he said, "How about sugar?"

"No." She shook her head, her blond hair flying around her face. "We got molasses. Will that help?" She pointed to the other cupboard which did indeed hold a tan ceramic jug of molasses and a few strips of dried beef.

Well, he had sugar in his saddlebags. Okay, it was a weakness. He'd never learned to drink his coffee black—and like it.

He was thinking about making some sort of tea for Molly. Honey was soothing to the throat, but maybe the hot liquid would be enough. He could try a little molasses in it. He never liked the taste but most folks did.

"How about some tea?" he called to the woman. "Might help warm you up and ease your throat a bit."

"Sounds nice," came her less than enthusiastic reply.

Ethan turned to Katie. "Okay, kid, here's what we're going to do. I'm going to start some water boiling for tea, then cut some of this ham, make some biscuits and eggs. There are eggs, aren't there?" he asked, remembering the chickens.

Katie screwed up her face. "I don't know."

"Well, go look."

"Mama doesn't let me get the eggs." Her face was all frustrated.

"Why not?"

"She says I break 'em and we can't sell broke eggs."

Ethan chuckled. It made sense but right now selling eggs wasn't his top priority. "Are you afraid of the chickens?"

"Naw, they don't scare me." Katie puffed out her chest.

"Good, then you check to see if there's eggs while I go get some water from the stream. Okay?"

"Okay." Katie grabbed a small basket from the counter and rushed for the door. Ethan picked up the nearly empty water bucket and followed.

"We'll be back in a minute," he told Molly.

"Okay."

Ten minutes later he had water boiling. Katie had indeed retrieved five eggs and hadn't broken one. Ethan was appropriately congratulatory. With the kid's aid, he got the lunch going, ham frying, biscuits baking and finally the eggs frying. He was no fancy cook, but he knew enough to stay alive on the trail.

He brewed a pot of green tea and put a big spoon of molasses in it, then stirred.

Molly slipped lower in the covers, the flannel warm but the sheet cold against her bare feet. A cough rattled around in her chest and the inside of her nose burned. With all that, the only thing she was thinking about was a man in her kitchen making tea for her. A man was taking care of her. Odder yet, she was letting him.

Her head kept spinning and she closed her eyes against the motion and throbbing in her temples. A cough. Then another. She rolled onto her side. Her eyes drifted closed.

Ethan tasted the tea and made a face, which made Katie laugh. "I hope your mother likes molasses." With that he started toward the blanket-draped bed.

"She does," Katie confirmed, and again he noticed the kid's missing bottom tooth.

"When'd you lose the tooth?" He walked to the bed where Molly was resting. His spurs jingled and left light scratches in the rough pine planks.

"Yesterday. You wanna see it?"

"Uh, yeah, sure, I guess." He stopped at the blanket and without looking over said, "Ma'am?"

No answer.

Cautiously he peered over the top. She was asleep. Her hair fell across her cheek and he could tell by the shape of the quilt that she had her knees drawn up as if she were cold. He wanted to touch her face, to check, to help somehow. He decided against it.

Putting the steaming tea down on the table, he sat down. "Katie," he said softly, "your mother's asleep so we'll eat quietly, then we'll go outside. Okay?''

"Okay, Mr. Ethan," Katie responded enthusiastically, then, as though she'd realized what she'd done, she repeated herself more softly. "Okay, Mr. Ethan. I can be as quiet as an Indian."

"Please don't even mention Indians. That's all I need right about now." The Sioux were raiding north of here. He helped Katie get settled in her chair.

"Can we play a game after lunch?"

"How about you show me your tooth?" He didn't care about teeth but games weren't his strong suit unless there were cards involved.

Katie's eyes brightened. "Okay." She gobbled lunch like a cowhand fresh in from the range. Ethan was enjoying the last of his biscuit when she jumped up and started pulling him outside.

Licking his fingers, he went along. "Where are we going?"

"To my secret place."

"Secret, huh?" Kids were always stashing some useless thing somewhere and expecting adults to get all excited. So, okay, he figured he could make an appropriate fuss.

Outside those thunderheads still looked threatening. The day was gray and ominous. He'd have to remember to get the horses inside soon. And there was the wagon.

The list kept growing.

Right now he was about to be treated to the revelation of Katie's secret place, which turned out to be near the stream. A piece of folded red flannel that was kept in a scraped out spot covered by a rock was her version of a Wells Fargo safe.

Katie made a big show of sitting Indian style on the ground and motioning for Ethan to sit opposite her and do the same. The wind stirred the leaves of the cottonwood trees, making a sort of clatter. The stream gurgled and tumbled over the small rocks that dotted the bottom, creating little waterfalls and whirlpools.

Ceremoniously, Katie unfolded the cloth one corner at a time until the contents were revealed.

"See here, this is my tooth." She held the white enamel square out for him to inspect, which Ethan did with what he hoped was great solemnity.

"Nice," he said, handing it back to her. "But why didn't you put it under your pillow for the tooth fairy?"

Katie cocked her head to one side, her little mouth drawn up in a serious expression. "What's a tooth fairy?"

Uh-oh. Now he'd done it.

"Well, the tooth fairy comes at night after you're asleep and puts a penny under your pillow." At least that was the story the nuns at the orphanage had told him. Why hadn't someone told her about it?

"Why'd the fairy do that?" Katie's face looked very serious, her eyes bored into his.

"Ah." He rubbed his beard-stubbled chin. "Because the fairy takes the teeth back to…ah…to…ah… heaven, yes, that's it, back to heaven so that they can be used again for some other little girl or boy."

Katie's eyes narrowed as she looked at the tooth

in her hand, then at Ethan, then the tooth again. "How come I never heard 'bout this before?"

"Don't know." Ethan lied as the realization came to him. *Maybe because your mother doesn't have the penny to spare.* "What else have you got there that you're saving?"

Katie put the tooth back in the flannel. "This is my favorite rock." She held it up to him. "See how the colors are so pretty? When you wet it it shines really nice."

"I'll bet it does."

"You wanna see?" Katie was already dashing for the creek edge.

"Be careful." The creek was only ten feet wide but pretty deep and running fast from the spring melt in the mountains.

"I do this all the time."

Katie dipped the rock in the water. "See," she announced, beaming. "See the colors?"

"I sure do. Let's look at it over here." He'd feel better if he got her away from the stream. Standing there, looking at the rock, his mind instantly flashed back fifteen years. He'd had a secret stash filled with odd bits of treasure he'd collected. His was kept in a handkerchief that he'd stuffed behind a loose brick in the chimney of Saint Anne's.

He wondered if it was still there, since he hadn't bothered to retrieve it the day he'd left. An odd feeling moved through him, nostalgia perhaps, sadness for sure. Anger, too.

"Mr. Ethan? Mr. Ethan?"

He realized the kid was talking to him. "Yeah."

"I also got a penknife, but it's broke and don't open so good."

He gave it a cursory once-over. The metal blade was rusted and the wooden case was cracked. "Maybe we can fix it." Assuming he could even get the blade open.

"You think?"

He gave a one-shoulder shrug. "We'll see a little later."

"And I got this." She held up a piece of jewelry. A few blue beads and a metal cross.

He knew what it was instantly. "Where'd you get the rosary?" He'd spent a lot of hours on his knees saying prayers, usually in penance for some transgression—everything from missing mass to missing his work assignment.

Ethan had made a lot of transgressions so he knew his rosary well, not that he said it anymore. Oh, he believed. He just believed in himself and Billy and cold hard determination more. That's another thing war will do to a man.

"I got the beads from my mama," she shouted over her shoulder as she darted on ahead after a big yellow butterfly. "Come back here, you!"

Her laughter carried on the increasing breeze. The sky turned darker with every passing minute and there was no longer any doubt that it was going to rain, just how soon. The child disappeared around the side of the cabin and Ethan smiled. Quite a bundle of energy. If he could harness that energy he could run a dozen trains without steam.

Yup, quite a kid. The wind picked up and swirled dust in his face so that he had to turn his back for relief. Standing there, looking at the pitiful excuse for a ranch, well, this was sure as hell not the way he envisioned things going. Who'd've figured a hard case like him would get all tangled up with a kid and a woman. All he wanted was his land, yeah, *his* land, and he was outta here.

Of course, he hadn't counted on the woman's being sick. Or, most especially, the fire in her hair.

Chapter Four

This day was never going to end. It was barely after lunch and the girl was running him more ragged than any crew of rail layers. At this rate he'd never make it to dinner. It was time for a little action, he decided.

"Hey, Katie, what say you give me a hand bringing back the wagon?"

The kid appeared from around the side of the house. "Really?"

She looked skeptical, her hair falling wildly across her face. "Can we ride your horse?"

"Yeah. We'll ride him."

"Ride the horse" seemed to be the deciding factor, which was pretty much what he'd figured.

Ethan was still watching that ever darkening sky. He hoped it held off until they got back.

In the corral, he saddled Four and plunked Katie in the saddle. Ethan knew he could trust Four not to move, and this way he would also know exactly where she was.

A few more minutes and he had the team hooked

to a lead, had borrowed a bottom rail from the corral to use as a drag, and was about to swing up behind Katie. Just then he realized he'd better tell the woman what was up. There was that temper of hers to consider. A hint of a smile quirked the right side of his mouth. He liked fiery women.

"Ma'am?" He spoke in a hushed voice as he entered the cabin in case she was asleep. Evidently she was, because she didn't answer, so he scrawled a note—penmanship never being one of the things he excelled at—and left it propped against the lamp on the table.

It took them about twenty minutes to reach the wagon, Katie bouncing up and down in the saddle the entire time. Wind swirled and stirred the dusty road. Ethan had to settle his hat a little tighter on his head.

Once at the wagon site, Ethan used the wagon jacks to prop up the rear end. He removed the broken wheel and lashed the corral rail to the hub. It was hard work but he didn't mind. In fact, he was glad to be doing something. It kept his mind off other confusing thoughts.

"Okay," he said to Katie when he was finished. "You and I will sit up here and drive."

"But I wanna ride Four some more." She flounced around in the seat, her arms folded tightly across her chest.

"You can, but not now." He didn't wait for her to agree. This was one time he was in charge. The girl decided to sulk, so jaw clenched, arms crossed and feet swinging faster than the horses were walking, they headed back.

The wagon creaked and groaned all the way and Ethan kept a close eye on that drag. If the damned thing broke he'd really be up the creek.

Fortunately, the fates were with him and, about an hour later, he pulled turtle-slow into the yard and stopped near the entrance to the barn so that he wouldn't have to walk so far between tools and wagon.

Ethan jumped down first, then held out his hands to Katie, who hurled herself at him as if she were flying.

The sky left no question of the fast approaching storm. Ethan put the horses up in the barn. There were no stalls so he tied each to a peg or post near the back wall, whatever he could find, leaving the rope long enough for them to reach the hay on the floor.

That was when he noticed that Four was favoring his front foot.

"What's the matter, boy?" Ethan asked as he lifted the horse's hoof to rest on his slightly bent knee. He clawed the compacted dirt and straw out with his hand. "I don't see anything but then it's so damned dark in here…."

There was a lantern hanging on one of the two uprights that supported the roof. He lit the wick, scraped a bare spot on the floor with his foot, and put it down. Now, examining Four's foot again, he could see there was a small stone wedged tight under the horse's hoof.

"That musta made things sore, huh, boy?"

He used his pocketknife to carefully pry the stone free. "That's better, isn't it, fella?"

He checked for damage. Bringing the lantern closer everything looked fine, as best he could tell. When he released the animal's hoof, Four stood on it squarely. That was a good sign.

"You'll be fine now, boy." Ethan gave the horse an affectionate rub on his neck. Just then light flashed bright and sudden, illuminating everything and disappearing. Four shied at the sight, as did the other horses.

"It's only lightning, not cannon fire," Ethan told his horse. "You know the difference." Four settled down as if he really had understood.

Ethan walked over to the doorway of the barn and leaned one shoulder against the frame. He watched the sky as another bolt of lightning zigzagged its way to earth in the distance. He liked storms. He liked the power and yes, the wildness of it all. He was still staring up at the sky when, out of the corner of his eye, he saw something move.

Glancing around, he spotted her, the woman, outside, struggling to close the cabin door.

"What the hell?" he muttered, thinking she might be sicker. That possibility sent him running for the little cabin which stood like a fierce citadel against the storm that soon would engulf it and the woman.

"What's wrong? What are you doing out?" he shouted as he closed on her but his words were evidently drowned out by a clap of thunder as loud and fierce as a war drum. White-edged clouds rolled and tumbled against each other as they moved east, blocking out the last bit of sunlight.

Ethan came to a halt beside her and grabbed for the doorknob she was holding on to so tightly. "Are you sicker?'' His hand covered hers for an instant. Molly pulled free of his touch and clutched her nightgown up close at her throat as though to ward off his nearness.

''Let's get you inside,'' Ethan shouted, and nudged her with his free hand. She obeyed.

He slammed the door and turned and there she was. She stood in the middle of the room looking as pale and scared as anyone he'd ever known. Her blue print nightdress flowed out around her like a tent. It could have been a fancy ball gown—she was that beautiful.

''Where's Katie?'' Molly shoved the wild length of her hair back from her face.

''Katie?'' he mumbled, trying to get his mind to focus. Ten feet away and he could still see that she was shaking. She oughta be in bed and he—his body—stirred. *Never mind that,* he commanded himself. ''Isn't she with you?'' He scanned the cabin. No luck.

Molly held up his note in her fist. ''You said she was with you!'' Her blue eyes sparked with anger.

''She *was* with me!'' He snatched off his hat and ran his hand through his hair in an agitated gesture. ''She took off after we got back.'' He slapped his hat back on his head.

''You're *supposed* to be watching her!'' Another cough. Clutching her chest, she bent over, obviously giving in to her illness. He refrained from helping her or even offering to help. The woman was so damned stubborn.

His temper was up a bit when he snapped back, ''I am watching her, dammit. Hell, do you expect me to follow the kid around like some blood-hound?'' About that time Molly coughed again and swayed, and he had to help her to sit down before she fell down.

"For God's sake, woman, go back to bed. I'll find her.''

"She's afraid of storms, of lightning!'' Another flash of white light lit up the inside of the room. The boom of thunder was close behind and that meant so was the storm. He realized by her sudden shake that Katie wasn't the only one who didn't like storms.

"Don't worry. She's around here somewhere. I'll find her.'' With that he walked out and slammed the door.

For a full minute, Molly sat there, staring at the closed door, hugging herself from cold, but mostly from fear as the thunder hammered overhead.

Katie was out there. Alone!

Her daughter was alone.

Any fear she had was outweighed by that one thought. No way was she sitting here. Barefoot, Molly ran to the door and yanked it open, the glass knob cold in her hand. The sky had turned gunmetal dark. The wind swirled in the tops of the cottonwood trees and cut through the flannel of her nightgown to chill her body beneath. She didn't care. Her child was missing. Nothing else in this life mattered.

Ethan was nowhere to be seen but she heard his voice calling Katie's name. She was thankful for him once again no matter what she'd said.

The wind came in wild, tree-bending gusts and it took both hands for her to pull the door closed. Her nightgown molded to her body and her hair streamed out along her shoulders.

"Katie!" she yelled as loud as her aching throat would let her. "Katie! Where are you?" Instinct sent her toward the barn, the earth hard and cool against her bare feet. A shiver skipped across her body and she knew it was from stark terror, not her illness.

Another bolt of lightning speared the earth, this time close but blessedly not too close. A loud bang of thunder followed. Molly saw the wagon by the barn doorway, heard the horses neighing in their own protest of the approaching storm.

She paused outside and craned her head up to the loft opening. The kittens were there and Katie loved those kittens. "Katie! Answer me!"

No answer, but, out of the corner of her eye, she saw Ethan loping in her direction. His mustache made his frown look even more serious. That meant he hadn't found Katie. Her heart sank. She'd been hoping like crazy that he'd come waltzing in with Katie in tow. She wouldn't even have minded an "I told you so."

As he approached, wind tugged at his shirt and jeans and he had to hold on to his hat to keep it from blowing away.

"I thought you were going back to bed."

"Not while Katie's missing!"

A small, shrill scream carried on the wind, and both Molly and Ethan turned at the same time. Black smoke boiled out of the doorway of the loft and there, silhouetted in the hay-stacked loft opening, was Katie.

Everything else forgotten, they both rushed the last few yards to the barn.

"Mama!" Katie called, waving a hand in front of her face in an obvious effort to clear the smoke away. "Mama, there's a fire. I can't get down."

Molly's hand flew to her chest. "Oh, my Lord, Katie."

Ethan stared at the barn. Fire. His brain kept repeating the word. But how? There'd been no lightning strikes here. Another thought flashed in his mind but was quickly gone. It didn't matter. The barn was on fire and Katie was trapped, in danger of dying. No. Not dying—not if he had anything to do with it.

"Mama, help me. I'm afraid!"

Molly made a dash for the doorway.

Ethan grabbed her arm and brought her up short. "Where do you think you're going?"

"In there," she snapped, yanking free of his grasp.

"Oh, no you're not."

"Oh, yes—"

"I am. You stay here." No way was he letting her go in there. He'd lose them both, and that was something he couldn't think about.

So instead, he pulled off his bandanna, ran to the horse trough and dipped it in water, then tied it masklike around his face. He shoved his hat in Molly's hand as he went past. "Whatever happens, don't move," he instructed. At least he knew one of them was safe.

He gulped in one deep breath of clean air before he plunged into the smoke-filled structure.

It was as though he'd stepped into a pitch-black room. He couldn't see his hand in front of his face the smoke was so thick. The floor felt hot on his boots and ankles. He knew that small flames were devouring the thin covering of straw and about to do the same to him.

"You'll be fine, honey," he heard Molly's voice calling to her daughter. "Ethan is coming for you."

Soot filled his eyes. Blinking and wiping were no help. Okay, the ladder to the loft was on his left. Moving carefully, hands out, he inched along. He could see flames licking up the front side of the barn. This wasn't good. Not good at all. A little farther and he should be at the ladder. But the smoke got thicker than day-old coffee and breathing was more than an effort, it was impossible. His throat closed as though he were strangling.

He couldn't see, couldn't breathe.

"Dammit to hell."

Reluctantly, he staggered out of the barn and fell to his knees while he struggled to catch his breath.

Molly was instantly there beside him, kneeling in the dirt. "Katie? Did you see Katie?"

Ethan shook his head. He was busy trying to wipe the soot out of his eyes with his bandanna.

When he looked up from the cloth he looked straight into her eyes, blue, tear-filled eyes. Eyes that were trouble any way he sliced it.

"Are you all right?" she asked quietly, taking the bandana from his hand and wiping his face for him.

It felt good having someone fuss after him. He forced the barest trace of a smile. "I'm okay but it's bad in there."

Ethan got to his feet and helped Molly up. He gave her hand an extra squeeze as if to say, "Don't give up yet."

"Mama!" Katie called again from her place in the loft opening, and Molly's gaze was immediately fixed on the child.

"Stay there, honey," Molly told her slipping her hand free of his. "It'll be just a minute and we'll have you out."

She looked at him a long moment, her eyes searching his face as though to make him understand something she couldn't say. Wordlessly, she started past him again. This time it was his words that stopped her.

Ethan understood and yet he couldn't let her give up her own life and probably lose the little girl, as well. "Don't even try it." He coughed. "The smoke is so thick you couldn't find an elephant in there."

"I have to," she said in a tone that was eerily quiet.

Looking at her, his gut clenched. "Molly. Please don't do this. Give me another chance."

She was shaking her head. "Don't worry, Katie. I'm coming."

"Please," he said. "Please. Let me go around. I need a tool, a rope, something to use so I can reach her."

Molly glanced up at Katie still in the loft opening. Still safe. But for how much longer?

Struggling to breathe, he ran full out to the back of the barn and came face-to-face with a solid wall. Where the hell were the goddamn doors?

"Stupid! Stupid!" he cursed himself six ways to

Sunday. He had known there was no door back here. That son of a bitch husband of hers had taken the easy way out...and the cheap way. Now it was liable to cost his daughter's life.

Ethan kicked at the boards and pried at them until his fingertips were bloody. Hardly a budge. He could hear Katie's voice calling to her mother and though he couldn't hear the words, he didn't have to.

Do something.

Do something!

He scoured the area and found a broken axe head with a portion of the splintered handle still in place. He rushed back to the barn and using the chipped edge of the blade he managed to get one board loose. Soon he had six free.

Smoke poured out of the opening like water out of a damn. Forgetting to use his handkerchief, Ethan plunged in. He freed the horses and sent them out through the opening. He tossed his gear out then he searched around for the rope he'd seen earlier.

His hand found it before his eyes could see.

"Ouch! Son of a bitch!" He jerked his hand away.

The rope was on fire. Okay, there was nothing for it but to find another way and he didn't have much time. That was when he spotted the lantern or the dimmest outline of it. He knew. It hadn't been lightning that had started this fire. It had been him. Ethan Wilder. He cursed himself every way he knew and he knew a lot.

Stupid! Stupid!

Now a kid's life was at stake.

Wilder, you better make this come out right or die trying.

Inching along, he worked his way to the front of the barn. This time he found the ladder. It was on fire. Still he stepped on the lowest rung on the off chance it hadn't burned through yet.

It had. The wood gave way with a sharp crack.

Smoke filtered into his lungs with every breath. ''Katie?'' he called.

''Yes.''

He heard her high, frightened voice but didn't see her.

''Stay over near the opening, okay?'' He coughed. ''Don't try to come down the ladder.''

''But I'm scared, Mr. Ethan.''

''I know, but it'll be all right.'' He hoped like hell he wasn't lying.

Carefully, he retraced his steps until he cleared the barn.

Molly rushed to him, grabbing his arm. ''Are you all right? Katie?''

Ethan bent over, his hands braced on his knees as he tried to catch his breath. ''She…'' He coughed. Slowly, he straightened. He said the words she most didn't want to hear. ''I couldn't get to her.''

Molly's eyes were frantic. Her color winter white. For what seemed like the longest minute in the world she just stared at him. Her eyes searched his face as though she wanted him to say this was all a joke, a bad dream. He couldn't.

Then she made a bolt for the barn and once more he stopped her. This time she fought back. She kicked and punched and clawed the side of his face.

"Let me go! My daughter's in there! Let me go!"

Her eyes filled with tears and Ethan pulled her into his embrace for just a second, just a heartbeat. Then he grabbed her by the shoulders and held her slightly away from him.

"We'll get her out," he said fiercely, head lowered so that he looked at her eye to eye. "We'll get her out."

Overhead, lightning and thunder competed for ownership of the sky.

He had one last idea. He leapt into the wagon. The wood creaked as his boots made a loud thud. Lightning sizzled overhead. The hair on his arms prickled with electricity. His heart raced in his chest, but not from the storm, from dread.

"All right, Katie," he said, trying to mimic Molly's calm tone. "I'm here. You're fine."

"Mama! Mama!" was the kid's only reply.

"Don't look at her!" Ethan demanded, muscles tensing in his back and arms. "Look at me!" It was an order, sharply given.

Slowly she complied, as though seeing him for the first time. "Help me, Mr. Ethan," she cried, and he could see where the tears had smudged the soot on her face.

The wind picked up. The flames were now clearly visible. Orange-and-red flames dancing to their own unique tune, closer, closer to their prey. The scent of burning wood and hay was pungent in the air. The sky was nearly black. Clouds rolled and tumbled and slammed together with a force that produced more lightning.

Feet braced, the wind whipping at his shirt and

hat, Ethan shouted up to the child. "I want you to jump."

Katie stopped stock-still and looked down at him as if he'd spoken in a foreign tongue.

"Come on, Katie." He held out his arms. "You remember how good I caught you when you jumped off the wagon."

There was a slight nod.

Molly was right behind him on the ground. "What are you doing? You can't—"

He spared her a glance. "I'd better. It's the only chance she's got."

"I'm afraid, Mr. Ethan."

Flames were getting dangerously close to her, licking at the top of the door frame.

"Jump, sweetie," Molly encouraged. "You know how you love to slide and pretend to fly. This'll be like flying."

That seemed to intrigue her and she inched closer to the edge looking down. "Okay," she said in a less than enthusiastic voice.

Ethan held out his arms.

She closed her eyes but didn't move. Then she did something Ethan hadn't counted on. She disappeared back inside the burning barn.

"Katie!" Molly and Ethan screamed at the same time.

Just as suddenly as she'd gone, Katie appeared at the opening, this time with her skirt pulled up in front of her. The wind swirled and twisted through the barn, making the smoke billow out the front until Katie almost disappeared from view.

Then, miracle of miracles, the kid moved closer to the edge. He'd say a prayer tonight!

Head and neck craned back, feet braced, he was ready to move in either direction. He couldn't miss her. He wouldn't.

"Now, Katie," Molly hollered, and Ethan could hear the strain in her voice, from the cold and from sheer terror.

Small flames scampered around the edge of the opening. As they fed on the wood, the flames would become bigger and bigger until the opening would be blocked.

Suddenly a bolt of lightning slammed into one of the cottonwood trees near the creek. The tree split and fell apart, one half falling into the stream and the other side crashing home on the bank.

Katie's eyes flew open and she jumped.

"Ohhh!" she screamed as she sailed toward Ethan.

A couple of long desperate steps and he was able to catch her. The impact sent him sprawling on the wagon floor. Lord knows how, but he managed to keep Katie balanced on top of him.

"Katie, sweetie," Molly called over the edge of the wagon. Her hand reached out for her daughter and the grin on her face was like a kid's on Christmas morning.

Ethan breathed a very deep sigh of relief when something sharp, like a couple of dozen straight pins, penetrated his shirt and dug into the skin across his stomach.

"What the hell?" he muttered and as he lifted Katie to her feet he saw that he was looking straight into the eyes of a cat, a teeth-baring, claws full out, take-no-prisoners mother cat and all her kittens.

"Is this what you went back for?" He pried the cat loose, refrained from a brief impulse to send the animal flying in the direction of the stream and instead unceremoniously tossed it over the side. Of all the damned fool things. "Do you know you coulda died?"

She looked at him and at the cat who sat grooming herself on the ground and then at her mother.

Ethan saw it coming about two seconds before it hit. Tears. Lots of tears. A damned raging torrent by the time they reached her eyes. Oh, yes, there were sobs. Great big sobs. Here he was, going out of his mind trying to save her, and she was worried about some damned cats.

Females. All the same. He got to his feet, his boots making scuffing noises on the planks. He was covered with soot from head to toe. His boots were singed around the edges and so were his pant legs. Then there was his burned hand.

By this time Molly was crying, too. Great. Just great. Why were women always crying when things went well?

Molly helped Katie over the side of the wagon. Ethan aided a bit.

"I had to save Queenie, Mama. I had to," the kid said with a pouting face that could win a prize. Who the hell cared about some damned cat when a person's life was at stake? Life was what mattered. Staying alive had become his prayer during the war. When he looked down, mother and daughter were in each other's arms. Crying. Laughing. Hugging. Just like that, any anger he'd felt vanished.

"I know honey, I know." Molly hugged the little girl tight, really tight. Oh Lord, no one ever felt so good. The child's face was blackened from the smoke and there in her arms, Molly could feel her shaking. "You're fine now." She got down on both knees. Tears streamed down her cheeks. "I was so scared." She managed a shaky smile. She couldn't stop touching her daughter. "What would I do without you? I love you."

"I love you too, Mama."

Still hugging Katie, Molly looked up at him. "Thank you." Her voice was ripe with emotion and it tore at him like an unexpected kiss.

"I'm glad I helped." He jumped down from the wagon bed. It was all he could say, considering he was the one who'd set the barn on fire. Now she'd never understand why he was here. Yet if he hadn't been…

Katie suddenly turned and barreled into him, hugging his legs. "I love you too, Mr. Ethan."

Oh, great, he thought. The guilt inside him turned into something the size of Pike's Peak. Things were going from bad to worse. First he'd lied to the mother and now he'd almost killed the kid.

Okay, he forced a smile, like a kid who's being praised for cheating on his test paper. Lightly, he stroked the top of Katie's head with his good hand. "You're not hurt, are you? Not burned?" His voice was a husky whisper.

She shook her head as she spoke. "I was really scared. Jumping was *really* scary." She hugged him again. "You saved me, Mr. Ethan. That's why I love you." She hugged him tighter and pressed her face against his denim-covered thigh.

She loved him. He was touched, genuinely touched. He liked the kid, though he figured all this love would last until they found out his real purpose for being there. It was a purpose he wasn't in quite such a hurry to tell them now that he'd gotten to know them both.

Looking at the woman, he selfishly decided this was not the time to tell her anything. No, instead he was thinking that he'd never seen any woman more beautiful than Molly Murphy at that precise instant. Her hair blew free and wild, back from her face. Her nightgown clung to her body, outlining every curve from her full breasts to her flat belly to her long legs. He knew that he'd carry her image with him all the rest of his life.

"Molly? You okay?" he asked gently.

At the sound of his voice, Molly's head came up. Their eyes met and held in a look of understanding, of relief, of something else she didn't know how to name.

Thank you, God, was her first thought. *Thank you for sending me Ethan,* was her second.

Chapter Five

There he stood, Katie clinging to his legs, covered in soot from head to toe. His mustache disappeared into the blackness that coated him. He looked awful. Awful yet wonderful, and without thinking or caring she walked to him. She needed to touch him to make sure he was all right but words like *marriage, vows, commitment,* circled in her head and she came up short, even though she was starting to believe Jack was never coming back.

"Are you...?" She stopped inches in front of him. The hem of her nightgown brushed the tops of his sooty boots.

But she was held by his gaze. Soft and inviting, as though he had the answers to questions she had yet to ask. Surely no man had ever looked at a woman so and made her feel the sudden heady warmth that surged through her.

"I'm okay," he said matter-of-factly. "Just burned my hand a bit is all."

He held it out for her to see and that need to touch

him drumming inside her in an ancient rhythm made her cup his injured hand in hers.

She noticed his flesh was warm and his fingers long and tapered, before making herself focus strictly on his injury.

"This looks bad." She tipped his hand this way and that. Lightning and thunder shook the sky above them but they seemed lost in a world that didn't include such things.

"I've had worse things happen."

She wondered briefly what he meant by that and glanced at the small scar over his right eye. "Let's get you in the house. We need to get a bandage and some salve on that hand."

At the sound of a sudden snap of wood, they both turned at once. The front side of the barn was fully engulfed by flames. Though the roof showed no sign of fire, if the walls went, then...

"I'm sorry," he muttered, his gaze fixed on the building.

"Thanks," she said, still cupping his hand in hers. Touching him seemed to give her strength and comfort at the same time. It was silly but true. "I just can't imagine how it got started. I mean, it wasn't struck by lightning—that I would have heard—but somehow..." She shook her head in wonder. Another cough punctuated her words.

A crack of lightning sliced through the air, followed by a clap of thunder. Then, the sky opened up like a torrent. Drops hit the ground and splashed up against her nightgown and his pants, big drops, huge drops, like pebbles in a pond.

"Rain!" shouted Ethan. Grinning, he repeated himself, "Rain!"

Molly stood by, staring at the barn, and then the sky and then the man, this incredible man dancing in her yard.

"Rain!" he shouted again. "It'll put the fire out. It'll save some of the barn at least."

Without warning he grabbed her around the waist and lifted her into the air, spinning around as he did. "Rain! I love rain!" he kept repeating, thinking somehow he was saved…maybe.

"Stop!" she ordered even as she smiled and buried her face against the side of his neck. She clung to him, her arms wrapped tight around his shoulders as the rain soaked their clothes. It felt so good to be held, to be cared for.

Suddenly, Ethan was very aware of her body pressed against his. He was very aware of what he was doing and what he shouldn't be doing. Unfortunately they were the same thing. Right this second he didn't care about right and wrong, only about how good she made him feel.

"Mr. Ethan. Mr. Ethan." Katie tugged on his pant leg. "Swing me next."

Ethan lowered Molly to the ground, her face craned up to his. Water, like diamonds, beaded on her lashes and in her hair. All he could do was stand there and look at her. Lord, she was beautiful, and that beauty soaked like the rain into his mind and senses and heart.

Then she coughed. A long racking cough that doubled her over. This time he *was* thinking when he said, "Let's get both of you into the cabin. Right now."

She held his gaze a fraction of a second longer. It was a look filled with questions and longing. Oh, yes, longing. He knew it because he was feeling the exact same thing. Abruptly, she turned and walked away. He wanted to go after her, to tell her, to ask her—

Katie's voice interrupted his thoughts. He looked down at the little girl who'd come so close to dying and now danced playfully around him, her earlier trauma evidently forgotten. "What about me? Aren't you gonna swing me?"

"Uh, sure."

Yet Ethan's eyes were fixed on Molly even as he scooped Katie up under the arms and twirled her around once, being careful of his burned hand.

An earsplitting crash of thunder sent them both running for the cabin. Katie darted ahead while Ethan followed more slowly, his mind on Molly and the intimate moments they had just shared. Rain saturated his shirt and his skin beneath, making him shiver. At least he thought it was the rain.

Katie barreled inside, leaving the door open for Ethan. Rain poured off the brim of his hat. Mud caked the bottom and sides of his boots. He hesitated in the doorway. Those nuns had drummed good manners into him with a firm hand appropriately placed.

Molly glanced up. "What are you waiting for?"

"I'm a mess," he returned, motioning down his front as though to confirm his statement.

Molly shook her head. "For heaven's sake, I'm

not worried about a little mud—not after what you just did.''

Their gazes found each other across the room. Soft gazes. Inviting gazes.

Ethan took a step, then another. He wasn't sure if it was toward her or away from the storm. Three steps inside he stopped. Rain still dribbled off the edge of his hat. His shirt was wet through, as were his trousers. At least his boots were dry inside.

''Close the door, will you?'' she asked.

''What? Oh, sorry.'' He obliged.

So there Ethan stood, feeling awkward and tense, not knowing what to do now. Rain pounded on the roof like the drumbeats of a walking charge. A quick glance through the window and he could see the rain coming down so heavily it blurred his vision of the trees and the road beyond.

There was a long silence.

Katie sneezed. One of those not-bothering-to-cover-her-nose sneezes that kids are so famous for, followed by wiping that same nose on her sleeve.

The sound propelled Molly into action.

''Katie Louise, you're going to catch your death.'' She crossed to where the little girl sat on the end of her bed. ''Let's get you out of these things right—''

Molly coughed and sneezed, and coughed again.

From his place near the door, Ethan could see that Molly was just as wet—wetter.

''Hey,'' he spoke up. ''I think both of you are going to catch your deaths. First of all it's freezing in here. Where's the wood?''

He was already walking in the direction of the

kitchen stove. His clothes dripped and his boots made muddy marks with each step.

"It's got a couple of logs," Molly told him as she continued to undress Katie. "I forgot to fill it today. I was—"

"You were sick is what you were," Ethan interrupted her words. "Still are. Where's the wood?"

"Outside. Next to the house under the overhang."

He put one log in the stove and waited until the flame took hold. Funny how fire could be a friend or an enemy...sort of like people.

With that, Ethan tugged on the brim on his hat as he headed out the door. By the time he'd gone a couple of steps he was soaked even more, if that was possible. He was used to the hard life but he always hated to be wet. He'd forded too many rivers in the war, he supposed, or slept in too many rain-filled ditches praying.

Lightning flashed overhead and he spared it only the barest of notice. The wood was wet but not soaked through. He gathered as many pieces as he could carry, wedged from chin to extended arm. Balancing the pile, he strode back to the cabin, not bothering to knock.

"You all right?" Molly queried as he crossed the room and dumped the wood into the box.

"Sure." *For a drowned rat,* he thought but didn't say. He tossed his hat on the counter. "It's raining cats and dogs out there. The good news is, the fire is out."

"Really? How bad is the barn?"

"We'll be able to tell better when we get a closer

look.'' The front was mostly gone…he couldn't tell about the rest.

''Am not.'' Katie's voice interrupted his thoughts.

''Are too,'' Molly countered.

''Not,'' Katie returned.

''What's the trouble?'' Water pooled around his pant legs and dripped off his elbows and cuffs.

''There seems to be—'' Molly pulled Katie's camisole over her head and dropped it on the floor next to her dress ''—some refusal to take a bath.''

''Am not,'' Katie piped up as though to confirm her steadfastness.

Well, this test of wills seemed to be getting nowhere fast, so Ethan did what came naturally. He took charge. *''Stop!''*

''What?'' they both said in unison.

''You heard me. I said 'Stop!' ''

''But—'' Molly tried to protest but he stopped her with an upheld hand.

''This is what we are going to do. Crazy as it sounds with this storm going on, there's not enough water for baths here in the bucket. Waiting for several to fill will take way too long and I'm *not* going to the stream and back to haul water.

''So I *suggest* we boil half the water and give Katie a sponge bath. In the meantime, Molly, you need to dry off and change nightgowns before your cold gets any worse.''

Molly came slowly to her feet and faced him straight on in that stubborn way of hers he'd come to know so quickly. ''Have you got any *orders* for dinner?''

''As a matter of fact, I do. I put beans on to soak

this morning and while I'd normally let 'em soak overnight, well, I think if I bring them to a boil for a while they'll do.''

Leaning back against the counter edge, he crossed his feet at the ankles. "Got any better suggestions?''

Molly stared him, this man, this hero who'd saved her child, nursed her through her illness and had been a godsend. He was soot-covered and rain-soaked. She'd seen hounds that looked better. Still leaning up against her counter he seemed to be right at home, in her home…their home. No. That was wrong.

"I have no objections," she said softly and surprised them both.

Two hours later, Katie had been bathed and dressed in her summer nightgown, then wrapped in a blanket from the rope partition like an Indian squaw. Molly had done the same. All of them had eaten a filling bean soup and the two ladies were seated a few feet away from the stove, which Ethan kept feeding with logs periodically.

Ethan had stayed in his clothes since he had nothing to change into.

"Mama, do you think the cats are all right?'' Katie asked.

"Yes, they're fine,'' she replied, and spared a brief gaze up at Ethan who was obviously struggling to hold his tongue.

Outside the storm raged on.

Dinner dishes were cleared. That meant Ethan dumped them all in the sink for tomorrow. The heat coming off the stove was just the right temperature, as though he had some way of controlling it.

Or maybe it was just him. In either case it felt damned good.

"You warm enough?" he asked both Molly and Katie, who were perched on chairs behind him, their blankets pulled tightly around them so that only their faces, their adorable faces, showed.

A smile tugged at the corner of his mouth.

"I'm warm," they said in near unison.

Ethan stirred the wood in the stove, then dragged a chair over and sat down next to Katie. "You scared the bejeebers outta me," he said, giving her thigh an affectionate pat. "Don't do that again."

Katie's blue eyes rolled up at him above the edge of the blanket. Slowly, she lowered it. "I won't," she said with great solemnity. Another bolt of lightning speared the ground nearby, followed by a resounding bang of thunder.

Before he realized what was happening, Katie scrambled out of her chair and into his filthy wet lap.

"Katie. No. I'm a mess." He tried to lift her away from him but no use. She'd managed to get her hands around his neck and was holding on for dear life.

"But the thunder scares me, Mr. Ethan, and I want you to protect me."

Finally, he gave in. "Sorry," he mumbled to Molly, referring to the blankets and the mess he was about to make of them.

There they sat silently listening to the storm outside. Katie had snuggled up to Ethan, her arms still around his neck, her legs supported behind the knees by his arms.

"Tell me a story, Mr. Ethan." Katie rolled her head back to look up at him. A small yawn escaped her lips.

"What? I don't know any stories." At least not the kind he could tell a five-year-old.

"I'll tell you a story," Molly spoke up. "Come over here to me." She reached for her. Katie squirmed tighter against Ethan.

"I want Mr. Ethan to tell me one." She tugged gently on the tip of his mustache. "You must know one story," she coaxed.

Ethan and Molly exchanged knowing glances. Sort of permission asked and permission given.

Ethan's brain was in overdrive trying like hell to come up with a story. Okay. He was gonna have to wing it.

"I know one about a little girl."

Katie yawned again then smiled contentedly. He, on the other hand, was trying to figure out what he knew about little girls. Nothing.

"Okay. Once upon a time there was a little girl. She was an, ah, witch, the most beautiful witch in the world. She had blond hair and blue eyes and her name was Katie."

"Like me!" Katie said before snuggling lower in the blanket, her eyes blinking fast in an effort to stay awake.

"She lived with her mother, the beautiful queen of their country, and they had magic powers...."

He wasn't more than halfway through when he noticed that she was sound asleep.

He gestured with his head and Molly leaned over

to take a peek. She smiled. "Poor little thing. She's had a tough day."

"I'll just put her to bed."

Clutching the blanket around her, Molly turned down Katie's bed and Ethan carefully slid her in, maneuvering the blanket free as he did. She barely roused.

As he pulled the coverlet up around her, a flash of lightning and a loud clap of thunder reminded them that the storm still raged outside. Katie stirred.

"Shh, honey," Molly said, brushing the child's forehead with a soothing hand. "Go to sleep."

Katie settled down and was soon making what could almost be called snoring noises.

Ethan chuckled.

"She's humming in her sleep," Molly told him.

"Humming, huh?" He chuckled again, and so did Molly.

"Well, it wouldn't do for a lady to snore now would it?"

"Oh, I've known a couple who did. It didn't seem to bother them any."

The instant the words were out he realized what he'd said. *Damn, Wilder, when will you learn to keep your trap shut?*

Molly was very busy looking at the floor, though she did spare him one quick glance out of the corner of her eye before she headed off in the direction of the bureau. The blanket dragged behind her like a regal train.

"I was thinking that maybe you'd like to get out of those clothes, Mr. Wilder."

Her back was to him.

"Yes, but my clothes are in my saddlebags getting soaked in the rain."

The top bureau drawer made a scraping sound as she pulled it open. "I'm sure I can find you something of my husband's for you to wear."

Her husband's? Just what he wanted—to be wearing that fool's clothes. "That's okay. I'm not very clean and—"

"That water Katie used for her sponge bath shouldn't be too dirty. You can use that to wash off."

She seemed to be intent on this...this project of hers.

He was equally intent on not obliging, though he suspected their reasons were entirely different.

"Naw. It's okay. I don't need—"

She turned around and held up a pair of faded red long underwear. "These should do."

She sorta held them in front of herself as though doing some sort of test fit. "There's no sense you spending the night wet and dirty and miserable. Is there?"

Well, she had him there. What was he going to say: "Yes." That would make a fine lot of sense.

"Uh, okay, but I'm not quite sure how we are going to work this." After all the place was one room, one small room with no walls or partitions or even a hat rack to hide behind.

"How about," Molly started, "if I simply go over by the window and wait until you say I can turn around—assuming you trust me?"

"I think if you can trust me all day, I can sure as hell trust you. Besides—" she heard the rustle of clothes as though he were taking off his shirt, "—there's not much worth looking at these days, dressed or undressed."

Molly heard the clink of his gun belt buckle and the thud of it being put down somewhere, kitchen counter, she guessed. Then his boots hit the floor with a small thud. Another metal clink and she realized he was taking off his trousers.

Molly stood there trying not to think about him, about what he was doing there a few feet behind her. Now, suddenly, she realized he was naked or perhaps he was wearing long underwear, too. But he was going to have to take those off to put on the new ones.

Naked.

There was a naked man in her cabin. Not just any man. No, this was a very special man and she couldn't help wondering what he looked like. Did he have muscles in his arms and shoulders? Yes, she decided, he did, the kind a woman could put her head against late at night when they were alone in bed. Her eyes fluttered closed. His chest would be broad, strong, the kind a woman would feel safe with.

His legs would be long and lean and corded from years in the saddle.

All in all, this was a man who would take care of a woman.

This was a man who already had.

"Just about ready." His deep voice interrupted her thoughts.

"Tell me when," she managed to say, pleased that her voice sounded so calm.

"Uh, well, this is as good as it's going to get," he said by way of telling her to turn around.

There he stood. The legs were about six inches too short and the sleeves about four. The long underwear was pulled tight across his chest so that there was a dangerous-looking tug happening at each button.

Ethan looked down at himself, laughed, then quickly covered his mouth with his hand so he wouldn't wake Katie.

"Well, Mr. Wilder, I'm sorry to inform you that you will not be on the cover of *Harper's*."

Ethan made a show of adjusting his sleeves, not that it did any good, and said, "All things considered, I'd say I'm grateful."

Molly chuckled. Since he'd been around, she chuckled a lot. Sick as she was, the man made her laugh.

"Why don't you take the quilt off my bed and wrap up in that?" she asked.

"Good idea." Barefoot, he hurried across the room, scooped up the quilt and headed back for the warmth of the stove.

Molly was already there, seated in one of the chairs they'd dragged over earlier. Ethan gave the stove a check and put another small piece of wood in.

He sat down next to Molly.

"That feels good, huh?" he said, staring at the stove.

"Good," she murmured, and he could hear her teeth chattering.

"My God. You're still cold, aren't you. Why didn't you say something?"

"Because every time I try to talk I—" She coughed and coughed. She coughed until she had to bend over. It seemed the most natural thing in the world for him to rub her back in what he hoped was a soothing gesture.

She waved him away and slowly sat up. "Thanks," she croaked, her voice still raw from coughing. Even cast in shadows as she was, he thought she looked pale except for the high color in her cheeks. Her hair, that liquid fire hair, fell seductively over one shoulder and covered her breast, hidden beneath her flannel nightgown. The collar was turned up on one side, the side she'd been sleeping on, he supposed. The buttons were done up all the way to the throat—out of habit or because he was there, he wasn't certain.

Either way, his first thought was that she was something to look at, sick and all. He couldn't help thinking that this was how she'd look in the mornings. The faint stirrings of lust brushed over nerve endings in his skin.

"Thanks." She shifted, adjusting the blanket.

Ethan felt strangely intimate. After all, they were a man and woman alone late at night in her, ah, bedroom, so that was a natural feeling, he supposed. He suddenly realized that he had nowhere to sleep tonight, no barn, no wagon, not even a dry spot under the stars. Things got a lot more tense.

"Thanks for telling her a story."

"You're welcome. I was scrambling there for a while."

"Are you going to tell me the ending?"

"That'd be like reading the end of the book first, wouldn't it?" Especially since there was no ending—not yet, anyway.

"Well, I've been known to do that." Molly rubbed her temples, her eyes closed.

"Headache?"

"A little," she murmured, then opened her eyes to him and made a weakhearted attempt at a smile. "I want you to know I only read the end of books to make sure there's a happy ending. I like happy endings, don't you?"

"Yes, I suppose I do." Though the happy ending he was thinking of was most likely not going to be so happy for her. That thought didn't settle well but he was trapped and there wasn't a damned thing he could do. He had a job to do, obligations, promises to keep.

As he watched, she went back to rubbing her temples.

"Here. Let me," he ordered, and she obliged. Ethan settled himself on the edge of a chair behind her.

"What are you going to—"

He rubbed her shoulders, lightly but firmly, letting his thumbs trace up along the tendons of her neck where they disappeared into her scalp. Her hair was like silk, soft and smooth and radiant. Fingers splayed, he let his hands glide up, trace the curve of her head before settling on her temples.

Slowly, rhythmically, he rubbed her temples while her hair slipped back and forth between his fingers and over the tops of his hands.

"How's that?" he asked, wondering what it would be like to have that same silken beauty brush against the side of his neck, pool on his bare chest before sliding off his shoulder.

"Hmmm," Molly murmured, lost in the feelings, the tenderness of his touch, the delicious perfection of having her ache massaged. His thumbs rubbed the base of her skull, then out along her shoulders. "Heaven," she said, not really realizing she'd spoken out loud.

"I'm glad," she heard him say, his voice suddenly deeper, richer, a bit more hoarse. "I'll do this for you again if you like."

It was on the tip of her tongue to say yes, to say that she liked it very much but reality washed across her sensitized nerves like cold water. Her eyes flew open and she sat straight up and away from him though his hands still rested on her shoulders in a way that was much too familiar, much too pleasant.

"Uh, thank you, Mr. Wilder. I feel better now."

Ethan didn't move for a moment, allowing himself one last touch of her hair.

She glanced back at him. "Thank you for the, uh, rub."

Ethan stood. "You're welcome. When you're sick you deserve special treatment. But when you're better…" He made a poor show of frowning.

"I'll remember," Molly said, and she wondered if she was talking about the admonition or the massage?

Ethan knew that he'd remember, too. "Can I get you something?"

"No, thanks. Nothing." She dragged in a deep breath and he watched her let it out slowly.

"Sure?"

"Sure. Now about that story," she prompted, obviously changing the subject. He went along.

"You'll have to wait." *For a great many things, judging by the look of the place,* he thought sadly and with a bit of temper for the man who would leave her here to fend for herself and for the child.

She chuckled. "Okay, I'll—" Her chuckle brought on another coughing spell and he felt somehow responsible, which was silly, but he felt it all the same. Maybe it was just that he felt sorry for her, for her suffering.

You don't have time to get involved here, Wilder. Get the land and get out.

Yeah, he knew, but she looked so pitiful, her hands cupped over her mouth to muffle the sound. He was totally and completely helpless, a feeling unfamiliar to a man used to being in charge, making things happen, making things happen *his* way.

He waited until her coughing stopped.

"Besides the coughing, how're you feeling? Maybe I shouldn't ask."

"Cold but better, I think." She straightened, hooking her hair back behind her ears. It didn't stay there, but fell in lush waves around her face again.

"Fever down?"

She felt her own forehead. "I can't tell."

Ethan could've taken her word for it. A smart man would've. What the devil did he know about fevers and such? Not a darned thing, but he reached out and touched her cheek anyway. Maybe because she was so close and looked so fragile. Maybe it was simply that he wanted to get closer, to touch her. He let his knuckles brush lightly along her cheek, then trail down to her jaw. Her skin was soft, warm and dry. She never flinched, never moved away at all, and his hand lingered there a moment or two longer than it should have. Long enough for black eyes to seek blue ones. Long enough for there to be a sudden stillness in the room, anxious, ripe with anticipation.

Blessedly, she coughed and broke the spell. She turned away, her hands covering her mouth. Ethan rubbed her shoulder. Not that it would do any good, but it made him feel better, as if he were doing something to help. Suddenly, it was important that he help her.

As he rubbed her arm from shoulder to elbow and back again, he was assailed with memories from earlier today, memories of her in his arms as he'd carried her into the cabin, to that very bed. That thought brought a whole other rush of memories, the slenderness of her frame, her head resting on his shoulder, her arms around his neck.

Wilder, where are you going with this? Business, remember?

He let his hand fall away to rest on the patchwork quilt of the comforter that was his cape. Absently his fingers traced the crisscross stitching. "I'm no good at nursing," he told her, ashamed and surprised by the direction of his thoughts.

"You're doing…fine."

Molly's coughing tapered off. A couple of deep

breaths and the ache in her chest eased. The scratchiness in her throat remained.

The coverlet pooled in Molly's lap as she sat Indian fashion in the chair. She let her chin rest on her chest. She needed a minute. Just a minute to put things all to rights.

"Can I do something for you?" she heard him ask, though she didn't bother to open her eyes. She knew he was there, close. She could sense his nearness, almost as though she were touched by him. That was the trouble—well, part of the trouble. She *had* been touched by him in ways that she was totally unprepared for. It had been a long time, a very long time, since anyone had shown her the concern, the thoughtfulness, the kindness that this man had.

Slowly, she opened her eyes and her gaze immediately sought his. He looked dark and imposing and totally out of place in her little cabin. His expression was serious, almost grim. His mustache seemed to add to his frown. She had the silliest impulse to reach out and touch his mouth, to coax a smile, the smile she'd remembered from earlier today.

She slammed her eyes shut and swallowed hard. It was the fever making her have these foolish thoughts. Yes, that was it. Fever. Lord, it was hot in here.

"Water," she said suddenly. "I need some water." She *needed* some distance. She surged to her feet intent on getting to that sink. Unfortunately, a wave of dizziness washed over her and she sank down on the chair as though someone had put a lead weight in her pockets.

Instantly, he was there, beside her, one arm around her shoulder in a way that was at once protective, comforting and more than a little exciting.

"Take it easy. You'll fall flat, and then what will I do?"

The question was more, what was *she* going to do? She angled her head around to look up at him, his face close, very close, his breath warm on her cheek. Their gazes locked. Why was it so hard to breathe?

"Molly," he said in a husky tone that sent shivers skimming over her skin. For a heartbeat, she thought that he would kiss her. More importantly, she thought that she would let him.

Thankfully, reality got a fingerhold on her fever-clouded brain. Awkwardly, she tore her gaze away and shifted so that he released her.

"Well," he muttered after what seemed an incredibly long time, "I'll get you that water."

She was still sitting on the edge of the chair when he returned.

"Here you go." His voice startled her and she actually jumped. She managed a shaky smile and took the offered cup.

"Thanks." The metal was cool against her fingers, the water equally cool, and she drank it down, needing something to quench her thirst, to distract her from the man who was tall and powerful and altogether too handsome.

"More?" he asked, and she nodded her answer, not entirely trusting her voice to work. What the devil was the matter with her? She was not some silly girl; she was a woman, grown and married, for heaven's sake. Not much of a marriage, granted, but married just the same.

Fever.

It was the fever making her behave so strangely.

"Don't spill," he said gently as he handed her the refilled cup. "I got it a bit too close to the top."

She did spill, though. Water sloshed over the rim and soaked into the green cotton of her nightgown, turning it a darker green. She kept her eyes and her thoughts fixed on that water, the cup, and just about anything else but him.

After draining the cup for a second time, she handed it back, careful not to let their fingers touch. "Thanks. I guess I was thirstier than I thought."

"Fevers do that." He lifted the cup away from her.

"I wouldn't know." She slid back in the chair. "Usually I'm as healthy as a horse. Mama always said I was gonna live to be a hundred."

Ethan chuckled. "I wouldn't compare you to a horse by any means." No, he could think of a great many things to compare her to, most of them having to do with dreams he'd had on lonely nights.

He pulled his chair up alongside of hers. "I'm glad you're doing better. I was worried earlier today."

Her expression turned very serious. "I was worried myself. I've watched too many fevers sweep through a gold camp faster than an avalanche and take out as many people in a matter of no time."

"I had no idea you were afraid," he said, and covered her hand with his. "You didn't have to worry. If it had come down to it I'd have gone to

Cheyenne and back for a doctor.'' He realized in that instant he would have. He would have done more to keep Molly Murphy safe.

''I believe you would have, Mr. Wilder.''

The silence stretched taut between them. Their gazes locked, the room breathlessly quiet. After what could have been a few seconds or several minutes, she slipped her hand free of his and he sat back a bit.

''So,'' he began, looking for something to say. ''What were you doing in a gold camp?''

''I grew up there.''

''In a gold camp?''

''Not one camp. There must have been a dozen, maybe more. I can't remember offhand without counting 'em up.'' She coughed, then managed a shaky glimpse of a smile. ''Looking for gold is worse than looking for a rainbow on a sunny day.''

Katie stirred in her bed and Ethan stood to check on the child. The lamplight flickered, casting strange shadows on the ceiling.

''She's still sleeping,'' he said, sitting down again.

Molly nodded.

Ethan went back to their discussion. ''Someone must be finding the gold or people wouldn't keep looking.'' He leaned forward, elbows to knees. Her foot brushed against his in a way that seemed provocative yet comfortable.

She cocked her head to one side, her red hair spilling over one shoulder in a way that definitely caught his attention. ''That's the trouble. What you just said.''

"Huh?" he muttered, holding back those suddenly erotic thoughts of his. "What?"

"Everyone goes around saying, 'Someone has to find it and it might as well be me.' Only 'me'—" she thumbed her chest "—is never the one."

"I take it, then, that your family was looking for gold and never found any."

"None much. Papa found some dust from time to time. Once when I was about eleven, it looked as though he'd really hit it." She smoothed the blanket on her lap.

"That must've made it all worthwhile."

"For about two weeks. He'd found three, no, four nuggets, pretty good size and a fair amount of dust."

"Then what?" Ethan tried to imagine what it was like to grow up in the bleak conditions of a gold camp.

"Then nothing."

"What do you mean?"

"Mama wanted to take the gold, sell the claim and leave. Find a house somewhere so Papa could go to work and we—my sister and I—could go to school."

"I have the feeling there's a 'but' coming here."

She nodded as she spoke. "Papa was sure there was more to be found, only there wasn't. *But,*" she emphasized the word for his benefit, "he kept looking."

"And the gold he'd found?"

"He spent it on food and new tents and supplies so that he could keep looking for that bigger claim, the bonanza."

"Where's your family now?"

"Gone," she told him, her voice sad and a touch wistful. "Mama died almost six years ago now."

"And your father?"

"Last year. Mining accident. There was a rock slide on a loose hillside. Papa and Ned both were lost."

"Who's Ned?"

"Ned was Katie's father. My sister Annie died in childbirth and I had been raising Katie for Ned. When he and Papa were killed…"

"You mean you're not her real mother?" Somehow he was glad. Not for what she'd suffered but that the child wasn't hers—that she hadn't born a baby with that no-good husband of hers.

When he looked again she was shaking her head. Tears glistened in her eyes. Instinctively, he scooted closer. His hand covered hers, his fingers tightened around her cool skin. "I'm sorry. I didn't mean to make you sad. I know it's hard when you have no one."

She pulled free of his grasp more quickly this time.

"What about you, Mr. Wilder? You never said what brought you to War Bonnet."

"Business," he answered vaguely, hating that he couldn't tell her the truth, wondering what she would say when he did. "Speaking of business, did you say your husband was gone on some business trip?"

She looked away, then back to him as though making some decision. "He's gone back to the gold fields. He left six months ago and I haven't heard from him since. For all I know, he could be dead,

too.'' There, she'd said it, and was glad for the telling. It was her worst fear, yet now that she'd said it
she felt more relieved than frightened. Was it the
telling or the man she'd told it to that made the
difference?

''I see.''

''No, you don't see. He—''

''Left you here alone. Yes, I see that quite
clearly.'' A surge of anger washed over him at the
callousness of the man. ''Do you have any idea
when he'll be back?''

She shook her head. Another cough erupted and
he waited patiently until she recovered.

''Okay?''

''Uh-huh,'' she muttered, her cheeks flushed from
the effort.

''So then you've been here...''

''Not quite six months.'' She pulled the coverlet
up to her chin, stretching the material taut from her
toes over her body.

''So you came in January?''

''The gold had run out in Calico Hill and with all
my family gone, Jack, well, Jack was a godsend. He
took care of us, Katie and me, and then we got married. He's a good man, Mr. Wilder, just got the gold
fever like so many.''

''Why did you buy *this* place?''

''Well, that was the strange part. We didn't buy
it. Someone owed Jack some money and talked Jack
into taking this land as payment. Of course, Jack
didn't want to do it, but I thought it was the answer
to a prayer.''

''This place?'' He didn't try to keep the incredulity out of his voice. "Sorry, but you'll have to admit it's…it's…"

"Poor. Sure, I know. But I can fix it. There's lots of potential here."

He frowned. "Potential for disaster. There's no grass or damned little. It's too dry for crops, not to mention too cold in the winter and too hot in the summer. You'd need a place fifty times this big to raise cattle, assuming you can afford to buy breeding stock and wait several years for a herd to take hold. Sheep's pretty much the same story."

She sighed. "The men from the railroad said the same things."

"Railroad?" he repeated.

"Yes. They're building one to War Bonnet. But I told them I wouldn't sell. This land may not seem like much but it's mine. The funny thing is that from the first moment I saw the place, it was as if I'd come home. Did you ever have that feeling? A place where you feel instantly calm?"

"Can't say that I have."

Another coughing spell.

"Well," Ethan continued, "I've heard that sometimes you can make a nice profit from the railroad."

"I know it sounds foolish." She looked directly at him, her blue eyes dark and intense. "This isn't just a cabin. This is my home. Can you understand what it means to have a home?"

"Yes," he told her honestly, thinking of the orphanage. "I can." It was an odd thing they had in common.

"Besides," she continued, "I couldn't sell even if I wanted to."

"Why not?"

"The land is in my husband's name."

"I see." Ethan stood. This just kept getting more complicated. He needed to think. He needed to think about business and not beautiful flame-haired women. He needed some distance. "You need to get some rest." He helped her up and to the bed.

Molly was feeling kinda tired. When she scooted down in the bed, a round of chills skimmed her body, making her bones ache. Her eyes fluttered closed as he covered her with the quilt that he'd been using. She could still feel the warmth of his body in the cloth.

"I'm gonna bed down over here on the kitchen floor." He spread a blanket near the stove and stretched out, using his arm for a pillow.

"Good. Do you need anything?" Molly's voice was hushed.

"No, nothing."

"Good night, Mr. Wilder, and thanks for...everything."

"Good night, Molly," he whispered. He did one more thing. He slipped a shiny penny under Katie's pillow.

Chapter Six

Two days later Ethan was still at the ranch. He rolled over in his blanket. The floor squeaked beneath him as he did. The sun was up an hour, judging by the look of it through the front window. The morning was clear with enough heat already to make a man hope things weren't going to get much warmer. How could it go from raining to blasting heat?

Sitting up, he yawned and stretched and flexed muscles in his shoulders and back. Stiff muscles. He'd gotten those working on her barn yesterday. Once the rain stopped he'd been able to assess the damage. The back and one side were a little scorched but otherwise untouched. The third side was partially burned, more in some places than others. The front though, the front was gone. Whatever was left would have to be pulled down. At least there was something left, something she could use.

Of course there would have to be major repair work if it was really going to be right.

But who was gonna do the work?

Who? Ethan thought. *Who?*

So he'd spent the day dragging wood away, assessing what, if any, was usable. There wasn't much. His guilt gnawed at him again.

He put his saddle on the corral fence and spread his clothes out to dry.

There were places in this country where a man could get lynched for burning another man's barn. Of course, this had been an accident. Accidents happen. But would she believe him?

He made a derisive sound in the back of his throat as he stood, rolling his head around, then rubbing the spot where neck meets shoulder top.

Soft, Wilder. You're getting soft.

He should have been gone yesterday. That's what he'd promised himself when he'd started this. One day. That was it. Sure as hell, he'd never thought about building barns, especially barns he was only going to tear down eventually. So what had happened?

Molly Murphy had happened, that's what.

Barefoot and shirtless, he strolled a few steps over to the open window. His denim trousers had been washed but they still smelled of smoke.

In the yard, a pair of gray doves settled on the ground behind the cabin, poking around for their morning meal. In a few minutes he'd wake Molly. He glanced over at her sleeping peacefully…finally. The cough had changed from constant to occasional. That was good, really good. So how come he felt kind of sad knowing he had no more excuses to get down to business and take off?

In the other bed, Katie was burrowed in like a

bear in winter. Nothing showed. Not the top of her head or the bottom of her feet, just a big bulging mound in the center. She was still making that little snoring sound—what had Molly called it? Oh, yeah, humming. A smile threatened. *Humming.* Sure. He'd remember that next time he was in camp. The men were just humming. His smile got a touch bigger.

He dragged in a deep slow breath. The scent of last night's stew lingered lightly on the air. His stomach grumbled. Ethan was one of those big breakfast kinda men. None of this coffee and go business. Not if he could help it, not like Molly. Absently he rubbed his arms.

She wasn't eating enough to keep a baby sparrow alive. He'd have to work on that…assuming he stayed. He wasn't staying, was he?

Maybe just until he finished repairing the wagon and doing a little more with the barn. That barn was going to take more than a little something. This was crazy. He couldn't do this. There was no time. People were depending on him.

His gaze settled on her sleeping form. *Yeah, people were depending on him.*

He heard her cough and all thought was forgotten except getting to her. Three long strides and he was beside the bed.

"Feeling badly?" he asked as he sat down on the edge and she naturally moved over for him as had become their custom.

She held the corner of the blanket over her mouth even as she shook her head in denial of his question.

He touched her arm through the soft wool of the

blanket. "Take your time." He squeezed her arm some.

She braced up on one elbow. "I'm...okay... really."

"Sure you are," he agreed in a way that could have been taken more than one way. In his mind she was okay. More than okay. Lord forgive him, he kept thinking about the way she'd felt in his arms that first day when he'd carried her into the house, the way she had nestled her head on his shoulder. Then there was that night, sitting there quietly, talking with her, listening to her explain why this place was so damned important to her.

He should never have touched her. That was his downfall. Why the hell hadn't he left bad enough alone? But no, he had to go and rub her shoulders, slender shoulders, like the rest of her body. And her hair. That glorious hair that had glided seductively over his hand and arm and through his fingers. Even now his body stirred at the memory.

Molly, what are you doing to me?

It was lust. Pure and simple. He was a man and she was a woman, a damned attractive woman, and he naturally wanted to...

She's married, Wilder.

Yes, dammit, he was well aware of that fact. Every muscle and nerve in his body was aware of the fact!

But there was more here than lust and he knew that, too. He couldn't help admiring her spirit, her determination to survive. Hell, he knew what that was like, working, worrying, wondering every day if there'd be enough to eat.

He flexed his shoulder muscles then finger combed his hair, which fell back across his face again. He repeated the procedure with more force. The failure was almost as bad as the first try.

Molly smiled up at him. The man was something else. One minute he was all stern and bossy and the next he was boyish, almost playful.

Sunlight glinted through the front window and made Ethan blink and turn his head slightly. Molly, too, lay down again.

"Sun's bright," Ethan commented.

"At least it means the rain is over."

"Ah, that's true enough." He stood. "I think I'll get dressed and take a look at a couple of things before breakfast…if you don't mind."

She shook her head as Ethan crossed to the stove to get dressed. "Go ahead," she told him. "If you run across that team of mine see if you can move them in this direction—if it's not too much trouble."

Grabbing up his shirt, which had dried by the stove, he gave the blue cotton a couple of sharp shakes—a cowboy cleaning—before he put it on.

He rifled both hands through his hair again, this time more agitation in the gesture than concern for appearance.

So, now what? he asked himself. Now nothing. He would round up the horses, finish fixing the wagon and the barn…. Jeez…he didn't want to think about it anymore.

He had to tell her, to ask her for her support. Yes, he knew the land was in her husband's name but if Molly said she would sell, Ethan was pretty sure the husband would go along—assuming he was still alive. Obviously, the man didn't care that much for ranching or he'd be here now, not off in some gold field.

Ethan had to do it now, today, before things got more complicated. He made a sort of chuckle in the back of his throat. As though things could get more complicated.

Determined, he stuffed his shirt into the waistband of his trousers and did up the last couple of buttons. He snatched up his socks then boots, shoving on one, then the other.

He paused. She'd be upset when she found out the truth. He'd have to deal with that. It was his sincere belief that he was doing the best thing for her. All he had to do was make her see that.

But looking at her, somehow the words dissolved in his brain and all he could say was, ''I'll be back in a little while.''

''I'll be here,'' she replied with a smile.

Outside the day was clear. A few white billowing clouds drifted across the sky as a last reminder of the storm. But Ethan didn't need any reminders. There was the barn and the partially burned wagon.

First things first. He needed to find the horses. He gave a sharp whistle, figuring that if Four was within hearing distance he'd come. Sure enough a couple of minutes later the big brown horse trotted around from behind the house and walked slowly up to Ethan where he stood looking at the burned wreckage.

The horse gave Ethan a shove and Ethan stepped back into place and stroked the horse's face with his open hand.

"So you doing all right, boy?" Ethan asked absently while in his mind he was trying to decide just how much work it was going to take to get the wagon going. "Let's have a look at you." He checked Four's shoulders, back, chest and haunches. "Well, you look fine. You wouldn't by any chance know where those two dumb draft horses are, would you?"

He waited for an intelligent answer. Hell, he'd settle for any kind of an answer but none was given. Too bad. Now he'd have to hunt those two up the hard way.

No sense daydreaming. He had horses to find. The saddle was too wet so there was nothing for it but to ride Four bareback. Grabbing a handful of mane, Ethan swung up, Pony Express style.

As Ethan settled in, the horse craned his neck around and stared.

"Well, don't stare at me," Ethan admonished. "Your back's not so tender that you can't put up with me for a little while."

The horse seemed to consider this, then looked away. When Ethan gave a nudge with his heels and tugged right on the mane, the horse complied.

Ethan figured that the horses would seek some kind of shelter but where was the question. He knew he had to find those animals; they were all Molly had…two horses and one railroad owner living a lie.

No. He wasn't going to think about that until the last possible second. He checked by the stream. Nothing. Scanning the distance, he couldn't make anything out so he started west in the general direction of town. About a half a mile from Molly's place he spotted a track, just one, which was a miracle considering all the rain. It was deep, really deep in the mud and that must have been the only reason it survived.

Ethan kept going, his hat pulled low on his forehead against the sun that drifted in and out from behind the clouds. Another mile or so and he spotted another track. He jumped down and looked closely but he couldn't be sure if this was the same as the last track or if either one belonged to those draft horses. But the tracks were large and moving in the direction the storm had moved.

He dragged in a deep breath and let it out slowly. God, he hated this. He also hated that the storm had come, that he and Molly had talked, that he'd gotten to know her too damned well and that he'd burned down her barn…sorta.

He swung up on Four's back again. "Okay, boy, let's find those critters."

He kept riding. Off in the distance to his right he could see the town. He needed to go there, to talk to people about business. He needed business to make money. That was the idea behind this scheme of his…to make money.

He kept riding, feeling Four's muscles move under him, knowing that it only took a touch of his knee or a shift in body weight to make the animal respond.

Judging by the sun he'd been at this a couple of hours. The house up ahead was off the beaten path as the saying goes. The white paint was peeling and the roof looked as though it'd been a while since anyone took a deliberate hand to it.

As he got closer he could see that the place was deserted. No curtains at the windows, rotting wood on the front stoop. He hopped up and moseyed around, peering in the windows. Yup, sure enough, empty. Not a bad place if someone fixed it up.

Great Wilder, you wanna fix up two places now? Maybe you're in the wrong business.

Suddenly he heard a sound, the distinctive sound of a horse neighing.

Ethan leaped down from the porch and strode for the small barn. The door was open, one of the hinges broken. And there, believe it or not, were his missing equines.

"There you are," he pronounced while he walked up to them. "What the hell are you doing here? Never mind," he amended.

"Hell," he muttered again.

Finding a couple of ropes in the barn, he made halters and led the team back to where Four waited patiently.

With the two horses in tow, Ethan headed back to Molly's cabin…and to Molly.

He put all the horses in the corral. The water trough was definitely full. He'd worry about their food later. He could always hobble them and let 'em graze if it came to that.

He started for the cabin.

Katie opened the door. "Hello, Mr. Ethan," she said beaming. "You come for breakfast?"

"I've come to *make* breakfast," he answered, happy to see the kid. Two steps inside he stopped. The sweet smell of bacon frying reached him the same instant he saw her. "What the—"

"I see you found the horses. You were gone so long I was getting worried." Molly turned to look at him. Their eyes met and it was the night before last all over again. For a heartbeat, it was as if all the oxygen had been sucked out of the room. "I was wondering what was taking you so long."

Ethan didn't trust himself to move. "What are you doing?" What do you know, the man could talk.

"I'm making breakfast. Have a seat." She gestured with a fork toward the table.

He didn't. "You shouldn't be doing that."

"Sure I should." She went back to stirring the bacon, and the grease popped and spattered. "Ouch."

"You okay?"

"Oh, sure."

This time when she looked at him she smiled, the most radiant, make-you-want-to-sigh smile he'd ever seen. His heart took on a funny sort of rhythm, slow and heavy and he couldn't have moved just then if his very life had depended on it.

"Everything will be ready in a couple of minutes." She scooped up the bacon and put it on a plate, then poured eggs into the hot grease. She looked bright and chipper and well. She looked like he'd want a woman—his woman—to look like in the mornings. Her hair was down, loose around her shoulders and she was wearing her flannel nightgown, which was thicker than a nun's habit and just as long. She had a red wool shawl wrapped around her shoulders.

"Are you hungry? Mr. Wilder?"

The mention of his name jarred him out of this

stupor he'd fallen into. "Uh, yes. Hungry." He crossed the room and stopped next to her. "Why don't you let me finish this?"

She shook her head, and her loose hair slipped seductively over her shoulders. He watched the way it curled at the very ends, thinking he'd like to curl it around his fingers.

"Nope. You've been waiting on us." She angled her head around to look at him and softly amended, "You've been waiting on *me* for two days."

"I didn't mind," he said just as softly, lost in the depths of her incredibly blue eyes. "Really. You should go back to bed."

Each seemed lost in the other's nearness, the other's gaze.

"Mama. Mama! The egg's are burning!" Katie's voice broke the spell and both turned at once. She was pointing at the stove and the first puffs of black smoke rising from the pan.

"Oh, good Lord!" Molly shoved the skillet off the burner to inspect the remains. "I don't think it's *too* bad."

Her shoulder brushed against his arm. "I think it's fine." He got lost in her gaze again.

"Mama?"

Ethan rallied first. "Yes, short stuff?"

"I'm hungry. Are we gonna eat soon? I wanna go check on my kittens."

"We're going to eat." Molly got busy pulling down plates and serving up the extra crispy bacon and eggs she'd made.

"Here, let me." Ethan took the plates from her

hands and carried them to the table. "Come on, Katie. Let's eat."

He helped Molly with her chair as though they were in some fancy Chicago restaurant and Katie giggled. "Me, too," she ordered and, laughing, he obliged.

It seemed strange sitting down together eating breakfast. It was as though he'd come in from working and they were waiting for him, his family. The notion settled easy on him, too easy, he reminded himself, because, looking at Molly over the breakfast table, he also realized she was not his wife, and Katie was not his daughter.

Ethan ate in silence, looking up occasionally. He caught Molly looking at him once, at least he thought he did, but she looked away so quickly he wasn't certain.

"I'm sorry there's no butter," said Molly. "I had planned on going into town today to stock up, you know." She sipped her coffee. "We'll manage one more day without starving."

"I'll go for you," Ethan said before he could think about it. "Are you going to need much?" The wagon wasn't finished so he'd have to go on horseback.

Wilder, you're getting in deep here.

No, he wasn't. He was helping. The woman needed help and that's what she was gonna get. It was good for business. Yes. That was right. Helping had nothing to do with an excuse to stay around here and everything to do with business.

"Oh, no." Molly gave a dismissive wave of her hand. "I'll go tomorrow."

Ethan studied her over the edge of his coffee cup. "You aren't going to be up to riding into town for a few days yet and besides—"

"I know, the wagon isn't fixed."

"I'll work on it this morning but it'll take more than a few hours depending on how much wood I can find that's serviceable."

"Absolutely not. You've done too much already and besides, you've got an injured hand."

Ethan held up his bandaged hand for inspection. It didn't feel too bad today, more a throbbing than actual pain. It reminded him of a powder burn he'd gotten at Bull Run. He'd survived that; he'd survive this.

"What about the wheel?" she asked.

He sighed. "Well, I can fix it temporarily but you're going to need another one."

Molly grimaced. "It's going to be expensive, isn't it?"

"Depends," he hedged. It was relative to the amount of money a person had at the time. With her, he figured she didn't have much.

"Mr. Wilder, you are a real friend. I don't know what we would have done without you these last few days."

Oh, great. He was a real true friend all right. A friend who wanted to take her home away. Somehow this didn't seem like the right moment to mention that fact.

"Make a list," he said. "I'll ride into town and stock up. It won't take me long."

"Can I come, Mr. Ethan?" Katie asked.

"No. You stay here and help your mother." He turned back to Molly. "I'll be back by afternoon."

"You really don't have to do this." Molly picked up her plate and Katie's and headed to the kitchen and the large metal basin she used as a sink.

Ethan brought his plate along. "I'll do the dishes." He gently elbowed her aside. "You sit down and make out that shopping list." He was already pouring water from the bucket into a saucepan on the stove to heat. "Don't forget honey."

She produced a piece of brown wrapping paper from a drawer for the list. "Honey's too expensive." She retrieved a pencil from the bureau and set to work.

Twenty minutes later, he'd heated water, washed and rinsed the dishes and set them to dry on the wooden counter. Molly had finished with the list, which she handed to Ethan.

"Is this it?" he asked.

"That's it."

"Not much to feed a growing man," he commented as he tucked the paper into his shirt pocket.

"Well, normally I don't have to feed a growing man and I wasn't sure how long you'd stay." Molly didn't want him to leave. She chose not to examine her reasons too closely.

He looked at her for a long minute as though thinking about something then said, "I'll go to town right after I finish a couple of chores."

He hadn't answered her question, Molly realized. She didn't press the point. He was going to stay at least long enough to get supplies. She was grateful. She liked him.

Ethan's voice startled her. "Katie, you wanna help me?"

"Sure." She raced out the door. Even Katie, Molly realized, had taken a liking to the man. "Can I feed your horse?" was the last thing she heard from her daughter.

He laughed. "I don't know how you hold up."

"I wonder that myself sometimes." Molly pulled her shawl around her shoulders, feeling a little chill prickle over sensitive skin.

"I'll let you know before I leave." With that he strode for the door and she wondered if he meant for town or for good.

Two hours later, Ethan had managed to find a little unburned hay for the horses. He'd checked them each over thoroughly to make sure none was injured.

Katie was busy playing with those kittens she seemed to hover over more than the mother cat.

Ethan led Four out of the corral and made quick work of saddling him up.

"See my kittens?" Katie dragged the washtub full of meowing cats in his direction.

"I sure do," he answered absently, more concerned with checking the cinch and the condition of the rain-soaked leather. Stitching looked good, he thought as he ran his hand over the cantle and forward toward the horn. This saddle represented one third of everything he owned, the other two thirds being his clothes and one almost completed railroad.

Interesting how that railroad came last on his list. Coincidence.

"So can we? Huh? Huh?"

Katie's voice interrupted Ethan's thoughts and he looked down at the little girl who was tugging on his pant leg. "Ah, sure."

"Great!" Katie did a little jig. "Mama hates worms so she won't never go but you don't hate worms, do ya Mr. Ethan."

His brows drew down in a frown. "No," he started cautiously, "I don't hate worms. What kinda worms?"

"For fishing, o' course."

"Fishing?" He shook his head adamantly. "I don't have time for fishing."

Her bottom lip came out. "But you said."

"When?"

"Just now. I said can we, and you said sure."

Great. Just great. What was he going to do now, tell her to forget it? She was growing up without a father and practically without a mother. He knew what that was like.

"Okay. Okay. When I get back we'll fish." With that he led Four toward the house.

"You won't forget?" she prompted.

"No, I won't forget. But it's up to your mother. Okay?"

"Okay."

While Katie went back to playing with the kittens, Ethan stopped near the front door.

Molly was seated at the table, her eyes closed. He said, "I'm ready to go."

She opened her eyes and smiled at him.

"Before you go..." She went to the bureau where she rummaged around in the bottom drawer.

"Here," she said, her back still to him. When she

turned around she was holding a small white porcelain jar. It looked like something a woman would
keep doodads and such in.

"What's that?"

She dumped out the contents into her hand.
"Money for the supplies."

"I don't need any money." That was his guilty
conscience talking.

"Of course you do. We don't have an account at
the store. I don't like running up bills."

"Me, neither." She was coming toward him with
money in her outstretched hand. He was backing up.
No way was he taking money from her.

"Take the money. How are you going to pay for
the supplies otherwise?"

"I have money." He was out the door, still backing up. "Later. Pay me later. After we know how
much."

He swung up on his horse as though to put distance between them.

She followed him outside. Sunlight glinted on her
hair. The morning breeze swirled the hem of her
nightgown around her ankles and he thought in that
second that she looked more wild, more vulnerable
than any woman he'd ever known.

"When will you be back?" she called to him, her
eyes shaded against the light.

"Midafternoon, I think. Not later."

She smiled then, a warm, lush smile that had his
breath lingering in his chest.

Then she turned away, and the moment, the spell,
was broken.

Strangely, he hated to leave. It felt as though it

were for the last time, as though he'd never see her again. He would. But for how much longer?

Abruptly, he snatched his hat off and settled it lower on his forehead, then nudged Four into an easy trot.

"Bring me somethin', Mr. Ethan," Katie called as she came running to catch up to him. She ran alongside for a few yards.

"Like what?" he hollered down to her.

"Candy!" she shouted and waved as he pulled away. "Peppermint candy!"

Chapter Seven

The trip to town was slow. He took it extra easy since the roads were a quagmire from the rain. Besides, he was in no hurry. He needed time to think.

So what just happened there, Wilder? What happened to telling her about the land, about the railroad? You remember the railroad? The thing you've sunk every cent you've got into?

Yeah, he remembered all right. Though, looking at Molly he sometimes wished he didn't. As for telling her, he would. Yes, he would tell her as soon as he got back from town. But…she was still sick and he had burned down her barn. Oh sure, it was an accident, him leaving the lantern there on the floor, but he'd done it just the same. So he owed her. He glanced at his injured hand and smiled remembering her concern as she'd bandaged it for him, the gentle touch of her fingers as she'd spread the salve on his blistered flesh. So gentle. So soothing. So intimate.

Wilder, are you out of your mind?

He didn't want to think about that too closely.

Afraid of the answer?

Damned straight!

Around the curve in the road, War Bonnet came into view a quarter mile ahead.

As he rode into town he could see there was only one street. But there were survey stakes driven into the ground at the south end of town, and he knew they were marking the perimeter of lots, new lots. Red ribbons fluttered like flags from each stake.

So the locals were already trying to sell land. War Bonnet might be small now, but it was well situated on the road to the newly discovered gold camps in northern Wyoming and Montana. From here, supplies could be dispatched to army forts like Laramie and Benton and Kearney, and it provided access for the cattle ranches to the booming meat trade in Omaha and Chicago without having to drive the herds miles south to Cheyenne. All this was exactly the reason Ethan had chosen War Bonnet as the destination for his first railroad.

Ah, yes, first railroad, the first of many he hoped to build. Of course, all that pretty much depended on how well this one went. Right now, it wasn't going at all.

He knew his best friend Billy was back at the end of track working hard, driving the men to go faster, to make time because they needed to be done and shipping before the first loan came due on July 15. If the railroad wasn't in operation by then, he'd lose it all. It was as simple as that.

He reined up in front of Hadley's Livery and jumped down from the wagon.

A big-bellied man with shoulder-length brown

hair wandered out to greet him. "Can I do something for you?"

"I need a new wheel."

The man raised his eyebrows and made a show of walking around Four. "All his wheels look fine to me. Which one is it?" he asked with a split-tooth grin.

Ethan chuckled. "You've got me there." He thumbed back his hat. "The wheel's for a wagon."

"Buggy or work wagon?"

"Work."

"Well, I got a couple back here. You wanna take a look?"

The two men walked through the barn and out the other doorway. There were several wheels propped against the red-painted wall.

"Think any of these will do the job?" the man asked.

Ethan looked them over. Most were too small. Finally, with an experienced eye, he found one. "This one I think."

The man nodded his understanding.

"How much?"

"Oh—" he rubbed his chin with his well-callused hand "—eight dollars."

"Looks kinda weathered. I'll give you five." Ethan was already pulling out his money as an indication that the negotiations were over.

The man took the money and shoved it in his pants pocket, then he hefted the wheel free of the others. "How you gonna get this home?" he asked as he rolled the wheel along the ground toward where Ethan had tied up his horse.

"Good question." He hadn't really intended to buy the wheel but he was here and Molly was going to need the wheel and so...

"Look," Ethan started. "I'm gonna be buying some supplies, too. How much to rent a buggy?"

"Three dollars," the man answered with a definite twinkle in his eye.

Ethan made a sound in the back of his throat. "You're gonna get that eight dollars one way or another aren't you?"

"Appears so," he answered, grinning.

"Okay," Ethan threw up his hands in surrender. "You hitch the buggy and tie the wheel on the back while I get my supplies."

"Say, I didn't ask you where you were headed with my three-dollar buggy."

"I'm headed out to the Murphy place," Ethan said over his shoulder as he started across the street toward the mercantile.

Along the way he passed Mrs. Haggerty's Boardinghouse, and took note of a sign in the window proclaiming Meals Served Daily. There was a feed and grain with a wagon out front, a man and a young boy loading sacks of oats.

Across the street, next to the El Dorado Saloon, was Brinsfield's Mercantile, according to the large blue sign that was displayed over the double doorway. Paint was peeling from the white clapboard walls and the wood on the front porch was curling from winter rains. The displays in the front windows were of cloth—everything from calico to red satin, and he wondered briefly just who in town was going to be decked out in that.

He opened the door, which squeaked. A small bell announced his arrival to anyone who hadn't heard those complaining hinges. Inside, the place was long and narrow, two sides lined with glass cases that served as counters, the walls behind filled with everything from bright-yellow cans of Coleman's Mustard to white-labeled canned milk.

The back of the store was stacked with blankets, both for horses and people. Burlap sacks of feed took up one corner. In the opposite corner, several wooden barrels were filled with brooms and mops and rakes, looking like some strange bouquet.

"Morning," Ethan said to the narrow-faced man behind the counter as he reached for the supply list in his pocket.

"Morning," the man returned with a smile. "What can we do for you today?"

"I'll be needing a few things."

The clerk scanned the list. "No problem. This everything?" He glanced up. "We've got a sale on sugar."

"Sugar, huh?" There wasn't any sugar on her list. Ethan strolled along the counter, taking stock of the goods displayed and remembering the pitiful condition of her larder. "Maybe a couple more things."

His couple more things turned into half a dozen, then a dozen, including canned milk and honey—a personal favorite of his—sugar, coffee and butter. The clerk made note as Ethan indicated the amounts of each item.

"I think that's about it." He'd nearly bought out the store.

"You wanna wait or do you wanna come back?"

He thought maybe he'd head on over to the restaurant he'd spotted in the boardinghouse, have a little lunch while he waited. "I'll come back."

"It'll be ready, Mister..."

"Wilder." The clerk scribbled it down as Ethan walked outside.

Standing on the plank sidewalk, he was about to check out that boardinghouse restaurant when he noticed the post office sign on the front of the stage depot. Might as well see if there was any mail. Billy, his superintendent, knew he'd been headed here, of course.

His spurs jingled as he strode across the street. A buckboard rattled past, a couple of local cowboys perched on the seat, the back stacked with several rolls of rope and sacks of oats. Ethan skirted around behind them and jumped up on the high sidewalk.

As two women strolled by, he touched two fingers to the brim of his hat. "Ladies."

They nodded in response.

He went into the stage depot. It turned out to be a small square room with a scarred wooden counter running across the entire front like a barricade that left little room for customers and lots of room for the freight that was stacked there.

A tall, lean man in a faded blue-plaid shirt and shiny black trousers ambled up to the counter. "Yes, sir?" He let fly a stream of tobacco that hit the brass spittoon with practiced expertise.

"Any mail for Wilder? Ethan Wilder?"

The agent scratched at his chin thoughtfully. "Yeah," he finally said, "I think there was somethin' come in on yesterday's stage. Let me hunt 'er up.''

"Fine."

Ethan kept thinking about Molly, about her land. He knew Billy was expecting things to have been handled. He gave a slight shake of his head. What the devil was wrong with him? Why didn't he tell her what he wanted and be done with it? Trouble was, once he told her there was no more reason to stay. There was a funny feeling, a sorta pain that moved through his chest every time he thought about leaving, about never seeing Molly again.

Ridiculous. Absolutely ridiculous.

Lust was what it was. Or was it?

Get your mind back on business.

Yeah. Business. That was a nice safe topic, not to mention an urgent one.

"Here's that letter," the clerk said, and Ethan blinked hard a couple of times, surprised that the man was standing right there in front of him.

"What? Oh, sure. Thanks." He ripped open the pale-yellow envelope.

It was from Billy all right. He recognized his scrawl without having to look at the signature. Quickly, he scanned the lines. "…be in War Bonnet in less than thirty days…trouble with suppliers…rain delayed but picking up the pace…see you soon."

Ethan scanned the letter one more time just to make sure he hadn't missed anything. He hadn't. He didn't understand what the trouble was with the suppliers, but Billy would handle it, he knew that. He'd been relying on Billy since, well, hell, since the army.

It seemed that Ethan had spent most of his life in one kind of institution or another. Before the army it had been the orphanage.

Orphanage. Now there was a place that seemed a world away. Brick and wood, it was three floors of wall-to-wall kids. It seemed the good sisters of charity could never say no to a child in need. Guess a woman has to have a big heart to want to be a nun.

Ethan had been twelve when his mother died and his father ran off and Ethan ended up with the sisters.

Days were long and there wasn't much to do once schooling was done. But they had been near the railroad tracks so it had been only natural that he would watch the trains go by, make up games and stories about where each was headed, then pretend he was on board, off to a great adventure. Trains were his escape, his promise of better things to come, of the future.

One day, he'd simply run away. Good sisters or not, he wanted to be on his own, to find all that adventure he'd been talking about. Ethan had been sixteen.

After a year of living from hand to mouth, he'd joined the army.

A year later the war had broken out.

Four years of blood and gore that somehow he'd survived without permanent injury. He'd left the army right after the surrender, without a place to go or a plan to get there.

Ethan glanced at the clerk. "Thanks."

Holding Billy's letter, Ethan went outside. At the end of the street he could see his horse tied up and the wagon wheel propped against the hitching post.

He leaned one shoulder against the porch post. He took off his hat and wiped his forehead with the curve of his elbow before settling his hat back on his head. He let his mind wander back.

Right after the war, his old commander had taken on a job with the Union Pacific and he'd asked Ethan if he wanted to come along. Well, sure he did. Work with trains, work on the railroad? All those kid's dreams and fantasies had come rushing back faster than he could say, "Sign me up."

Colonel Bridges was eastern bred, old money, college educated. He'd liked Ethan from the first and had taken Ethan under his wing, taught him about engineering, about surveying and planning and budgeting. That's where Ethan had again met Billy, who was the superintendent of the men.

By the time the tracks met in Utah, Ethan had built what some called an impressive reputation as a man who knew how to get things done, and with Billy as his partner, well, they'd figured there'd be no stopping them.

Ethan had put together a plan to build his own railroad, a spur north to cattle country, to War Bonnet. Investors had been willing based on Ethan's reputation and help from the Colonel. He'd seen to it Ethan had met the right people. Why, he'd even invested, and that was pretty much enough of a guarantee for everyone else.

Everything had fallen into place and he and Billy had figured they couldn't lose.

But that was before Molly Murphy.

Something had happened almost from the first, from seeing that flame-red hair of hers, from feeling her curled so helplessly in his arms as he'd carried her into the cabin, from seeing how scared she'd been that first night.

Something. But what?

A couple of blackbirds settled in the middle of the street, squawking and flapping at each other over some slight, he supposed.

Like the blackbirds, Ethan needed to settle things and get on with business. He had obligations to Billy and to the investors. He had made a promise to himself.

"Mr. Wilder?" a male voice interrupted his thoughts.

Ethan looked up.

A tall, barrel-chested man dressed in a tan-striped suit held out his hand. "Ed Bartel, head of the businessman's association here and owner of both saloons. You are Ethan Wilder with the railroad?"

"Yes," Ethan responded, thinking the man had the slick look of a devious horse trader he'd once known.

Bartel was busy still shaking Ethan's hand. "We've been expecting you, Ethan. You don't mind if I call you Ethan." It wasn't a question and Ethan was half tempted to say he did mind just to see what the man would say. He didn't. Bartel here was part of Ethan's customer base and there was no sense riling up the customers.

"How'd you know—"

"Oh, I was over to the mercantile," he interrupted Ethan's question. "They said you was here, at least someone with your name...." His grin widened and he kept shaking Ethan's hand.

It was like pulling taffy to get his hand free, but Ethan managed, flexing his fingers as he did. He adjusted his hat more comfortably on his head. "Yes, Mr. Bartel, we've corresponded." He'd written to Bartel discussing various business plans, encouraging him to put the word out to the local ranches that the railroad would be available for their spring shipping and that he'd negotiate rates with them. "I appreciate all your work."

"Nothing to it," Bartel replied, his voice booming so that people on the other side of the street glanced their way. "Think nothing of it, Ethan. Glad to do it. Glad to do it."

Sunlight inched up on the porch and the two men took a step sideways, closer to the wall of the stage depot. "When you got to town, you should've come on over to the office and looked me up. Now, you come along with me. I'm gonna show you around, introduce you to a few folks." He gestured broadly, that horse-trader grin of his firmly in place.

"Some other time, Mr. Bartel. I've got—"

"No time like the present," Bartel countered, and the next thing Ethan knew the man had him by the arm and was propelling him along the sidewalk. "Now, we'll get you a room at the boardinghouse. Nothing fancy, but clean and good food. Mrs. Haggerty is a mighty fine-looking woman too, which ain't a bad way to start the morning, if you know what I mean." He winked at Ethan.

Ethan understood but wasn't interested. "I'm not staying in town, Bartel." The man was beginning to irritate him. "I'm picking up a few supplies is all." He didn't mention Molly or the land or his staying with her. He knew full well how quickly a woman's reputation could be ruined and he wouldn't do that to her.

"Supplies? You hauling supplies for the railroad?" His blue eyes widened in excitement and he slapped Ethan on the back. "Hot damn! So the line is that close, huh? I didn't know. How come I didn't know?" he said out loud, as if someone would be held accountable to his being uninformed.

Ethan corrected his impression. "No, it's not that close. I'd say—" he glanced at Billy's letter again "—about a month if the weather holds and supplies are on time. Maybe two." *And if I buy the key piece of land to make the whole damned thing happen,* he thought, but didn't say.

"Sure. Sure," Bartel said in a dismissive tone. "Sounds mighty close to me. Wait till the boys hear this." Bartel had Ethan by the arm again and was ushering him along the sidewalk. "You know this railroad's gonna make this town prosper. That's why we're selling lots already." He skidded to a halt and in a conspiratorial tone, said, "I can make you a good deal on a couple of prime parcels, and if you want a place with a house on it I got one out the other end of town—porch, fireplace in the parlor and even a white picket fence." His bushy eyebrows inched up and down his forehead a couple of time.

"You want land, you see me. No one but me, now, you hear?"

Ethan nodded. "I hear." He wouldn't buy a bucket of water from this guy if he was on fire, and he pitied the people who were going to have to deal with him in the coming months.

The afternoon breeze ruffled Bartel's hair and he flattened it against the top of his head with the palm of his hand. He kept walking, half pushing, half dragging Ethan along with him.

The next thing Ethan knew, they were standing in front of Evans' Feed and Grain. It was a plain storefront next to the town's other saloon, called the Bull Dog.

"Ralph," Bartel called out, and the man inside the store came onto the sidewalk to join them. He was shorter than Ethan, and thin, with a graying fringe of hair.

"Ralph Evans, this is Mr. Wilder, our railroad owner," Bartel said.

Evans wiped his hand on the dirty white apron he wore over his light blue shirt and brown trousers. The men shook hands.

"Mr. Evans."

"Wilder. Is this your first time here?"

"Yes. My partner surveyed this route a year ago."

Bartel spoke up. "Ralph, Ethan here says the railroad's about a month away."

"Maybe two," Ethan corrected.

Evans nodded. "Any chance you might be here sooner than that? The spring roundup is getting started in a couple of weeks. It's a little late this year because of the heavy snows we had.''

"Yeah, I know," Ethan said. The snow had delayed the railroad too, which had worked a real hardship on their finances. It was gonna be tight.

Feeling suddenly anxious to get back to Molly, to get this land thing resolved once and for all, he said, "Look, I've really got to go." He glanced over at the mercantile. "I've got some supplies to pick up and—''

"Fine. Fine," Bartel interrupted again. Didn't the man ever let someone finish a sentence?

Bartel continued. "So now, when can I set up a meeting with the local ranchers?" His expression turned thoughtful. "How's next Monday?"

Ethan didn't know about next Monday. He didn't know about tomorrow. "Look, I'll have to get back to you on that." He swung down off the sidewalk and started across the street. The men hurried to catch up.

"But," Bartel was saying, "we have to talk about rates and schedules and—''

"Later." This time it was Ethan who cut in.

"Now, passenger service will begin at the same time, right?" Evans asked.

"Uh, right. Passenger service from Cheyenne. Mostly I think that'll be miners, soldiers and their families—''

"And investors," Bartel added. "Investors in our town, Ethan. Don't forget investors. Why, we've advertised in the *Cheyenne Leader* about the train and our town." Bartel gestured broadly. Obviously the man had a lot of money sunk in the locale and was chomping at the bit to cash in. It wasn't wrong, but it irritated Ethan.

"Gentlemen, I really have to go."

"Now," Evans piped up, "we'll be putting together a celebration for you. The whole town will want to meet you and thank you for what you're doing."

"It's too early for celebrations," Ethan told him. "Let's wait until the train actually gets to town."

"Yes. Yes," Bartel agreed, nodding as he spoke. "How about a drink before you go?"

"Go?" Evans cocked his head to one side. "Aren't you staying in town?"

"Uh, no. I'm doing some surveying. You know, looking things over along the route and such." It was kinda the truth. "So I came in for messages and supplies, then I'm headed back out again."

The men seemed to accept his explanation. He was relieved.

The three of them walked over to the mercantile together.

"Here's your order, sir," the clerk said as they walked in.

Ethan went to the counter. "Thanks. How much do I owe you?"

"Six dollars will cover it."

Ethan counted out the money in silver coin then hefted the crate and was heading for the door when he spotted a large peppermint stick in the glass case. He remembered Katie's parting words. "Let me have one of those, too." He gestured with his head.

"One of these?"

"Yeah. The peppermint sticks."

The clerk wrapped the candy in brown paper and tucked it in the top of the crate. "Sweet tooth," Ethan said in answer to the men's questioning looks.

"Ah," Bartel mumbled. "I have one of those myself." He rubbed his rounded stomach as proof of his words.

"How much?" Ethan asked the clerk, shifting to balance the crate on one hip.

"It's on the house."

"Thanks."

The men trailed after him as he went outside en route to the livery.

Even before he spoke to the man there, he could see that the buggy was hitched and the wheel tied on the back. He put the crate on the seat beside him.

"We're all square. Right?" he asked as the liveryman approached.

"Sure are."

Ethan climbed up on the wagon seat. Looking down at the men gathered, he said, "I'll be around the area. We can talk more later."

With that, he slapped the reins on the horse's rump and the wagon lurched forward. He turned around and headed back out the way he'd come.

The three men stood near the corral gate at the livery stable and watched him go.

"Well, that was strange," Bartel said after a minute. "The man sure was in a hurry to leave."

"Yeah, I thought so, too," Evans said. "What's the wagon wheel for?"

Old Harry, the livery stable operator, rubbed his face with his hand, "Don't know exactly."

"Well, what do you know?" Bartel demanded, obviously exasperated.

"All I know is where he's going."

"Well!" Bartel snapped. "I swear, Harry, trying to get information of you is like trying to get water out of a rock."

The men looked at him.

"He said he was headed out to the Murphy place." With that Harry turned and walked away.

Evans spoke. "What would Wilder be doing out there?"

Bartel watched the wagon pull away. "Maybe we should find out."

Chapter Eight

It was midafternoon by the time Ethan rolled up to the cabin. Katie was playing a few yards away, drawing some kind of designs in the dirt with a long switch.

"Hello, Mr. Ethan," she called, running toward the wagon.

Ethan reined to a stop. "Hi, yourself." He smiled at her. Dirty dress. Dirty face. He was getting to love this kid.

"How's your mother?" He climbed down from the wagon seat. He figured he'd unload first then take the team and buggy back to town.

"She's fine. She's resting and I'm waiting for you. Whatcha bring me?"

Ethan walked around the buggy, Katie hot on his heels. "What makes you think I brought you anything?" he asked, trying hard not to smile.

He grabbed hold of the crate, his bare fingers digging hard into the soft pine as he hefted the heavy box. The cabin door was open enough that he could push it the rest of the way with the toe of his boot.

Muscles along his back and shoulders tensed as he went inside and headed for the table. Either he was getting weaker or he'd bought more supplies than he'd figured on. Maybe he should have stuck to that short list after all.

Katie danced and skipped alongside.

"You brought me something," she told him. "You said you would. Remember?"

"Remember?" He pretended to be confused. "No, I don't think so." He plunked his hat down on the table beside the crate and wiped his forehead with the curve of his elbow. Sweat turned his green shirt a darker shade.

"Candy," she announced, lifting up and down on her toes as she spoke. "You was supposed to bring me candy."

"Are you sure you said candy? I thought you said castor oil." He made a show of rummaging in the box as though to find the liquid medicine hated by man and child alike.

Katie made a face as if she'd just eaten a raw frog. "No," she moaned, shaking her head adamantly. "Mama made me take that once and…" She stuck out her tongue then wiped it with the hem of her dress, revealing dirt-stained legs and pantalets. One thing Katie knew how to do was get dirty. There'd be a bath tonight, unless he missed his guess, knowing Molly as he did. Funny how he felt he did know her. Speaking of which, the lady was nowhere to be seen.

"Delivery!" he called out.

"I'll be right there." Her voice carried from the other side of that blanket curtain she'd apparently restrung. For a second he remembered sitting with her that night, watching her face, her deep-blue eyes, while she tried to pretend she wasn't scared. It had been a strange feeling, being strong for her, trying to comfort her. But he'd liked it, liked that he could help.

Almost like a vision, she seemed to appear before his memory-clouded eyes and he had to blink twice to return to reality. But reality was worth the effort. As she came out of the enclosure to greet them, she was doing up the last few buttons of her green-flowered shirtwaist. Her hair was partially up, the sides were at least, tied back with a comb or ribbon he couldn't see. Her face was soft, almost radiant. Her skin was still silver-moon pale and there were traces of shadows under her eyes. With all that, she was lovely. Lust stirred in him and he shifted from one foot to the other, surprised at the sudden reaction of his body. Perhaps not so surprised.

"Uh. I just realized I probably woke you. I didn't mean to."

"No." She did up the last button and straightened her collar before her hand skimmed down the front of her shirtwaist. A simple gesture that was somehow very provocative.

"I was getting dressed," she said.

"So I see."

She smiled then. A gentle, lush smile, like a woman with a secret. "My fever is gone. I don't like to lie around." Her smiled moved up a notch.

"Are you sure? No sense overdoing." He was almost sorry to hear she was well because it meant she wouldn't be needing him anymore...except for the wagon repair and the barn, he amended. Yeah, that would keep him here a while.

Yeah, that's what you need. Let's see, build a railroad or fix a wagon?

He didn't want to think about the lunacy of it— not just now. Maybe a little later. Maybe tomorrow.

"I'm feeling much better." She nodded as she spoke, making her hair slide over her shoulders. Sunlight glistened in the coppery strands.

Ethan made a big mistake then. Without thinking, he went to her, touched her forehead in a way he'd done many times in the last two days. But this time, his fingers lingered a few seconds longer than necessary. This time he brushed back a nonexistent lock of hair from her cheek, feeling the silk of her skin against the backs of his work-roughened knuckles.

He saw her eyes slam shut for a heartbeat, then open quickly. As though she'd felt the sudden longing he was feeling now, she stepped clear and went around him to the table and that crate of supplies he'd hefted inside.

Ethan dragged in a calming breath, then turned to face her. "Your skin is...cool," *and smooth as wet silk,* he thought to say. He kept trying to remind himself about business and goals and the lady being married. None of it seemed to take hold in his brain.

"Yes," she agreed, barely turning her head, "I'm relieved to be past the worst, that's for sure."

"Mama, does this mean you're all better?" Katie asked eagerly, her eyes wide with hope.

"I think so, honey." Molly cupped her daughter's chin. "I'm a little tired but on the mend. Definitely on the mend." She coughed. "Though there is this cough and a runny nose." She chuckled. "Runny nose. So attractive." Now why the devil did she say that? Who was she trying to impress?

Katie hugged Molly around the hips and Molly held the child close needing the support, the reminder of who she was and what she wanted. She was Molly Murphy, she needed nothing and no one except Katie and her home. She did not need or want any handsome cowboys with midnight eyes deep enough to drown in.

What she did need was something to take her mind off the man standing enticingly close. She gave an extra squeeze to Katie against her hip and moved in on that crate parked on the table. The size of the thing dawned on her slowly. Crate? Wooden crate. Not bag. Not basket, but crate. It was filled to overflowing with cloth sacks and items wrapped in brown paper. What was all this? No way was this what she'd ordered. Why, her few requests would've fit in a saddle bag.

This time when she looked at him, there was nothing warm or friendly in those snapping blue eyes of hers. Ethan, being a man of some experience, knew when he was in trouble with a woman. This was definitely trouble. He sighed inwardly and braced for the inevitable. He didn't have to wait long.

"What's all this?" she demanded, releasing Katie and inching closer to the table until her black skirt pressed into the edge. Sunlight poured into the room through the opened door settling white and warm on the dusty floor.

"Supplies," he replied, walking around the other

side of the table and stopping in the square of light. There was a sudden chill in the room and he figured he needed a little warming, though looking at her was warming him in an entirely different way.

"I can see that it's supplies," she countered. "Whose?"

With the tips of two fingers, she pushed paper and cloth to one side or another, peering in, obviously reading labels and trying to decide what was concealed in the wrappings.

"The supplies are yours. Who do you think they belong to?" he said, feeling a little short-tempered, perhaps at his unexpected attraction more than her attitude.

She arched one brow in surprise. "This isn't what I asked you to get, Mr. Wilder."

So they were back to "Mr. Wilder" again. "I picked up a couple of things you forgot." He emphasized the last two words. Here he was trying to help and she was getting all uppity.

Katie tugged at his sleeve, distracting him momentarily. "Like candy? Huh?"

"What? Oh, maybe."

"Can I see? Huh?"

"Sure." He hoisted Katie up so she could get a better look. "If you can find some, then..."

She squirmed in his arms and he held her while she leaned in closer still, her feet sticking out into the room, her hands rummaging in the crate's contents. Brown paper crinkled and creaked as she pushed it aside looking for the telltale distinctive shape of candy. Never mind that it came in all shapes and sizes, children always knew where it was. He always had, when he was her age.

"There's gotta—" She grabbed the brown wrapping paper and tore it free of the peppermint stick it concealed. "Candy!" she shouted. "Look Mama, candy! Ethan brought me peppermint candy!" With that she threw her arms around Ethan's neck and gave him a hug. He got a clunk in the back of his head with that candy stick. "Oh, thank you, Mr. Ethan." She shoved the candy into her mouth, her lips instantly red from the coloring. Her blue eyes danced with excitement.

"Katherine Louise," Molly scolded. "You don't eat candy this close to dinner. In fact—" her hard gaze flashed up to Ethan "—you shouldn't have candy at all. Not that anyone asked me."

Okay, Ethan had heard that tone before from more than one woman, that self-righteous indignation sort of tone that made him cringe a bit, made his temper rise. He let Katie settle lightly to the floor. Well, if the woman wanted a fight, he figured he was up for it. Maybe fighting was safer than the other emotion he'd been feeling, the one that was heating his loins.

"Katie," he said, his gaze fixed on Molly, "why don't you go see if you can dig up some worms by the garden so we can go fishing?"

Katie's gaze flicked from Ethan to Molly and back again. Quietly, as if sensing there was trouble brewing, she put the candy down on the scarred table surface. "Okay, Mr. Ethan." With that she went outside.

Ethan and Molly stared at each other for a long moment, then Molly went back to looking through the supplies. "You're going to have to take all this back, Mr. Wilder." She swept her hand over the crate in a grand gesture.

"Why?"

"I didn't ask for this and I can't afford it." She took the flour out of the box. "I'll keep the things I need, but the rest—"

"You *need* everything there and more. You need help. You need to get off this place and into a decent home and—"

"I'm not interested in your opinion of what I need or don't need, Mr. Wilder. I asked you to do us a favor. No, I didn't ask. You insisted, as I remember."

"Look, your cupboards are practically bare. I got a few extra things. I'll pay for them. I'll pay for the whole order. In fact, I already did." He started for the door before he said something he'd regret. He was trying to help. He was trying to soothe his guilty conscience.

She grabbed him by the arm, her fingers digging hard into the flesh just below the rolled-up cuff of his shirt. "Now, hold on there, one minute. I did *not* ask you to buy my food. I did *not* ask you to buy these extra items. I do not need or accept charity, and furthermore—"

"Charity! Who the hell's talking about charity?"

"Evidently, you are. You said you paid for my food and I won't allow—"

"Well, somebody better pay for supplies. What are you planning to live on? Cornmeal mush and water?"

"What I live on is none of your business!" With

a flounce of black cotton, she turned back to the table. Her stomach clenched and unclenched she was so darned angry. She removed the items one at a time from the crate, sorting them out as she went, mumbling under her breath, "Who ever heard of some stranger paying for my groceries? Why I wouldn't... I never... What the devil is this?" With sharp motions, she pulled the brown paper free, opened it and went instantly still.

"Now what?" Ethan demanded, seeing her reaction.

All she was doing was standing there, staring at the half pound of butter he'd bought.

"What's wrong? The butter rancid?" His tone was sharp.

She didn't answer.

"Hey, don't tell me this is the silent treatment because if it is—"

"It's butter," she barely breathed and sank down in the nearest chair. "You bought butter."

"Yes," he snarled, "I bought butter and dried apples and cream of tartar and canned milk—"

"Milk?" she said on the thready tone again. "Milk?"

"Yes! Milk! You got something against milk?"

She shook her head, looking suddenly pale and shaky. Instantly, his anger was replaced by concern.

"Are you sick again? Is your fever back?" He touched her forehead with the back of his hand.

Molly looked up at him, her eyes luminous.

"Do you know how long it's been since I've had butter?"

It was ridiculous for someone to go without something as basic as butter, Ethan thought. It was heart-breaking. And he realized, perhaps for the first time, how much it was costing her to stay here, in her home, the only home she'd ever had.

With the tip of her index finger she scraped the tiniest dab off the edge of the paper, not actually touching the portion itself. "Butter."

The delight in her eyes was something close to sexual. Hell, it *was* sexual. He watched her lick the butter from the tip of that finger. It was a simple gesture, and provocative as hell. His hand cupped the side of her face and she leaned into it for just a second, then straightened away. In that second everything changed.

"I haven't had butter since Christmas," she was saying, and he realized that was six months ago. "I love butter on bread, don't you?"

"Sure. Especially when the bread's hot and the butter melts and—"

"—runs all down your fingers."

They laughed together, easy, comfortable.

The cabin was very quiet. The room filled with white sunlight. The gentle call of a meadowlark carried through the open window near the kitchen. They were alone.

It seemed so natural for Ethan to drop down on one knee beside her. "I bought some honey to go with those biscuits and butter."

There was a huskiness in his voice that drew Molly, but she was already shaking her head in refusal, of the honey or the man, she wasn't entirely certain—and didn't want to think about it.

Move, the voice of warning called to her. She

didn't. Instead she looked into his upturned face. Such a handsome face, she thought, all chiseled angles and carved planes. Rugged, strong, like the country, like the man.

His hand rested lightly on her knee. She tried to make conversation. "Honey is...extravagant."

"A person needs to be...extravagant, at times."

His voice moved over her like a summer breeze, soothing, tantalizing. She touched his face, letting her thumb trace the line of his brow and the top of his cheek down to his mouth, then follow the line of his mustache. It was soft. She'd wondered.

"Extravagant is something I don't know much about." Her voice was hushed.

"It's not so hard," he told her, taking her hand and kissing the pad of each finger. "All you have to do is let go of your fears."

His mouth on her fingers was warm, moist, and sent tiny sparks of electricity skimming over her skin, making nerves pulse in anticipation. Her body tingled to life.

Don't do this, the voice of reason called, but it was faint and drowned out by the pounding of her heart. Yet, somehow she managed to pull free of his grasp.

Slowly, almost reverently, she closed the paper over the butter, one corner at a time. She was surprised to see her hands shake with the movement.

He must have noticed, because he reached over and took the package away from her, putting it on the table. Then, without a word, he took her hands in his. "Later," was all he said.

She stopped, letting him hold on to her hands,

feeling so safe, so secure in his touch. Their gazes found each other and locked. Pulling free of his grasp, she touched his cheek, brushing at his beard-roughened jaw. His eyes drifted closed. "Molly," was all he said.

"Yes," came her answer, the only answer she could think of at this moment.

When he looked at her again, he hesitated. She knew he was going to kiss her, knew he was giving her a chance to stop him. She didn't want to. She was married and still she wanted to kiss this man, and so she said nothing.

She waited for the first touch of his lips on hers. His mouth was gentle, as she knew it would be. Warm, easy, his lips skimmed hers. A tasting, testing, nothing more.

His eyes were open. So were hers and a look passed between them, of consent, of acceptance, of recognizing the inevitable.

His mouth settled more firmly on hers. The kiss deepened. His hands found her shoulders, his fingers curled over the tops, turning her more fully toward him.

She went willingly. Molly was lost in the world of heat and fire that his kiss ignited in her. He kissed her long and slow and deep and wet. He kissed her forever, or at least that was what she wanted him to do. Nothing and no one had ever made her feel the things she was feeling now. Nerves pulsed with longing she didn't know existed. Desire, blatant and lush, flashed lightning hot in her mind. Muscles tensed along her back and deep between her legs. A sort of purring sound came from somewhere deep inside her.

"Molly," he whispered against her lips as one hand glided up her ribs and cupped her breast. Instantly, her body responded in ways she didn't understand, ways ancient and carnal.

She gasped for breath, her mind struggling to catch up to the rampaging feelings drumming through her.

Stop this!

She struggled frantically against the desire that was drawing her in like a whirlwind, until, helpless, all she could do was surrender to the power and pray for rescue.

Perhaps it was the thought of rescue that first stirred reality in her brain. She tore her mouth from his and dragged in a long, slow breath. Their faces were mere inches apart. Passion darkened his eyes while her own body trembled with the wanting he'd stirred in her.

Yet she forced herself to take another breath and then one more. The world filled in around her, the cabin, Katie's little bed, the realization that she was married even if the chances were that her husband was dead.

Have you lost your mind, Molly Murphy?

Ethan leaned toward her again and she knew he meant to kiss her. Lord help her, she wanted him to kiss her more than she'd ever remembered wanting anything in her life. But from somewhere, from strength she didn't know she had, she managed to say, "Don't."

He went very still, his gaze locked with hers. She

had to get away from him, from the desire he created in her before…before she did something she'd regret.

She pushed at his chest, which was like pushing on a slab of granite. "We can't."

His grip loosened enough for her to twist around so that she no longer faced him. She only wished she could step clear of the heart-pounding longing that pulsed in her blood.

"We did," he countered.

"Don't do it again."

"Why?" he said, one side of his mouth quirking up in a semblance of a smile. "Didn't you like it?"

His smile was a touch too arrogant, a touch too confident. It sparked her temper and she fanned the flames with every gulp of air. She needed that temper. "No, I didn't," she lied, relieved that her voice was strong.

He sat back on his haunches. "What are you talking about?"

"I'm talking about kissing me. Don't do it again. I don't like it. I won't stand for it!" This time she moved toward the back wall near the kitchen as though searching for an escape, which was silly since she had nothing to fear…except perhaps her own quicksilver feelings.

"You're serious, aren't you?" he said, his expression incredulous.

"Absolutely."

He stood. His powerful presence seemed to fill the room, her room, dammit. No one intimidated her in her own house, especially not sable-eyed cowboys.

"I didn't do anything that you didn't know I was going to do, anything that you didn't *want* me to do."

What Molly wanted right now was to call him a liar, to deny what he'd said. She couldn't, and they both knew it. She could have stopped him. She should have stopped him.

The fact that she hadn't was bad. His knowing it was worse.

She was determined to bluff it through. "I never did any such thing."

Ethan gave a harsh excuse for a laugh. No way was he going to let her get away with pretending this was all his fault.

"Woman, you and I..." He rifled one hand through his hair. "You and I—"

"There is no 'you and I,' Mr. Wilder. I'm a married woman, remember?" she asked, clinging to what seemed only a faint memory.

"Yeah, I remember. I wish to hell I didn't." He knew he shouldn't have kissed her. He knew she was married and he respected her and the marriage and, aw, hell, he just should've controlled himself better. But when he'd walked in here, seen her looking more fragile and more tempting than original sin, he couldn't help himself. And neither could the lady, no matter what she said now.

"Mama! Mr. Ethan! Look at this!" Katie barreled into the room and skidded to a halt right in the middle of the ever widening chasm that separated them.

"In a minute, Katie," Ethan mumbled, his gaze fixed on Molly, on the look of shock and shame that shone tear-bright in her eyes. In a calmer tone he said, "We're not done talking about this."

She never acknowledged him at all. It was as though she were looking right through him, as if he'd ceased to exist.

Katie bobbed up and down like a rabbit on a string. "Look, Mr. Ethan. I got them worms."

She wiggled a dirty hand with two worms clutched in it in front of him. Ethan spared her a glance and a pat on the head, but he wasn't seeing worms or little girls. He was seeing one very beautiful woman—one he wanted very much. One he couldn't have, no matter what he did.

Sadness replaced his earlier lust and even anger.

"I'm sorry, Molly," he said, speaking to her as though there were no one and nothing else in the room or the world. "I never meant to…"

Molly went to Katie, cutting off all chance of further conversation. She bent down to inspect the worms. "Uh, nice, Katie. That's, uh, nice."

"See, Mr. Ethan?" Katie ordered. "Aren't they the best worms?"

"Yes," Ethan agreed absentmindedly. "The best." He was still trying to find a way to tell Molly, to explain.

Wilder, sometimes you can be an ass.

Katie tugged on his sleeve again. "Can we go now?"

"In a minute. I need to talk to your mother."

"Go now. Now is a good time," Molly said softly but firmly.

"Come on, Mr. Ethan." Katie had him by the hand and was pulling him toward the open door.

"Later," he said as he went out the door, Katie leading the way. "I'll see you later."

Molly stood motionless for a long time. At least she thought it was a long time, she wasn't sure. All she knew was that when Ethan Wilder had kissed her it was as though her whole world tipped on its axis.

She wandered over to the table and the crate of supplies still scattered there. Her hand lightly skimmed the package of butter where he'd put it on the table. It intrigued her, pleased her, that the man had thought to bring butter and milk. She picked up the can, inspecting the stark white label. They hadn't had milk for months. Jack had sold the cow to raise a stake to go back to the gold fields.

Poor Jack, he'd said he'd strike it rich in no time—two months at the most—and buy them two cows, three—a hundred. Fool's dreams. Just like her father. Both fools. Selfish fools because neither one cared about what happened to those around them.

Unfortunately, she hadn't figured this out until after she'd married Jack. When he'd ridden out, she made up her mind that she didn't need a man, couldn't trust a man. That plan had worked fine until Ethan Wilder.

It wasn't supposed to happen like this. She touched her hand to her lips and felt foolish so she let her hand drop away. But the memory of the kiss lingered. Ethan was all the things she'd thought a man couldn't be. He was all the things she'd ever dreamed of.

No one else would've stayed and cared for a sick woman, just because she had no one else. Lord, the man had not only taken that task he'd also looked after Katie, which was a full-time job all in itself. He'd watered animals and plants, fixed the corral fence, and the wagon, and cooked. The man had cooked for them!

No man she'd ever known had cooked, at least not more than opening a can of beans and dumping the contents in a skillet. Ethan had made biscuits.

A delicious shiver scampered up the backs of her legs. No. She could not be attracted to him.

Too late, her conscience countered.

Very well, then. She was attracted to him but she was not going to act on that attraction. Yes. That was the difference between honor and disgrace.

Oh, she was going to honor her wedding vows even if her marriage wasn't much more than a sham. She'd only married Jack because he was lonely and winter was coming and he wanted her. She had wanted to make a family for Katie and he had this piece of land. They both had their own reasons, she knew, but she'd hoped they would work them out together.

That had been her first mistake. Jack was never interested in families, just in a warm place and a warm woman for the winter.

She glanced out the window at the stream and the grove of cottonwood trees. To her eyes it was the most beautiful spot she'd ever seen. Clean and fresh. But as much as she loved this land, Jack hated it. He hated trying to repair the barn, fix the fences, work on the cabin. He grumbled and groaned and spent most of his time in town talking to anyone who would listen about gold and the latest strikes.

She'd kept hoping these last few months that Jack would come back, rich or poor. She told herself that she could still make this marriage work.

In truth, she didn't know if Jack was even alive. It had been four months since he'd left and she hadn't heard a word since. Why, for all she knew Jack was dead somewhere in a gulch and there'd be no one to tell her she was a widow…she was free. Free to be with someone else, someone like Ethan.

She snatched back the thought. No matter what, she didn't wish Jack dead. No. Never that.

She straightened and turned up her chin determinedly. Could that be possible? Just for a moment she let herself imagine if there was no Jack, only Ethan. The thought settled well with her but then she snatched it back.

No, she would not disgrace herself or Katie. As for that kiss, well, it was a mistake. An error in judgment. People made mistakes all the time. The important thing was to learn from them and move on. No sense fretting over what's done.

Ethan would leave. Probably not today since it was late and he and Katie were fishing together. Tomorrow. She was on the mend. He wasn't needed. She'd send him away…tomorrow. In the meantime, she would simply go on as if nothing had happened.

She and Ethan would go back to being…friends.

Chapter Nine

Two steps outside the cabin, she saw the dust cloud on the road before she heard the hoofbeats of several horses. As the men came into sight, Molly wondered if they were coming to her house or just riding past. The breeze caught her hair and whipped it across her face, blinding her for a moment before she pulled it free.

Shading her eyes from the sun, she could see that the riders were headed straight for her.

A few more seconds and she singled out Ed Bartel as the leader of the group. Normally, she wasn't a suspicious person, but a group of men, riding hard into her yard, indicated that this wasn't a social call.

She edged back toward the doorway and that shotgun she kept there. Better to err on the side of caution.

She knew Ed Bartel from when she and Jack had first arrived in town. He'd made a show of welcoming them. Of course, neither he nor his wife had called on them since.

Bartel reined up a few yards away, dust swirling

around the horses as he did. With him were Evans and Foster and three more men she didn't know by name but had seen around town a couple of times. Her throat ached from the dust which she had to fan away to get a good look at the men.

"Mrs. Murphy," Bartel said by way of hello, she supposed. He raked her with an appraising look. "Are you ill? You look under the weather."

"A little, Mr. Bartel." She brushed at the dust clinging to her skirt and shirtwaist.

Bartel made to dismount.

She stopped him. "As you've already mentioned, gentlemen, I'm not at my best. If you wouldn't mind coming back some other time... Bring your wives," she couldn't resist adding. "I'll make tea."

"Well, Mrs. Murphy," Bartel said, settling back in the saddle. "I appreciate the invite. And sure we'll do that...sometime."

"Sometime," she repeated knowing that meant never. Molly was not part of War Bonnet society and she knew the chances of them and their wives coming out here for tea were as likely as the moon turning pink with yellow spots.

Bartel's smile stayed fixed firmly on his face. "Now, Molly... Can I call you Molly?" He didn't wait for an answer. "I feel as if we know each other." He thumbed his hat back. "Like I was saying, Molly." That smile got a touch bigger. "We actually came out here because it's come to our attention that you haven't sold your land to the railroad that's coming through here real soon."

He rested his hands lightly on the saddle horn, the reins held loosely in his stubby fingers. In a voice that was calm and polite, he said, "Now, we know this is an oversight and we're sure you will be co-operating—"

"Why?"

His expression drooped a bit. "Why, what?"

"Why would you assume that I'd want to cooperate?"

Bartel lost all pretense of a smile. "Because them railroad folks will pay you nicely for your land, if that's what's worrying you."

"It isn't worrying me at all. I'm not interested in selling."

"What do you mean you aren't interested in selling? Everybody's sold."

"I'm not everybody. This is my home, Mr. Bartel. I like it here. I don't want to go somewhere else."

"You could move—"

"Not interested." This was the only home she'd ever had and, good or bad, it was hers. She'd put her whole self into making this a decent place to live. For the first time in her life, she had roots, she felt secure. She did not want to wander again, to be a gypsy the way she'd been all of her life.

"Now, look, lady." His tone was hard. "We need this land for the railroad."

"Are you threatening me, Mr. Bartel?" Molly took a half step toward that shotgun leaning just inside the doorway. Briefly, she wondered when Ethan and Katie would return.

"Woman, you can take it any way you want. All I'm telling you is that we ain't leaving here without this land." He reached in his jacket pocket and produced a folded piece of white paper. She figured it was a bill of sale.

"I want you to sign this," he told her. But this time when he made to dismount, she picked up the shotgun and held it cradled in her arms, the barrel pointed downward.

"I have no intention of signing your document, Mr. Bartel. I couldn't if I wanted to. This land belongs to my husband." For the first time she was glad the land was in Jack's name, not hers.

"Get your husband out here!"

"He's not here," she took great pleasure in saying.

"When's he coming back?"

"I couldn't say."

"What do you mean?"

She cocked her head to one side. "My husband's not here now."

Molly let her eyes move across the group of men, lingering on each man until settling on Bartel again.

His expression got tight and angry. "Now look, lady. This town needs that railroad and that railroad needs this land. It's that simple. They are gonna pay you and—"

"Get off."

"What?" Bartel looked confused.

"You heard me." Molly lifted the shotgun higher. "Get off my land. Now."

"There's no call for waving guns around," Evans spoke up.

"I'll be the judge of that. When I get confronted by a bunch of men, all wearing guns, who tell me

they want what's mine..." She let the implication
linger.

Disbelief was reflected in the faces of the men
gathered. Bartel stiffened but made no move to
leave. "I want you to sign this land over, do you
hear me. Just sign your husband's name." He waved
the document at her. "I'll pay you myself. Name
your price."

"That wouldn't be legal," she told them in a
sweet tone that held no warmth.

"Ain't no one here gonna say it was different, are
we boys?"

There was a general sort of nodding and mumbled
agreement.

"No." She pulled back the hammers on both barrels.

"Now, Mrs. Murphy. Molly. All we want is for
you to sign this deed for the railroad. That's all,"
he amended with a sly smile. "You know you aren't
going to shoot anyone."

Molly's expression remained fixed, her fingers
curled around the triggers. She didn't know whether
she would fire or not. She didn't think she could
actually kill anyone, but she was enjoying watching
the uncertainty on their faces.

The moment stretched tight between them and she
was afraid they were going to put her to the test.
But the test never happened. A male voice from off
to her right intervened.

"She might not shoot you, but I sure as hell
will."

Molly saw Bartel's eyes move over to the direction of the voice and she turned. Ethan was there,

leaning casually against the side of the cabin. In one hand he held his Navy Colt. She actually sighed with relief. Ethan was here.

Molly saw the surprise in Bartel's face but strangely he didn't seemed worried.

"Wilder. Thank goodness. Maybe you can talk some sense into her. After you left today, we checked at the land office and discovered that hers was the only land not sold, and when you said that you had unfinished business we naturally figured—''

"Don't say another word, Bartel." He closed on them in five angry strides. "Just turn and ride out of here."

"What? Why? She's a stubborn one. We'll back you up."

"I'm handling things. Now get the hell outta here." Ethan could see she was watching, listening. He saw her head come up sharply at the mention of the railroad. Lord, it wasn't supposed to be like this.

Bartel seemed to consider this for a moment, then a look of understanding softened his features. "Ah. Sure." His smile came back. "I see what's happening."

He turned in the saddle. "Well, men, I think we'd better go and let Mr. Wilder here handle this. If anyone can get this straightened out it's the owner of the railroad."

He touched two fingers to the brim of his hat. "We won't trouble you again, ma'am." He jerked his horse around and rode out, the others following.

Molly focused on the dust cloud and avoided looking at the man coming toward her. *The owner of the railroad.* The truth settled somewhere in the pit of her stomach, hard and cold and tight as a noose. Ethan Wilder owned the railroad.

Suddenly, he was there, in front of her, close. "Molly, we need to talk."

She put the shotgun down against the side of the house before she skirted around him and paced out into the yard. "There's nothing to say, Mr. Wilder."

"I think there is. I'd like to explain."

"About the railroad?"

He sighed. "Yes. I never meant for you to find—"

"—find out that you were here for your railroad? Too bad that Mr. Bartel let it slip. And just when you were so close, too. What was your plan? To sweet-talk me, kiss me, make love to me?" Molly's hands curled into tight fists. Muscles down her back knotted with barely controlled anger and shame. "How far were you planning to go with your little plan, Mr. Wilder?" She gave a harsh laugh. "Foolish question, huh?"

She strode in the direction of the corral because it was away from him. She didn't want to see him, to hear him. She didn't want to remember what she'd felt minutes ago.

Ethan caught up with her, grabbing her arm and spinning her around to face him. "It's not like that, Molly."

"Really!" She yanked free of him. "Do you deny that you own the railroad? My God, you own the railroad!"

"Yes, but—"

"Do you deny that you came here to get my land?"

"No, but—"

"Do you deny that you kissed me because you thought that would get you what you wanted?"

"Yes! Dammit! Yes! I deny it. I never used you. I would never do that to you. When I kiss a woman, it's because I want to."

"Oh, so you do this a lot then," she snapped back at him.

Ethan snatched off his hat and rifled one hand through his hair. "No. I do not go around kissing women. Certainly not to get their land. Billy was supposed to have taken care of this. Somehow he didn't, and I said I would come here and buy the land. That's all."

"Then why didn't you say so when you rode in?"

"Because you were sick. Because I felt sorry for you—"

"Felt sorry for me! I don't need you to feel sorry for me. I don't need anyone to feel sorry for me." She noticed Katie coming toward her with a fishing pole propped on her shoulder.

Ethan grabbed her by both shoulders and held her. "Oh, no you don't, Molly. You can send me packing if you want. But I won't go with you believing that I kissed you because I wanted this damned chunk of Wyoming wilderness."

She was as stiff as a fence post, unmoving. Not at all like the woman who'd melted in his arms such a short time ago. "I wanted to tell you. There never seemed to be the right time."

"How convenient for you." She easily pulled free

and straightened the front of her blouse, making a show of fussing with wrinkles.

"But when I kissed you... I know I shouldn't have, but I wanted to. I wanted to kiss you more than I've ever wanted anything in my entire life. Because in the few days that I've been here something has happened between us. You know and I know it and there's not a damned thing we can do about it. Every time we look at each other it's like lightning and I want—"

"I'm married!"

"Dammit, don't you think I know that! If I could find your husband I'd shoot the son of a bitch where he stands just for leaving you and Katie."

"Oh, I see. If you can't get the land by making love to me then you'll resort to shooting my husband."

This time it was Ethan who paced away. "You aren't going to listen, are you?"

"No."

"Molly," he said softly, reaching out to her wishing, praying she'd reach back.

She didn't.

"Leave, Ethan," was all she said.

"Molly..."

Tears glistened in her eyes and clogged her throat. "I am telling you for the last time to get out of here! Get away from me! Stay far away from me!" She swiped at the tears that shimmied down her cheeks. "Damn you, Ethan Wilder."

With that she went to the cabin.

Ethan watched her go. There was nothing else he

could do. He went to the corral, gathered his gear and saddled Four.

"Where you goin'?" Katie's voice startled him.

"Town." He snapped the cinch down hard enough to make Four shy and side step. "Watch out!" Ethan grabbed her out of the way. He was taking his sullenness out on the horse and the kid and it wasn't fair, he knew. So he hunkered down and said, "I've got some work to do."

"But we didn't catch any fish, and you said you was gonna help me make a house for the birds to live in in the wintertime." Her mouth pulled down in a frown.

"Katie, honey, I'll be around for a while, in town. Maybe later we can work on that birdhouse. Okay?"

"I don't want you to go, Mr. Ethan." She hugged his neck and he hugged her back. This was getting tougher and tougher. Was this some kind of punishment for not telling the truth up front? If it was, it was working. He felt like someone had just gut-punched him.

He pulled her arms from around his neck and set her back a ways from him. Brushing the hair back from her round face. Something moist was happening in his eyes and he blinked hard. "Honey, I have to go." He stood and checked the cinch and bridle and the tie on his saddlebags. He swung up in the saddle.

"You never did teach me how to ride your horse," Katie told him.

Ethan shifted in the saddle, the leather creaking. Four shook his head as though anxious to go. "You know, you're right about that." Leaning down, he hooked Katie under the arms, and in one motion positioned her in front of him.

"Okay, I'll take you as far as the road."

Katie beamed and bounced up and down as though they were already moving. Four looked back and Ethan chuckled. "Never mind, boy," he said, giving the horse a pat. "Katie's going to handle the reins this time."

They rode out into the sunlight together, Katie laughing and saying giddy-up as Four walked calmly along. He took her as far as the road. "Okay, this is where I leave you." He lifted her down and deposited her on the ground. When he straightened, his gaze naturally sought the cabin and, sure enough, Molly was standing in the doorway.

It was in his mind to go back there, to talk to her some more, to make her understand, believe him. He knew it was no use. She needed time to calm down. He needed time to sort out his feelings.

"Katie!" she called, and Katie ran to her mother. He paused to look at Molly a moment longer, remembering, wishing, and regretting, oh, yes, regretting.

"We aren't through," he called to her. She made no sign of hearing him. No matter. He'd be back. Yanking down hard on the brim of his hat, Ethan reined over and rode in the direction of town.

Inside the cabin, Molly was putting the last of the supplies away, trying to concentrate on making dinner, on what Katie was saying—anything except the one thing she did not want to think about.

Ethan.

"But why did Mr. Ethan have to go?" Katie asked for about the fourth time in the last ten minutes. "I liked him. Didn't you like him?"

"Yes, Katie, I liked him." *More than I care to think about,* she thought.

"So, can he come back?"

"Not right away." Molly stowed the milk on the shelf.

"Why not? Where's he going?"

"To town." She unpacked the last of the crate and put it down at the end of the counter on the floor.

"But we didn't get to finish fishing and—"

"Katie, why don't you go outside and feed the chickens?"

The little girl scooted down from the chair and started for the door. "Okay, but it won't be no fun without Mr. Ethan. He let me ride his horse. Did you see me riding?"

"Yes, I saw." She had seen him sitting atop that horse, tall, powerful, dark. He was as tempting as sin and, even knowing what she did, it had taken all her strength not to go to him, to let him explain, to believe simply because she wanted to believe.

"I'll be out in a minute," Molly shouted after Katie.

But for all her wanting Katie to stop talking about Ethan, being alone in the cabin was worse. It was strangely quiet without him.

Well, she wouldn't give in to this. She was strong. She'd been lied to and used by him. She should be angry. Dammit, she *was* angry.

Molly straightened. She was not going to think

about him in any way. She was better. Her fever was gone. She didn't need him or want him around. She was lucky she'd found out the truth when she had.

Yet, she seemed to feel his presence in the cabin. If she closed her eyes, Molly could see him standing in the doorway, filling the width of it, having to duck his head to come inside. Her hand naturally glided along the top of the chair. Memories of him sitting there, laughing with them over some silly thing Katie had said, came to mind. He had a nice laugh. An easy smile that lit up his eyes and made her want to smile back at him.

No. This was getting her nowhere. She shook her head against the lush memories. She stormed toward the blanket he'd tossed over her bed this morning. Grabbing it with both hands, she snatched it up, the wool rough and scratchy on her sensitive skin.

Molly stood there holding it against her, remembering him stringing it up that first night, remembering the fire and him risking his own life to save Katie's.

She'd been grateful to him for that. And more. Much more. Perhaps that was why she hadn't been as angry as she should have been when he'd kissed her, when she'd let him kiss her.

Why should he have this power over her? She needed to think about her husband. Yes, that was it. Think about Jack.

But every thought seemed to be nothing more than a comparison, and Jack came up lacking every time.

Molly dropped down on the edge of the bed.

The cabin was suddenly overbearingly small and confining. How could a man make such a difference in her life in such a short period of time?

She hurled the blanket down on the floor. "Leave me alone, Ethan Wilder!"

But he *had* left her alone. She had ordered him from the place and he'd gone. She wanted her life back the way it was before she'd met him, before he'd come in and taken over.

She ground the heels of her hands into her eyes. She would not cry. She *wouldn't*.

"Damn you, Ethan!" she shouted. "Damn you for doing this to me!"

Confused and desolate, she fell over onto her side on the hay-filled mattress. She curled into a small tight ball and cried.

Chapter Ten

There's two things a man wants when he sulks, whiskey and solitude. Ethan found the whiskey at the El Dorado Saloon in War Bonnet. It was a poor excuse for a saloon, as far as saloons go. It was long past its prime, judging by the faded wallpaper and stained pine floors.

The single room was long and narrow, with the required bar taking up half the length of the left side; a pair of spittoons punctuated each end. There was a mirror hanging behind the bar that was too dirty to reflect what light was coming in the equally dirty front windows. There was the distinct smell of stale tobacco and whiskey in the air.

Two men in suits occupied a table near the front.

Ethan went first to the bar. "Whiskey," he said. "Bottle and one glass."

"Three bits," the barman replied, his hand still around the neck of the bottle as though he weren't letting loose until he saw the money.

Ethan obliged, tossing several silver coins on the

scarred walnut top. Grabbing up the bottle, he went to find a remote table in the back of the room.

"Hey, you forgot the glass," the squirrel-faced man called, and Ethan retraced his steps long enough to snatch the glass out of the man's hand.

He settled into a chair in the corner, his back against the wall. Sort of like his life these days, he thought. When he moved, the chair's leg wobbled, and after a minute his dark mood wouldn't put up with such a petty annoyance so he changed chairs but not location.

He filled the glass with a slosh of whiskey and tossed it back in one swallow, taking pleasure in the way it burned his throat on its way down. Those men at the table near the bar kept glancing his way, then saying something low that he couldn't hear. Probably knew who he was. When he saw one of them get up, he fixed the man with a you'll-be-sorry-if-you-come-over-here look that must have worked because he went out the double doors.

Smart man, he thought churlishly. He poured another drink and tossed it back. Hunched over the table, he stared at the amber liquid in the bottle.

So this is what it's come to, huh, Wilder?

Evidently. Oh, he knew getting drunk wasn't going to help a damned thing but it seemed like the only thing he could do, at least do right. Damn, he'd really made a mess of things.

Another slosh of whiskey and another single swallow to take it in. So now what?

Try as he might, he knew he still had to have that land for the railroad and he knew now with crystal clarity that if he got it, then Molly would never forgive him. If he didn't, then he'd lose everything he'd ever worked for, everything he'd wanted, every promise he'd made to investors and to Billy.

So, what was he going to do? Damned if he knew! Ideally, he'd come up with some magical new route. Yeah, right, only if there was an earthquake big enough to move mountains in the next couple of weeks.

Not much hope there.

There was no other way around, not without going a hundred miles out of the way, not without losing time he didn't have. Bankers were a cold-hearted bunch when it came to loan payments.

So he had to have the land or give up on the railroad.

He poured another drink, the whiskey spilling over his fingers and onto the gouged surface of the table, pooling in a deep cut that someone had carved in the pine.

Absently, Ethan ran his finger back and forth over that scar, feeling the rough edges, watching the way the liquor seemed to cling to his skin, then fall away. Something within his grasp, yet he was unable to hold on to it...like Molly.

Shaking his head, he swallowed the whiskey. It didn't burn his throat anymore. In fact, he hardly felt it at all. He ought to be halfway to getting good and drunk. He wasn't.

The glass was smooth and warm in his hand and he turned it around slowly, back and forth, between thumb and forefinger.

He should never have kissed her. Yeah, that was

his big mistake. He should never have stayed there, never gotten to know her.

But Molly Murphy was the most enticing woman he'd ever met. She was strong and determined and honest—something he hadn't been. When she smiled at him, it was as though she ignited a flame inside him. Erotic fantasies merged with rich memories, stirring his body to life.

His fingers actually trembled when he reached for the bottle again.

Molly had been like fire-heated silk in his arms, all soft and pliant. Her mouth had been easy against his, warm and willing, and when she'd made that little sound, desire had overwhelmed whatever rational thought he'd had.

Dammit, she should have stopped him!

He stilled, the glass held out in front of him. Yeah, she should've stopped him. She hadn't.

He put the glass down. Truth be told, in the back of his mind, he'd thought she would. Instead, she'd kissed him back. There was no mistake about that. He was no novice with women and he knew when a lady was willing. Molly Murphy had been very willing.

That thought fed his male pride and something else. Thinking about her, another feeling stirred in him. Oh, there was lust there, but something else. Like a midnight shadow, like a ghost of a long-forgotten memory, a feeling circled in his mind just out of reach.

Dammit!

He snatched up the glass and slammed it down hard enough to draw everyone's attention.

"Hey!" the barman called out. "No trouble in here, you!"

Ethan frowned. "No trouble."

Still the question lingered in his mind. Why had she kissed him? Why hadn't she slapped his face?

He was pouring himself another drink when he heard the shuffle of men's feet and looked up in time to see Bartel and Evans and a couple of other men from earlier today come into the saloon. They made a beeline right for him.

"Ethan!" Bartel said loudly as he and the others closed in on him. So much for being left alone to sulk.

"So?" Bartel was saying as he dragged out a chair and sat down. The other three did the same.

"Wilder," Evans said by way of acknowledgement.

The others nodded their greeting.

"Have a seat," Ethan said with a sarcastic edge to his voice.

"What? Huh? Oh. You mind?" Bartel mumbled.

"No, why should I mind?" Ethan replied in that same tone. He was in no state of mind to discuss the fine points of brooding with these men. "Drink?" He nudged the half-full bottle toward the center of the table.

"Sure," Bartel said, then over his shoulder called, "Ben, three more glasses over here. I guess this means we're celebrating?"

Ben brought the glasses.

"You got the land?" This time it was Brinsfield doing the asking.

"Did I?" Ethan returned, pouring himself another drink. This one he sipped.

"How much did she finally take for it?"

The men all seemed to lean in at one time, as though he held the answer to the secret of life. He didn't, though he wished to hell he did.

"I didn't get the land."

Their faces all showed their surprise. "What the hell happened?" Bartel said.

"Nothing happened. I didn't get it. We're...in negotiations." He poured the whiskey, but didn't drink it. Suddenly he was losing his taste for it and for getting drunk. What he wanted to do was ride back out there, demand she listen to him, to reason. Fat chance.

"You can't leave it like that. What are you gonna do?" Evans asked. "We gotta have that land."

"Don't you think I know that!" Ethan snapped back.

Bartel turned to Brinsfield and said, "Maybe *we* better ride on out there tomorrow and—"

"Don't," was all Ethan said.

"Why? I'm sure if we explained things just right..." The sneer on his face was coldly chilling. "She can be *made* to listen."

There was something in that *made* that sent all Ethan's protective instincts to the fore.

"Leave her alone, Bartel."

Bartel lounged back in his chair and raked Ethan with an appraising stare. "Sounds to me like you've got your priorities mixed up."

"Leave the woman alone. My 'priorities' are

none of your business. I'll handle what needs handling.''

''And how much *handling*,'' Bartel emphasized the last word in a snide sort of way, ''does the woman need? Is that old Molly's price? A good roll in the hay? Why, Ethan, I figure you're up to the task. If you ain't, why I can sure—''

Ethan didn't even think. In one motion, he stood, reached across the table and grabbed Bartel by the coat front, dragging him halfway onto the table.

''A man never talks about a lady in a saloon, Bartel.''

Bartel's face was mottled red and he was digging his fingers into Ethan's, trying to pry loose his grip. He failed.

''Mrs. Murphy is a lady,'' Ethan ground out. ''You hear me?''

Bartel nodded.

Evans grabbed Ethan's arms. ''Let him go, Wilder. He didn't mean nothing.''

''I don't want to hear anyone mention her name, not in here, not anywhere…even in church. If I do…'' He released Bartel so suddenly that he sprawled on the tabletop for a second before staggering to his feet.

''Wilder,'' Bartel snapped as he fussed with and straightened his coat front. ''What the hell's got into you?''

Ethan looked at the faces of the men glowering at him. He needed these men. He needed their business, and yet here he was…

''I'll take care of the railroad. You take care of getting the cattlemen here.'' He snatched up his hat from the table. "Look, I'm a little short-tempered these days…"

Bartel stuffed his shirtfront into his waistband again and tugged down on the front of his vest. "Sure, I understand, but—"

"I gotta go." He needed to get out of here before he said or did something he regretted.

"When will you be back? The cattlemen will be here next Monday to talk about shipping schedules and rates and such."

Ethan was already moving toward the doorway, talking over his shoulder as he went. "I'll be back in a few days."

Ethan pushed through the doors to the outside. He was headed for the end of the track or, as it was commonly known, Hell on Wheels.

Ethan spent the night on the open prairie mostly because he wasn't up to facing Billy and the other railroad men yet. He'd kept a cold camp, just some water from his canteen and a piece of beef jerky for dinner. Sleep, what little he'd gotten, was filled with dreams about a blue-eyed woman with fire in her hair.

The morning dawned gray and cloudy, like his mood. That was the whiskey and regret. An hour or so later he rode into the sprawling hodgepodge that was the end of the track. It was a small city nestled against the treeless hills. They had close to eight hundred men on the payroll: graders, track layers, wood choppers, mule skinners and surveyors among others.

As Ethan made his way between tents, he spotted

the work train up ahead. It sat cold and black and silent with flat cars and bunk cars strung out behind it like a serpent's tail. A small herd of cattle grazed on the grass nearby. They, too, belonged to the railroad. Eight hundred men demanded meat every day and, when antelope or buffalo weren't available, steers were slaughtered.

Smoke rose steadily from the stove in the cook tent. In the distance Ethan spotted the survey team headed out on horseback to stake out the next leg of the track, while close at hand, graders were busy leveling the land in preparation for the ties to be set.

There was shouting and cussing, lots of cussing; words that would make a nun run for cover.

The men worked as a team, each knowing his job, each doing it almost without instruction. Except today, Ethan realized. While most men were working, there were some sitting around, lounging almost, on crates and barrel tops, sipping coffee as though they were in the lobby of the Inter-Ocean Hotel in Cheyenne, instead of building a railroad.

"What's going on here?" he demanded of one of the men sprawled on the ground near the telegraph car.

The man came quickly to a sitting position and had the good grace to look a little sheepish. "Waitin' on rails, Mr. Wilder," he said, touching two fingers to the brim of his woolen cap.

"Rails?" Ethan shifted in the saddle, scanning the area. Not a rail to be seen anywhere. What the hell? "Where's Billy?" he demanded.

"Over to his tent, I suppose," the man replied, nodding his head in the general direction.

Ethan didn't need anyone to tell him where Billy's tent was. But why was Billy in his tent when he should have been working, and more importantly, where the hell were those rails?

Ethan rode the few yards and dismounted quickly. Shoving aside the canvas flap, Ethan ducked inside.

Head down, Billy was seated at the walnut traveling desk they used for paperwork and keeping documents.

"All right, Billy," Ethan said, not bothering with polite civilities, "what's all this about no rails? I made arrangements and—"

"—and they aren't coming." Billy looked tired and drawn and old for his twenty-four years. His dark-blond hair fell over his forehead and brushed the collar of his brown shirt. "I was writing you a letter about it."

"A letter!" Ethan paced the two steps over to the tent opening and turned. "You shouldn't be writing me letters. You should be on the train back to Chicago to find out what's wrong. You should—"

"Don't tell me my job. I'm writing you a letter because *you* were supposed to be back here two days ago and there's no telegraph in War Bonnet!" Billy surged to his feet, his hands curled into tight fists below the rolled-up cuffs of his faded brown shirt. "I've wired Anderson's in Chicago and they say they are temporarily *out* of rails and they won't have any until the thirtieth."

"The thirtieth!" Ethan echoed. "That's too late. We've got to make the two-hundred mile mark by the fifteenth or that damned bank will be screaming foreclosure. I wish to hell we'd never borrowed from a bank and stuck with using investors.''

"We ran short. We didn't have a choice." Billy's round face was drawn down in a deep frown. "We've got fifteen days to lay ten miles of track."

"Well, what are *you* doing about it?" Ethan paced over to the tent flap and back again, all of two long strides.

They faced off like a couple of lions over a piece of meat. Each man glared at the other. As usual, it was Billy who broke the tension. He settled in his chair and, reaching behind him into an opened trunk, produced a bottle of Irish whiskey.

"A little early in the day for drinking, don't you think?" Ethan said, dropping down on the cot.

"It's not early. It's late. I haven't been to bed yet." Billy poured a hefty amount in a tin cup and offered the bottle to Ethan, who refused.

Elbows on knees, Ethan willed himself to be calm. "Tell me what's happening?"

"I wish to hell I knew." Billy sipped the whiskey, winced and put the cup down on the desk. "A few weeks ago we were having trouble getting spikes. You remember."

"Yeah, but we took care of that," Ethan replied. "I wired the San Francisco foundry and they said they had mistakenly overshipped to another buyer. The spikes showed up."

"A week late." Billy came around the desk to stand by the tent opening, his back to Ethan. He lifted the flap and looked out. "Since then," Billy continued, "there's been more trouble." He let the flap fall and turned back to his friend. "Think about it, Ethan. That last shipment of tools, saws and such never did show up. The supplier swore up and down they had been shipped but no one could find them. We finally had to buy stock from a different company.''

Ethan snatched off his hat in an agitated gesture and rifled his hand through his hair. ''Yeah. Cost us twice as much.''

''Burt Hockmyer over at Anderson's says they lost our order.''

''Ridiculous. Anderson's have been shipping to us since we started this job almost a year ago. I could practically set my watch by their deliveries.''

''Exactly.'' Billy went back to the desk.

''Well, we damned sure can't build a railroad without rails.'' Ethan was looking at the canvas-covered floor trying to figure out how he was going to overcome this latest in a string of obstacles. He was so close to winning—except for a certain piece of land.

''I know that.'' Billy toyed with the metal cup of whiskey, but didn't take any. ''What I'm wondering is, how come we're having all this trouble sudden like?''

''What are you saying? You think there's some kind of conspiracy or something?'' Ethan met his friend's gaze straight on. ''Why? If we don't make this thing go and the banks have to foreclose, they stand to lose. Everyone loses if we don't finish.''

''I know all that. I've sat here all night trying to figure the damned thing out.'' Billy came over and sat down beside Ethan on the cot. ''It just doesn't make sense.'' He glanced over at Ethan sitting shoulder-rubbing close. "At least you got the land, so that much is taken care of."

"I might as well tell you..." Ethan looked down at the floor again, then back to Billy.

"Tell me what?"

"I didn't *get* the land."

Billy sat unmoving for a long minute. "Okay," was all he said.

"Okay?" Ethan paced away, spurs jingling. He knew he'd failed and he wanted someone to tell him so, penance, he supposed. The tent fluttered in the morning breeze. The sound of a couple of mule skinners discussing the fine points of wrangling with a couple of mules, carried through the tent walls. "We can't do without that land and you sit here saying, 'Okay'?"

"What the hell do you want me to say?" Billy straightened. "I know it's my fault. You put me in charge of buying the land in the first place and I missed that one." He went to where his saddlebags were piled in the corner with his saddle. "Let me get a few things together and—"

"What the hell do you think you're doing?" Ethan demanded.

"I'm going to get the land."

"If Molly won't sell to me, what the *hell* makes you think you can do something I can't?" Ethan paused. "I'm sorry, kid."

"I know."

Ethan sat down beside Billy again and gave his partner an affectionate pat on the shoulder. "We'll work it out."

"We always do," Billy agreed, straightening as

he spoke. "There's no way we're gonna let this dream slip away from us now, not when we're so close. We've been planning this a long time."

"Yeah, kid. A long time." It was true. They'd talked of building a railroad ever since that first week working on the U.P. Two men who had nothing and no one in this world, except a railroad, a dream, a thing to give them identity.

"If I have to build the last fifty miles with my own damn hands," Billy told him fiercely, "that's what I'll do."

"Not while I'm around you won't." A smile tugged at Ethan's mouth. "You think I'm gonna let you have all the fun? This isn't any worse than Gettysburg, and if we can get through that alive…"

Billy slapped his knee and stood in the way of men who want to change a subject before they got too emotional. "Okay. First things first. We want to tackle the supply problem or the land problem?"

"Supplies," Ethan told him. "If we don't get 'em, the land won't matter. Molly would be glad to hear me say that, I suspect."

Billy was busy rummaging in the camel-backed trunk behind the desk. "Molly? Who's Molly? You mentioned that name a minute ago."

"Molly Murphy," Ethan replied, instantly thinking of the woman and the kiss. "She owns the ranch we need, or rather her husband does."

"What's he say?"

"Nothing. He's not there."

Billy produced what appeared to be a clean shirt from the trunk. He tossed it on the end of the cot, the red plaid dim from too many washings. Billy pulled his shirttail free of his trousers and started working on the buttons. "When will the husband...Murphy, be back?"

"Don't know."

"And the wife, does she know?"

"She doesn't know, either." Ethan glanced over at his friend. "Can you believe it? That son of a bitch ran out on her months ago. He left a woman and a kid to fend for themselves while he's off chasing gold. She's raising chickens and selling the eggs and growing vegetables and doing a damned fine job of surviving against the odds." There was an unmistakable note of pride in his voice.

Billy shrugged out of his dirty shirt and reached for the clean one. "Sounds like you got to know her pretty well."

Ethan's head came up with a snap. "What the hell's that supposed to mean? Look, Billy, if you're saying something—"

Billy stopped him by holding both hands up in unconditional surrender. "Whoa! I only meant she sounds special. You're not usually so...patient about things. What's got you so riled?"

"Nothing!" Everything: taking a woman's land, having no choice about it, remembering the look in her eyes when she'd ordered him off the place, knowing he'd have to go back there and see her and...

Ethan stormed outside and headed for the campfire by the cook tent. He needed some coffee, some breakfast. He needed distance from these memories.

Billy followed along, tucking his clean shirt in as he went.

Ethan snatched up a cup and a gray metal plate from the stack on the end of the plank table before getting in the chow line. Billy joined him.

The day was warming fast and there was a sage-scented breeze out of the north. Overhead the sky was pale blue, dotted with puffy white clouds that would probably turn into thunderheads late in the afternoon.

Breakfast was cornmeal mush, bacon, biscuits and coffee. "I hate cornmeal mush," Ethan told the cook sharply.

"Since when?" Mulroon, the camp cook asked, looking surprised and more than a little annoyed.

"Since always," Ethan retaliated, holding out his plate for the mush just the same. He'd been eating it every day for the last seven months.

"Well, we ain't in New York and this here ain't no Delmonico's, you know," Mulroon said in the way of sharp-tongued cooks, waving Ethan along with the business end of a ladle.

Ethan helped himself to some extra crisp bacon and three biscuits. There was no honey, but there was butter. Butter. Molly loved butter, she'd practically cried when—

"Hey, Ethan, you gonna stand there all day or what?" Billy nudged him with his elbow.

Ethan snapped out of his musings. "No."

There were a couple of dozen men seated at the picnic-style tables. Ethan headed for the far side of the eating area and settled on a makeshift bench made of a plank, straddling two empty nail kegs that was out of earshot of the men. Ethan held his plate out in front of him. His cup of coffee rested beside his right hip near his .44.

Billy sat Indian fashion on the ground, leaning back against one of the barrels. "When do you want to leave?"

"Right after breakfast." Ethan ate the mush because he was hungry and because it was there. He'd learned to do a lot of things he didn't like over the years. "I'll go to Chicago and see what's wrong at Anderson's, then I'll go by the bank and see if we can get an extension on the loan payment."

"We're gonna need it. There's no way we can lay ten miles in five days. All we'll need are a couple of weeks. Even one would make the difference," Billy added. "Shouldn't be a problem. Like you said, it's better business for them if we finish than if they foreclose. Sure you don't want me to come?"

"No. You stay here. Keep the men working. Have them keep grading and readying the roadbed." The day was already warming, the sun made Ethan squint. He pulled the brim of his hat down lower and shifted around a bit until the sun fell on his shoulders and back, warming muscles through the dark-green cotton. A herd of antelope grazed about a mile away, well out of rifle range. Animals always seemed to know exactly how far that was.

A couple of workers strolled past. "Mr. Wilder. Mr. Trumble," they said almost in unison.

"Boys," Ethan answered with a nod. To Billy he said, "Once we get the supplies moving again, I'll go back and get the land."

Billy craned his neck around to look at his partner. "What are you going to do different? I mean you were gone four days and—"

"I don't know. I'll figure something out." He had to figure something out, some way to redeem himself with Molly and get the land. It was untenable but it was the hand he'd been dealt.

Ethan cleared his throat and straightened. Needing to change the subject, he said, "I met with the businessmen in town. That guy Bartel is a blowhard of the first order, but enthusiastic. He sees dollar signs in his sleep, I'll warrant. Land is already going up in price and I wouldn't be surprised if he owned most of it."

"Well, railroads do that for a town," Billy muttered, tossing a chunk of biscuit toward a flock of sparrows pecking at crumbs nearby. The birds fluttered away but came immediately back. "Don't I remember you writing to Bartel?"

"Yeah. Anyway, he's got the cattlemen organized for us, which is good...assuming we're there in time for the spring calf shipping. Otherwise..." He let the implication linger.

Billy scrambled to his feet enough to perch on the bench beside Ethan. "I still don't see why you don't let me go see this Molly person about the land while you're in Chicago. Luke Thompson could handle things here."

Yes, Ethan thought, Thompson was a first-rate foreman and could probably run the work just fine. It made more sense to let Billy do what he'd said, but Ethan had his own unfinished business with Molly Murphy that had nothing to do with the railroad. Fleetingly, he thought about sending Billy to Chicago, but most of the suppliers had made their deals with Ethan. He wanted to look them in the face when he explained what the hell was going on.

Chapter Eleven

Billy stopped midmotion. "I'm gonna argue this one with you, Ethan. I can handle Chicago."

"I know you can, but you can handle this work better. You know the men better than I do. They trust you and you know who to count on…when to push and when to back off. We're a team, right?"

"Yeah, but I need to help."

"I know. You've been helping ever since that day at Brandy Station."

When the war had started lots of men on both sides had formed their own companies, but, as the war had raged on, the ability to get the job done became more important than family connections.

Ethan got the job done. He'd led an elite band of hand-picked cavalry that had raised havoc with Lee's forces at Five Forks, Brandy Station and Gettysburg, to name a few. Ethan had risen through the enlisted ranks all the way to brevet major and Billy to brevet lieutenant. They'd been ordered into a joint flanking mission in support of General Stoneman.

Ethan had been in charge and when they'd been

ambushed, he'd given the order to scatter. It had
been his last order before being shot twice. He'd lain
there, unable to move, feeling the life flowing out
of him. He'd known with certainty that he was going
to die.

But he hadn't counted on Billy Trumble. When
the few survivors had gotten back to camp, they'd
reported Ethan dead, along with about three dozen
others but Billy, thankfully, had refused to believe
it.

Disregarding orders, risking his own life to go
into enemy territory, Billy had spent hours searching. When he'd found Ethan he'd been so close to
death he still swore he could hear the angels playing
their harps. Billy had literally dragged, then carried
Ethan until he'd gotten Ethan to a hospital tent. He'd
found out later that Billy had hovered over those
doctors like Gabriel, watching, coaxing, threatening
them with their own demise if they didn't pull Ethan
through. They had. Ethan owed Billy his life.

He'd do anything for Billy. Anything. And that
included finishing this railroad.

Plate in hand, Ethan stood, picked up Billy's plate
from the ground and carried them over to the barrel
Mulroon was using for a depository until he could
wash them.

Billy caught up to him. "Okay," Ethan said,
walking toward his horse, Billy falling in alongside.
"I'll get the supplies moving again and see where
we stand with the banks. You put these men back
to work. Yes?" He grinned.

"Yeah. Yeah. We'll be ready by the time the rails
get here."

"Good. Listen, send a message to Bartel in town that I won't make that Tuesday meeting."

"Sure."

Ethan picked up Four's reins and led the horse over to the area they were using as a corral. There, he unsaddled him and turned him loose among the six dozen mules tethered there, waiting their turns to pull the wagons that hauled the ties down from the local mountains.

Dust filled the air and mixed with the acrid scent of horses and mules. The familiar hiss of steam surged from the locomotive they used for runs to Cheyenne and back.

Billy and Ethan walked over to the locomotive.

Sam Cory leaned out from the cab. "Hiya, Ethan, going to Cheyenne?"

"Yeah, Sam. One passenger today."

Sam grinned revealing a missing front tooth. "Climb on up here, then."

Ethan answered him with a wave as he turned to talk to Billy.

"We are going to build this railroad, aren't we, Ethan?"

"Damned straight, we are, kid. Believe it."

The ride to Cheyenne took the rest of the day. Ethan spent the night at the boardinghouse where he kept most of his belongings, sort of a home away from home.

Ethan caught the Union Pacific and took it east to Chicago at 9:47 the next morning.

As he stepped off the train, his first thought was how crowded it all looked. He might have been born and raised in the city, even if Pittsburgh wasn't near as big as Chicago, but he'd never felt comfortable until he'd gone west. There was something about those wide-open spaces that made him peaceful and calm.

Ethan hefted his carpetbag and made his way through the milling people. Evidently, people in Chicago didn't see men in cowboy hats and boots very often, judging by the stares he got. He wasn't interested in what people thought and, ignoring the looks, he went directly down the wooden stairs and through the cavernous train station. His boots' steps echoed on the cement floor as he exited outside onto the street where a line of horse-drawn cabs waited. The sky was gray but the streets were dry. There was the distinct smell of rain in the air and Ethan wondered briefly if he was in for a storm.

"Excelsior Hotel," he told the uniformed driver as he slammed the cab door shut. His carpetbag settled on the floor next to him.

"Yes, sir," the man replied and, with a snap of his whip, the horse stepped out quickly, the clip-clop of hooves like a rhythmic drumming on the cobblestone streets.

Ethan leaned back against the velvet-covered red upholstery, trying to find a comfortable position for his back and shoulders. Of course, he knew it wasn't the cab that was the problem, it was him. His muscles were tense. He was anxious. Hell, he was downright worried. He'd wired Anderson's from Cheyenne and had gotten no answer to his inquiry about his rails. Why?

He was damned well going to find out. He figured

he'd check into the hotel first, get cleaned up and head straight over to see Burt Hockmyer, general manager at Anderson's Foundry.

The cab pulled to stop in front of a small two-story hotel on a quiet side street. The structure was brick with white shutters and looked more like someone's mansion than a hotel. Ethan liked its remoteness.

"Excelsior, sir," the driver called out.

Grabbing up his bag, he let himself out before the driver could get down. A fine mist of rain started to fall.

"Fifty cents," the driver said.

Ethan fished in his pocket and paid the man, with a little something extra for his trouble.

"Thank *you,* sir," the man returned, looking at the silver dollar.

"I'm going back out and if you'd wait about ten minutes you could take me to Anderson's Foundry over on Fourth. Do you know it?"

The man looked down at the money clutched in his hand. "I'll find it. I'll wait right here for you, sir."

"Fine."

Ethan took the six front steps two at a time and paused only long enough to hold the door open for a lady and her little girl who were coming out as he was going in.

"Ma'am," he said politely, tipping his hat as he did.

The little girl grinned at him and giggled. "What kinda hat is that, Mama?" she said bluntly.

The woman looked a bit embarrassed but Ethan

said, "It's a Stetson, honey. Out where I come from it's the only hat worth having."

The woman smiled her thanks and for just a moment he stared after them, wondering what Molly and Katie would think of a place as large and bustling as Chicago? It was a big change from War Bonnet and surely a big change from those gold camps she'd grown up in.

What was Molly doing right now? Was she thinking about him as he was thinking about her? Was she missing him at all? Strangely, he hoped so, even though he had no right to hope any such thing.

The rain came down heavier and seemed to rouse him from his musings. Quickly, he went inside the ornately furnished lobby. The walls were white, the carpet a muted pattern of blues and greens, and the staircase that led to the second floor was highly polished walnut.

He went to the registration desk.

The narrow-faced clerk smiled politely. "Nice to see you again, Mr. Wilder. Room Fourteen is ready and waiting for you." He handed Ethan a brass key on a ring.

"Thanks," Ethan said hefting his carpet bag.

"Up the stairs. Third room on the right. I'll send the maid up with towels," the clerk called after him.

Ethan was already halfway up the curving staircase; the walnut banister glided smoothly beneath his hand. His footsteps were muffled on the thick carpeting. He was anxious to get his business done and get back to Wyoming. Even though he wasn't quite sure what he was going to say or do or...

All he knew was that he wanted to be there, not here.

Number Fourteen was a corner room with lace-covered windows on two sides overlooking the street. The walls were pale blue, the carpet darker blue and a little worn near the doorway.

There was a double bed, a bureau and a wardrobe cabinet, all of walnut. In general, the room was small, but as neat and clean as Ethan remembered from previous trips.

He tossed his carpetbag on the floor near the foot of the double bed. It landed with a heavy thud. That was his .44. He'd brought it along mostly because he never felt quite complete without it.

He poured a splash of water in the white porcelain basin and scooped a double handful up to his face, rubbing away the day's grim and dirt from travel. Blinking against the water, he remembered, too late, that there were no towels.

Necessity being the mother of invention, he shrugged out of his shirt and used it for a towel, then retrieved a clean one from his bag. He made quick work of doing up the buttons and tucking the white cotton into the waistband of his black wool trousers. He added a tie, vest and jacket as an accommodation to being in the city.

A glance in the mirror confirmed that he needed a shave but there was no time. He wanted to see Hockmyer today and it was late, nearly three.

Yanking open the door, the maid was standing there hand raised, obviously about to knock.

"You startled me, sir," she said, her arms full of clean white towels.

"Sorry. Put the towels down anywhere." Ethan moved past her and down the stairs.

The cab was waiting for him and that mist of a rain was now a heavy downpour. The sky was gun-metal gray but there was no thunder, no lightning.

"Anderson's Foundry on Fourth," he told the driver as he climbed inside the vehicle.

"I remember," the man returned and, with a crack of his whip, drove away from the curb.

Traffic was light, mostly delivery wagons and an occasional buggy. Folks were staying in due to the rain, he supposed. He reached the foundry in about fifteen minutes.

"Here you go, sir." The cab rolled to a stop in front of the dilapidated brick building. The storage yard surrounding it was already puddled in water. Smoke from the chimneys was beaten down by the rain. Even from ten yards away, Ethan could hear the sound of hammers clanging against steel and iron, and steam drifted from the copper roof as proof of how hot it was inside the shop. Behind the building, he could see the railroad tracks that were used whenever a large order had to be shipped.

Keeping his head down, Ethan stepped out of the cab and reached in his pocket for money. Rain beaded on the wool of his jacket and pelted the side of his face.

Rain poured off the driver's hat. "You want me to wait, sir?"

Ethan's brow drew down in thought. When he left here he was headed for the bank. "Well, yeah, that would be a help, but this might take me a half hour or so."

The driver pulled out his watch and checked the time. "How about I come back this way in about thirty minutes? If you're here then..."

"Sounds good." Ethan paid the man in paper money this time, again with a nice tip.

"Thanks," the man beamed. "See you in thirty minutes."

The rain was coming down harder now. Rain soaked his collar and cuffs and generally irritated his already short temper. Why the hell hadn't he brought his slicker? He hadn't been thinking clearly. No, he'd been thinking about a certain woman, not about work. That realization didn't help his temper one bit.

Ethan headed for the back, remembering a separate entrance up a flight of stairs. As he came around the corner, he stopped dead still. There, gleaming in the rain, like a mountain of silver, were rails, stacked like firewood near that siding. What the hell?

Rain pounded on his shoulders and soaked through his jacket, chilling his skin. He didn't care. Rails. These were his rails, he was sure of it. Slowly, he walked around the stack, his steps splashing water as he moved. Lightly gliding his hand over the smooth metal, his eyes searched for a tag, a mark, something to confirm what he was already certain of.

Then he saw it, a small, waterlogged piece of heavy brown pasteboard partially submerged in a puddle of water. Lifting the tag, he read, "Wilder—Wyoming Central Railroad."

These were his rails, but why hadn't they been shipped? Why had Hockmyer said they didn't have any? Anger merged with frustration inside him. Muscles tensed along his shoulders and down his back. "Hockmyer, if you're playing tricks, you've picked the wrong man," he said aloud, to no one.

Ethan strode for the stairs. Taking them two at a time, he banged into the office. The door slammed dangerously hard against the wall before springing back at him. He caught it absently. His attention was focused on the man seated at the desk not five feet away.

"What the—" Hockmyer surged to his feet then went white as a wash day bedsheet. "Wilder. What are you doing here?"

Hockmyer was a short, burly man, with a fringe for hair and a cigar that seemed to be permanently stuck in his mouth.

Ethan closed on him. "What the hell do you think I'm doing here? I came for my goddamn rails." Ethan braced his hands on the front edge of the desk and leaned toward Hockmyer.

"What rails? There are no rails."

"Then what do you call that mountain of steel stacked out there?" He pointed toward the wall with one outstretched hand. "Those are my rails and I want them now."

Burt Hockmyer dropped down in his chair. "I, ah, I don't know what you're talking about. I'm busy. Come back—"

Ethan slammed his fist down on the desk, papers lifted and fluttered then settled. Hockmyer came partially out of his seat. "Look, Wilder—"

"No, you look, you little bastard. I want my rails. I paid for them and dammit I want them!"

"There are no rails until the thirtieth," Hockmyer countered.

"Says who?"

"Says me, that's who." He thumbed his chest. "Now get out before I call my men to throw you out."

With one hand, Ethan grabbed the front of the little man's shirt and pulled him in close. "You lying son of a bitch. My rails are stacked outside. I saw them when I came in—"

Hockmyer pried Ethan's fingers loose from his shirt and took a faltering step back until his retreat was blocked by the wall. His face was mottled red. "Those aren't your rails. Those are..." His gaze darted to the desk and he reached for the papers scattered there. "Those are...are..."

Ethan slammed his fist on the desk again and Hockmyer jumped. "No use, Hockmyer. I saw the tag on them. Now what I want to know—" his voice got deadly soft "—is why you're lying. Who put you up to this? Did someone offer you more money for them? Who, Hockmyer?"

"I'm not lying." Hockmyer was inching toward the door on the far side of the small office. Ethan moved toward him when he realized what he was up to, but it was an instant too late. The man wrenched open the door and shouted, "Gunther! Gunther! Get your ass up here and bring a couple of men with you!"

Through the window that looked down on the foundry, Ethan saw three burly men start for the stairs, each picking up a piece of iron as he did. Anger rolled in him and he was halfway tempted to stand and have it out with Hockmyer and his goons. But getting his brains bashed in wasn't going to help things. Ethan knew when to retreat. He also knew there was a difference between retreating and giving up.

"All right, Hockmyer. You win...for now." With that, he left the way he'd come in.

"I'm sorry but I can't give you an extension on the loan," Nick Fraser, the bank manager said. He lounged back in his oversize leather chair that was behind a huge carved mahogany desk. The room and the man bespoke the stuffy arrogance of Chicago's First Central Bank.

Ethan, on the other hand, was wet and tired and feeling more than a little mean.

But he needed this loan to be extended and so he schooled his temper as best he could and said, "Why not? What's a couple of weeks going to matter? By then—"

The man held up one hand to stop him. His silver cuff links flashed in the light from the lamp on the corner of the desk. "Look, Mr. Wilder," he said in a voice that sounded high and nasal, "we aren't interested in making any changes or accommodations at this time."

There was something smug and irritating as hell about Fraser. Ethan's temper was moving up the scale fast.

If Fraser was aware of just how dangerous a man he was dealing with, he gave no indication of it. Instead, the manager leaned in, and with one finger—as though touching something unpleasant—

moved the papers in a file on his desk. One brow arched and he glanced up at Ethan. "Ah, yes, I see that your first payment is due on the fifteenth. Should you fail to make it the bank would have no choice but to…foreclose." His gaze flicked up to Ethan once again. There was a slash of a line on his face that Ethan supposed was a smile of sorts.

Ethan was thinking what he'd like to do with that smile but this was business. "Why?" he asked, demanded bluntly.

"Business, Mr. Wilder. Nothing personal, I assure you." He made a show of straightening the seam on the lapel of his blue suit.

Ethan had had about enough of this. You'd think he was begging for something he didn't deserve. Ethan never begged for anything.

In one motion he stood and picked up his hat from the corner of the desk. About the same time, he and Fraser noticed the water ring that Ethan's hat had left on the mahogany. While the manager suddenly frowned, Ethan had trouble keeping his smile in check.

Why, Wilder, you spoiled the nice man's brand-new desk.

Yeah, that wasn't the only thing he'd like to spoil. It was temper that made him give his hat, his very wet hat, a good shake and send water spraying all over the desk and the papers and the smug Mr. Fraser.

"Hey, you!" Fraser said sharply, momentarily losing his composure.

"Oh, did I get you?" Ethan said in all innocence. He pointedly didn't apologize.

As Ethan stormed from the office, he ran quite literally into someone he'd known a long time ago. Staring into the man's brown eyes, Ethan had the answer to all his questions.

"Hanscome," Ethan said, his voice as cold and hard as a sword's edge.

"Wilder." The man extended his hand but Ethan pretended to take no notice. He'd be damned if he was shaking hands with the man who was trying to put him out of business.

Ethan stared at the man for a long minute then said, "Since when is the Union Pacific interested in spur lines?"

"What makes you think we are?"

"You're here aren't you?"

The man straightened and the look on his face changed from denial to a sort of victory. "Oh, the U.P. is interested in anything to do with railroads. It's so nice if we can keep it all tidy, so to speak."

Yeah, "nice and tidy" translated to "no competition." Ethan had worked on the U.P. and knew firsthand how ruthless and how greedy they were. He'd just never thought his little line would come under their notice. He was wrong.

"So tell me, Hanscome, before I bother going to the other banks in town—"

Hanscome's mouth drew down in a frown. "Oh, I wouldn't bother. I'm sure you have more important things to do."

A plan flashed bright and clear in Ethan's head, and he smiled. "Actually, you're right. I do have more important things to do."

Chapter Twelve

Two men rode in the cab of the sleek black locomotive. It was well past midnight. Slowly, steadily, they moved through the night. Gray smoke drifted upward in the coal-black sky. The rain had slowed to an occasional mist.

Up ahead was Ethan's destination. He could see it clearly in the light of the three-quarter moon. Otherwise, all was dark and still. There was no guard, no houses or tenements close by that would allow prying eyes to see what was about to happen.

Arms braced, hands gripping the cold steel of the engine cab, he leaned out, feeling the chill rain against his face, sending gooseflesh prickling down his neck.

Muscles tensed, and he said, "That's it, Bob, about twenty more feet." The engineer slowed the locomotive to a crawl, steam whooshing out from vents as metal brakes scraped metal wheels. Another few feet. "Yeah. That'll do it."

They stopped in the yard and Ethan looked out, eyes straining in the darkness, scanning the building for signs of life, of someone working late in the office perhaps. Nothing.

Relieved, he swung down from the cab, landing in a small puddle. Muddy water splashed up against the side of his black trousers.

He wasn't worried about appearances. He was here to get what was his.

A quick glance at the engineer and he told his old friend, ''Keep the pressure up in case we have to leave in a hurry.''

''Just like old times, huh, Major?'' Bob replied, a grin on his freckled face. ''Don't worry, me and old Betsy here—'' he patted the locomotive affectionately ''—won't let you down.''

Four flat cars were strung out behind the engine; like blue shadows against a black background, they seemed unreal. But they were real. Ethan had called in a few favors. Men he'd known when he worked on the Union Pacific, men who didn't like to see a fellow railroader in trouble, men like Bob, who'd served with Ethan in the war. It was a nice touch of irony that he was using Union Pacific equipment.

So with a little help, he'd ''borrowed'' an engine for a couple of days—and flat cars. Workmen, the dozen on the flat cars, he'd hired with the last of the cash he had on him. It was surprising how few questions men asked when money was put on the line.

''All right, boys.'' Ethan waved them down to where he stood by the stack of rails. Nice of Mr. Hockmyer to be so considerate as to locate his foundry near a railroad siding.

The rainy mist wafted lightly on the breeze as the men gathered around him. He spoke in a loud whisper. "Quick as you can now, start loading the rails on the cars. You six stay up there to receive the rails." He motioned toward the flat cars. "You six do the carrying. We'll switch back and forth every so often."

"Right."

"You're the boss."

The men started off in the direction of the rails.

Ethan stood guard. His hand rested lightly on his Navy Colt that hung low on his right hip. He was taking what belonged to him—no more and sure as hell no less. He had a contract right here in his vest pocket to prove it, not that he was in the mood to argue the point.

"That's it boys, keep moving."

The work was slow and hard. The rails were heavy and harder still to lift up to the men on the flat cars. Metal clinked against metal, the sound seeming to echo through the night like the ringing of a fire bell. Ethan worried that surely someone would hear and wonder what a bunch of men were doing loading railroad ties in the middle of the night.

He strolled toward the front gate, now padlocked against intruders. A smile pulled up one corner of his mouth. This intruder always got what he wanted.

Three days later, a train loaded with rails rolled into camp forty miles south of War Bonnet. Ethan, grinning like a kid who'd just stolen a chunk of rock candy, grabbed the whistle pull cord and let her rip.

The sharp, shrill sound pierced the afternoon like an arrow. Not that anyone wasn't already keenly aware of the train. Ethan had wired ahead.

"Ethan!" Luke Thompson, the foreman, shouted, waving his hat and running alongside as the train came to a stop. "Hot damn! You did it!"

Steam spouted from the side vents, the roar nearly deafening. Grinning, Ethan swung down and the men exchanged one of those slap kind of hugs that men do sometimes. "Damn straight, I did it."

It was hard to tell who was grinning more. Ned turned and hollered, "You men, get started with these rails. We've got miles to go!"

"Yes, sir!"

Twenty-five track layers hustled to do as they were told. There was loud talking and more shouting, orders given and acknowledged.

The sun was bright and warm, too warm. Ethan snatched off his hat and wiped his face with the curve of his elbow before settling his hat snugly on his head again. "Where's Billy?" he asked, scanning the area for his partner. "I expected him to be here. I've got some news for him."

"Didn't you know?" Luke asked, but the engineer laid on the whistle again blocking out whatever Luke was saying.

Ethan winced then grabbed Luke by the arm and led him a few yards away. "Know what?"

Men shouldered past and Ethan and Luke had to dodge the crew.

"Billy," Luke began, then turned to holler at one of the track layers. "Not there, you idiot! Over there." He pointed and started away when Ethan snagged him.

"Billy. Where's Billy?" Ethan demanded, suddenly worried that something was wrong.

"What?" Luke looked momentarily confused then blinked and said, "Oh, he's gone."

"Gone? Gone where?"

Luke was moving away again. "You men, don't just stand there. Get those rails down." He glanced back at Ethan as though he'd just remembered what they were talking about. "Billy left yesterday. Right after your telegram came. He said since you did your job he was gonna do his, whatever that means. He rode out, headed for War Bonnet."

Ethan made the trip to War Bonnet in record time, assuming someone was keeping score. He'd been gone only ten days but the difference between the town he'd left and this one was nothing short of a miracle.

Everywhere he looked there were people. People on the street. People in wagons. People on horseback. He suspected that Billy had most likely confirmed what they all already knew. The Wyoming Central was close.

He spotted Ed Bartel walking with a young couple in the general direction of those lots he'd red-flagged near the edge of town. Good prospects no doubt. This town would be twice its size come this time next year, if things went well. "Things" meant the railroad.

He wanted to talk to Billy. Actually he wanted to do more than talk. He was intent on telling Billy in no uncertain terms that he, Ethan, would take care of Molly Murphy and getting the land. Ethan knew now that somehow he would make her see that he had to have the land. The trouble would be to make her believe it was the best thing for her. It was, too. He was convinced of that now. No more hesitation. No more excuses. He would make an offer and get the land. She'd said herself that her husband might be dead so then she could sign the deed. If he wasn't dead, then he'd probably be glad to have the money since he obviously wasn't interested in ranching.

Wilder, if only it were that simple.

Yeah, he thought, if only it were. If only he didn't feel… If only she'd never looked at him the way she had that night. If only she hadn't kissed him back. If only…

The world was filled with too many "if onlys."

He was actually shaking his head in dismay or disgust, he wasn't entirely certain, as he made his way along the south side of the street and he had it in his mind to keep on going. Just ride on out there to her place and…and…

What he wanted to do was take her in his arms again and demand to know why she'd kissed him back. What he wanted to know was why he felt this way about a married woman. It was wrong.

He needed to get his feelings under control before he saw her again.

The boardinghouse was up ahead on the right. He figured he'd stop and see if Billy was there. If he was—and Ethan was suddenly very hopeful that was the case—then he could find out what Billy had done or said or offered. He could find out if Molly had sold out to Billy.

Maybe she had.

That thought came as a surprise to him but it was possible. Maybe Billy had convinced her. Maybe she'd agreed and was packing right this minute. Maybe she'd be gone by the time he got there, if he ever got there.

Maybe he'd never see her again.

The sudden cold dread that curled in his chest quickly eased when he spotted her wagon parked in front of the mercantile.

Shifting the reins in his hand, he tied up at the hitching rail. A couple of horseflies buzzed his head and he waved them away as he walked over to inspect the wagon and team. It was hers all right. That new wheel was a dead giveaway.

Molly was here. Just like that, all rage or fear or worry disappeared. Molly was here. The three words were like a salve on a wound.

Molly was here.

Sunlight glinted on the sparkling clean front windows of the store and he had to shade his eyes close to the glass to see inside. He spotted her instantly, there, by the counter talking to Brinsfield. Katie stood close, clinging to her mother's black skirt.

A smile tugged at one corner of his mouth as he watched the way the little girl seemed to be playing some game known only to herself, her lips forming words he couldn't hear while she used the folds of Molly's skirt like some kind of veil.

Outside a pair of women stopped and looked into the window, also. They spared him a questioning glance as if to ask what he found so interesting.

Ethan straightened. ''Ladies,'' was all he said as he opened the double doors.

''Now, look, Mrs. Murphy—'' Brinsfield broke off in midword.

The wood creaked and the cowbell tied on the inside door handle rattled as Ethan walked in. All heads turned in his direction but he was only looking at one person.

"Hello, Molly."

A strange sort of silence seemed to engulf the room as Molly and Brinsfield and the customers stared at Ethan standing just inside the doors. He looked tall and powerful and more like an outlaw than a railroad owner, dressed as he was in dark clothes, complete with a black leather vest and chaps. For an unsteady moment, Molly thought he looked more handsome, more enticing than she'd remembered—and she'd remembered very well.

"Ethan." The word was a whisper or the answer to a prayer, Molly wasn't certain. She only knew that for an instant she was glad, very glad to see him.

He's come for me. The thought flashed in her mind, though why exactly she wasn't sure. He hadn't come for her but for her land, she knew, but knowing didn't seem to have the slightest effect on the gladness that bubbled inside her.

"How are you?" he asked in a husky tone that sent unwanted and most assuredly unexpected shivers prickling over her skin.

Perhaps it was the shivers that startled her out of those daydreams. Reality was harsh and cold in the bright light of the afternoon.

What was he doing here? She'd sent him packing. She'd thought he'd gone back to the railroad camp. She hoped like crazy he'd gone back to the railroad camp and that she'd never have to see him again.

Out of the corner of her eye, Molly noticed Brinsfield move a half step to the right. "Mr. Wilder," he said. "Nice to see you again. What can I get for you?"

Absently, Ethan gave a small shake of his head. There was nothing the merchant or anyone could get for Ethan. What he wanted he could get for himself—maybe.

"Molly," he said again as he closed the distance between them.

Judging by the set of her jaw and the anger in her eyes, he could tell she was upset. He'd heard the tail end of the conversation when he walked in and knew something was going on.

"Is there something wrong?" he asked her. She was more beautiful than ever. She wore a simple black skirt and white blouse with what looked to be a hundred buttons going up the pleated front. Her hair was piled high on her head, but tiny wisps escaped to brush against the side of her neck and her cheek. Ethan was assaulted with the memory of that same hair down around her shoulders, gliding like fine Chinese silk through his fingers when he'd kissed her.

Damn. He dragged in a steadying breath and ordered his wayward thoughts to behave. Too bad he couldn't order the pounding of his blood to cease as quickly.

Of all the things he'd expected to feel when he saw her again, this wasn't it.

Molly looked up at him. He stood so close, too close.

"Molly," he said and reached for her then stopped short. "Can I help you?"

His voice was so quiet, so tender that it was nearly Molly's undoing. *I won't let you do this to me. Not again.*

She was a woman of blessed common sense and right now that common sense was screaming to move away from him. She couldn't seem to comply but she did manage to turn back to Mr. Brinsfield.

"About my order..." she prompted, struggling desperately to control the frantic beating of her heart.

"Like I said," Brinsfield replied. "We're out of everything." His expression was smug. His statement was ridiculous since Molly and everyone else could see that the store's shelves were well stocked with every imaginable item under the sun, certainly everything Molly had asked for.

About this time, Ethan squared off on his side of the counter facing Brinsfield. "What the devil is going on?"

Brinsfield sidled a half step in Ethan's direction and in a conspiratorial voice said, "If the lady wants to shop, she'll have to go elsewhere. In fact, maybe it would be a good idea if the lady went elsewhere in general."

So that was it, Ethan thought, his temper suddenly rising. They were planning to starve her out. The thought of Molly going hungry, of Katie going hungry—and of him being responsible, didn't settle well with him.

"Look," Ethan started, "I understand what you're up to but—"

"Really," Molly cut in. "And just what *is* going on here, Mr. Wilder?"

Ethan's gaze flicked from the merchant to Molly and back again. "Mr. Brinsfield is mistaken about being out of supplies, aren't you?"

Brinsfield's expression drew down in a deep frown. "No, I'm not."

Molly gathered up her list and took Katie by the hand. As she turned to leave she said, "I trusted you, and this is how you repay me?"

"No," Ethan countered. "I never asked them to—"

"To what? Starve us out?" Molly started for the door, Katie following along.

Ethan caught up in a couple of long strides. He grabbed her by the arm and turned her around. Anger flashed hard and bright in her eyes and she stared at the spot where his hand gripped her elbow.

Feeling at once foolish and frustrated, Ethan released her. "I'm sorry, Molly," he said, referring to the way he'd grabbed her and more, so much more.

"Yes. I'll just bet you are. The only thing you're sorry for is not getting my land. Well, you can't have it, you hear me!" She shouted so that everyone heard her quite clearly. "I won't give up my home. Not for you. Not for anyone."

With that she yanked open the door and stormed outside onto the plank sidewalk. Ethan was hot on her heels. He made the mistake of grabbing her arm again but quickly released her. "Molly, I never meant for it to be like this."

She only glared at him but he could see the hurt

in her eyes and it tore at his gut. "Is that all?" she finally said.

"I—look, wait here and I'll get whatever supplies you need. I'll get more than you need."

"No, thank you." She turned and hoisted Katie onto the wagon seat. Hitching up her skirt, she made to climb up herself.

"Dammit, Molly, don't be like this," he told her.

"I'll be any way I want, Mr. Wilder, and right now I want to be far away from you."

That was it. Ethan wasn't taking this anymore. She was going to listen to him. She was going to understand.

"Woman, don't you turn your back on me!" he snapped, skirting around her and wedging himself between her and the wagon.

"Get out of my way, Mr. Wilder."

"Not until you listen to me."

Before Molly had a chance to think, she hauled off and slapped him, hard, across the lower part of his cheek and jaw.

Time seemed to stand still. It was as though someone else had done the terrible act, but the stinging in her hand confirmed that it was she who had slapped him, this man who had nursed her back to health, saved her child from a fire, cared for her crops and animals.

Tears welled up in her eyes and she reached for him again, wanting to touch the place on his face, wanting to sooth the redness and make it all go away. But Ethan took a half step back, enough so that her hand stopped midmotion.

"I'm sorry, Ethan. I never meant… You didn't deserve…"

"I should thank you. I was confused for a while about…things." He rubbed his jaw lightly. "I'm not anymore." With that he turned and walked away, leaving Molly to watch him.

Slowly, she climbed up on the wagon seat next to Katie. A tear slipped down her cheek, then another.

"Mama, what's the matter? Why'd you hit Mr. Ethan?"

Molly picked up the thick reins and turned to her daughter. "Because I'm a fool." With that she slapped the reins on the horses' rumps and the wagon rumbled out of town.

Ethan was just crossing the street when he spotted Billy coming out of the boardinghouse.

"Hey, Ethan," Billy called out to him, and Ethan grabbed up his horse's reins and walked in the direction of his partner.

"What are you doing here?" Billy asked.

"I could ask you the same thing," Ethan replied.

"I came to see about getting Murphy's land," Billy answered.

"I told you I'd take care of that."

"Yeah, I know, but when I got your wire about the rails, I knew there was no time to waste. Luke can keep the men working."

Ethan sighed. "You didn't get the land, though, did you?"

"No," Billy said. "She sent me packing." He glanced over at the El Dorado Saloon a few steps up the street. The tinny sound of a badly tuned piano carried out to the street. "Come on, you look like you could use a drink."

"Yeah," Ethan agreed. "I could."

They got a bottle of whiskey and settled at a table.

"Billy, there's more bad news."

Billy poured himself a drink as well as one for Ethan, which he slid across the table in Ethan's direction. "Great. Just what I need is more bad news."

Ethan picked up the glass and took in the whiskey in two swallows. "The rails are here and the men are working. I've told Luke to keep 'em working around the clock if necessary."

Billy arched one brow in surprise. "Look, Ethan, I know you're anxious to finish but with not much of a moon, working at night isn't safe."

"We don't have a choice." Ethan reached for the bottle and helped himself to another drink. "I didn't get the extension on the loan. It seems our loan has been frozen."

"What do you mean frozen? By who?"

"I couldn't find out exactly but it's pretty clear it's our old friends over at Union Pacific."

Billy stared hard at Ethan for a full five seconds then said, "I should've known." Billy drank the whiskey in a couple of swallows then put the glass down as though it were fine crystal. For a few seconds, he stared at the glass deep in thought, then he looked up, his gaze meeting Ethan's. "There must be someone we can talk to, some marker we can call in. What the devil do they want, the entire west?"

"I don't think you are far off. Besides I already

called in a few markers—how do you think we got the rails and the train to haul 'em?''

"We're running out of options…and time here."

"What do you think I'm telling you?"

"So you figure they've cut some kind of deal with the banks to take over when we default, something that will make it worthwhile to the banks…more worthwhile than us."

Ethan reached for the whiskey bottle again. "It's the men at the top who are determined to control everything and everyone. Come on, Billy, we saw enough of that when we worked there. Course, then their bullying helped us so we didn't complain."

"Speaking of complaining, who was that guy we used to go to with problems? Jefferson. Jeffers. Jedson! That's it. He always seemed to be able to make things happen. Maybe he can help us get our loan extended."

"Maybe. If we knew where he was and we could get to him in time and convince him it was in his best interest to help us."

"Oh, I can convince him all right." Billy laid his Navy Colt on the table.

Ethan was already shaking his head before his friend finished speaking. "Tempting as that is, I try to draw the line at murder."

"I'm not so squeamish, at least not when it comes to keeping what's mine."

"Yeah, but I'd like to get through this without either of us being hanged."

"Well, what do you want to do?"

Ethan toyed with the glass in his hand. "You need to go back to the camp and keep the men working. Work them in shifts if you have to. Do whatever it takes to make that two-hundred-mile mark.''

"And the land? My laying track won't do us any good without that land," Billy said with equal honesty.

"I'll get the land." Ethan stood, his chair scraping as he did. "Count on it. I'll get the land."

Chapter Thirteen

It was close to sundown when Ethan rode in to the ranch yard. There was smoke coming from the chimney on the east side of the house. Getting ready for supper, he supposed.

The wagon team was in the corral, the corral he'd fixed. Chickens strolled and clucked around the horses' hooves and they seemed to be unaware of the feathered creatures.

All was quiet. On the ride out here, Ethan had run over several dialogues in his mind—almost the way actors do for a play. He'd tried to figure the best way to tell her that he was right about the land, to convince her that she would be better off if she sold. But it always came around to the same point. He wanted the one thing she wanted.

With a deep breath and a small prayer of hope, he knocked on the door.

"Mr. Ethan!" Katie practically screamed with delight and hurled herself at him so that he had to catch her to keep her from falling on her face. He hoisted her up in the air high above his head. "Hiya,

Katie,'' he said, genuinely glad to see her. He settled her on one hip, her little arms almost reaching around his shoulders and neck.

"Mama. Mama," Katie called out. "Look who's here. Mr. Ethan's here." She bounced up and down in his arms. "Did you bring your horse? Can I ride him again?"

"What? Ah, sure," Ethan said, but he wasn't really listening to the child in his arms. He was more interested in the woman standing by the stove looking so intently at him.

"Can I come in?"

"I thought we had an understanding this afternoon," Molly said bluntly, thinking all the time how right he looked standing there holding Katie.

"Did we?" he asked innocently. Now that he was here, he knew he was staying, for a while anyway.

He let Katie slide to the floor and, holding her hand, he walked over to the table. There were two places set for dinner.

"Have I come at a bad time?" he asked.

"Yes." Molly went back to her cooking, a stew of some sort, judging by the single pot she had going. He thought about their meeting at the store and wondered how her supplies were holding out. He'd bought quite a bit before he'd left…before she'd ordered him gone.

"Mama, can Mr. Ethan eat dinner with—"

"No!" Molly snapped. More softly, she repeated, "No, Katie, not tonight."

Katie's mouth turned down in a pout. "But I want him to," she whined, twisting back and forth, her hem flaring with the motion. "Please. He can eat half of mine."

"No," Molly said. "No."

"It's all right, Katie," Ethan told her. "Your mother's right. There's not enough."

"Don't go, Mr. Ethan." Katie grabbed hold of his hand and held on tight.

"Oh, don't worry, Katie, I'm not leaving."

Molly's head came around sharply at his statement. Eyes met and locked. "I want to talk to you."

"I *don't* want to talk to you." She went back to stirring the stew.

"I'll wait." Ethan dragged out a chair and sat down. Katie was immediately in his lap, fiddling with the flaps on his shirt pockets.

"Did ya bring me anything, Mr. Ethan?" she was asking, peering into his pocket.

"No, Katie, I'm sorry, I didn't bring you anything."

Katie looked momentarily sad, then immediately brightened. "That's okay, Mr. Ethan, I'm just happy to see you. Mama's been real sad since you left and she cried—"

"Dinner!" Molly practically shouted. She carried the stewpan over to the table and put it down in the middle.

Ethan watched her. So she'd been sad, huh? A smile threatened, and when he tried to look at her, she pointedly looked everywhere else except at him.

"Katie, get the spoons, please," Molly ordered, and Katie slid down off Ethan's knee and did as she was told.

Moments later Katie returned carrying three

spoons and one additional plate. "Mama, why can't Mr. Ethan eat with us?" She put the spoons down and the plate in front of him. "There's lots of stew and he won't eat much, will you, Mr. Ethan?"

"No, not much," Ethan confirmed with an innocent expression, all wide eyes and drooping mouth.

Molly was trapped and she knew it. She'd known it since the moment he'd walked in...from the moment she'd first seen him. Yet she had to try. In a tone that held no warmth at all, she said, "Would you like to eat with us?"

"Yes, thank you, ma'am," he returned with great formality, "I would be pleased to stay."

They ate in silence. At least Ethan and Molly had nothing to say to each other. Katie, fortunately, was oblivious to the tension between the two adults. She brought Ethan up to date on the kittens and the chickens and the vegetable garden, which now had the first formation of beans on the vines.

"I can show you," she offered.

"Not now," Ethan told her, thinking they'd never see those beans sprout. "You need to finish your dinner first."

Katie nodded solemnly and went back to eating.

Ethan did the same, glancing up from time to time. Once he caught Molly watching him, but she quickly averted her gaze. "This is good," he offered.

"Thank you."

As he sat there, he kept wondering what or how he was going to convince her to forgive him and then give up the land. To achieve one goal he would have to surrender the other.

When they finished dinner, Ethan said, "I'll do the dishes." He picked up his plate and Katie's and started for the sink.

"That isn't necessary," Molly told him in a demanding tone. "I can do it."

"I know, but it's the least I can do since you were so kind and invited me to stay."

She gave him an I-did-no-such-thing look. With elbow and hip, she kind of moved him aside until she was in front of the sink and he was displaced entirely.

"Katie," she said as she scrubbed the first of the dishes. "Get washed and ready for bed."

"Aw, Mama, I don't want to go to bed." Katie was busy playing with her rag doll on the floor by the table.

"I know, but you were up early today and didn't have a nap. You need your sleep."

"But Mr. Ethan is here and I wanna visit."

"Mr. Ethan is leaving."

Katie shot him a questioning look. "Are you?"

"Ah, well, not right away." He leaned one hip against the counter. "I need to talk to your mother."

"See," Katie retaliated. "He's not leaving."

"That still doesn't mean you don't have to get ready for bed, young lady. Just let me dry my hands and—"

"I can do it. Katie and I are a pretty good team, aren't we, short stuff?"

"Yup," Katie agreed.

Ethan helped her with her dress, undoing the buttons down the back. She did her own shoes and stockings.

As he'd done several times before, he poured water from the kettle on the stove into a washbasin and added a splash of cold to make it just right for washing. The soap was brown lye.

He saw Molly watching them, but the expression on her face was unreadable.

"How am I doing?" he finally asked, as much to get her to talk to him as to get her approval.

"Fine," she responded in a tone that had an edge like glass.

This wasn't going well, he thought.

Katie washed quickly. "Mr. Ethan, can you tell me another story?"

"Another story?" Ethan had pretty much exhausted his story supply. "Ah, I—"

"Please?"

"If I do, will you go to sleep?"

"Uh-huh," Katie agreed, climbing between the sheets and settling down.

The only story, the only thing Ethan had on his mind, was Molly; so he began, "Well, once upon a time there was a beautiful lady with red hair. She lived in an old castle."

"Was there a prince?" Katie asked.

"Well, sort of."

"Was he handsome like you?"

"Sort of." He heard Molly make a derisive sound that he decided to ignore.

"You see, the princess was alone in the castle except for her little girl. All the soldiers and villagers had gone off to build a road."

"Wasn't the princess afraid to be alone like that?"

"I think maybe she was sometimes, but she was very brave and wouldn't let anyone know how she felt."

"Oh."

"So one day this prince—" There was that derisive sound again. He pressed on. "This prince—" this time he said it firmly "—comes to the castle. He says that the castle is old and falling down and that he will buy the castle from her."

"Does she sell her castle?" asked Katie.

"Not right away. You see, it was her very own home and she liked it there, cracks and holes and all."

Katie's eyes were beginning to droop.

More softly, Ethan continued. "But the prince wanted the castle because it was right in the middle of the road the villagers were trying to build. The road would make things a whole lot easier for them. They could get places faster. They could ship their goods to market a lot easier and make life better for themselves and their families."

"But where would the princess go?" Katie said, then punctuated her question with an openmouthed yawn.

"The prince was willing to pay the princess money for her castle and she would be able to buy another one somewhere else." He turned to look at Molly who was watching him openly. In a soft tone he added, "He hoped she'd buy a place somewhere close, so that the prince could see her sometimes."

It was true. Ethan knew it was wrong, but he wanted somehow to know that she was near.

The silence stretched between them, then slowly, like tearing flesh, Ethan looked away, glancing at Katie, who was sound asleep. A smile pulled up the corners of his mouth and he smoothed and straightened the bedclothes. A sound caught his attention and he saw Molly going out the door of the cabin.

Ethan followed her outside and found her in the shelter of the small porch.

The night was clear. Ten thousand stars glittered against the soft black sky. A lone gray cloud drifted slowly across the face of the silver-bright moon. All was still. Even the horses in the corral were silent.

Grabbing hold of the porch post, hand high above his head, he leaned against the rough wood. "Nice night, isn't it?"

"Yes." She never looked at him at all, but at least she'd answered him. It was a start.

"It's been a hot month," he said, struggling to find words to say how sorry he was, how much he missed her.

"Uh-huh." She started away from him and the cabin.

In a couple of long strides he caught up and fell in beside her. They walked toward the creek, the sound of the gurgling water getting louder. The night breeze stirred, ruffling the neckerchief tied loosely around his neck.

Molly had her hands behind her back as she walked, her head down, as though watching the ground for each step or as though lost in thought.

The cottonwood trees cast inky black shadows in

the grayness of the night and they strolled along the edge of the creek where Ethan had taken Katie fishing.

"How have you been, Molly?" he asked. The ten days since he'd seen her were like a lifetime.

"I'm recovered, if that's what you mean." She kept walking.

"I'm glad."

"Are you?"

"Of course, what did you think?" he said firmly, surprised by her tone.

"I don't know what to think about you," she told him honestly.

He stepped around in front of her, blocking her path. She paused, her head coming up as though she'd only half realized he was there.

"I'd like you to think that I'm your friend." He hooked one finger under her chin and lifted it up until her face looked directly into his down-turned one.

The cottonwood leaves clattered in the breeze and for a moment moonlight flashed on them like a streak of lightning, illuminating only these two in the world.

Then he saw the telltale tears in her eyes. Instantly, his hands went to her shoulders. "What's wrong, Molly?"

She gave a rueful chuckle. "What *isn't* wrong is more the question."

She started to move past him but he stopped her.

"Oh, honey, I never meant for any of this to happen. All I wanted was to buy a piece of land, to build my railroad."

"You've made that very clear."

Frustration warred with desire. "No, I didn't mean— Ah, hell, I didn't know you then."

"Would it have mattered if you had?" She angled her head around.

Ethan dragged in a deep breath. He wouldn't lie to her, not again, not ever again. So with absolute honesty he said, "Much as I wish I could change things—and Lord knows I wish it were possible—I can't. I have to build this railroad and I have to go through here."

"I understand."

This time as she moved to go past him, he let her, walking a step or so behind. His boot heels sank in the soft soil. He wanted her to know that he realized what it meant to have a home or, more importantly, not to have one.

"When I was a boy," he began, his voice low yet heard above the gurgling sound of the creek, "my mother died and my father left. I was raised by the Sisters of Mercy in Pittsburgh."

"An orphanage?" She stopped.

"Yes."

"You never told me that." Molly thought of all the times she'd felt like an orphan, her family all gone. Alone. So alone. What must it have been like for a child? "Was it hard?"

"Living there?"

"Uh-huh."

"It wasn't bad." They started to walk again. "The nuns were nice, except for Sister Helen—you had to watch out for her."

"Why?"

"Ah, she made sure we did our homework, and she used a long wooden switch to *make* sure her wishes were carried out."

"That sounds terrible. Did she... I mean did you ever... I can't imagine lifting a hand to a child."

He laughed lightly. "Well, in fairness, we were a handful and she was outnumbered. Anyway, she got the job done and no one, including me, suffered any long-lasting effects."

It was hard to imagine this strong, powerful man, so confident, as a small child...a child with dreams like hers, only his were about trains and hers were about homes.

"And what kind of home was it?" she asked.

"Oh, the place was clean and warm and they kept us well fed. What else can a kid ask for?"

"Someone to love them," she said quietly, reflecting back on the times her father had been too tired to talk, much less play, and her mother hadn't been much better. At least she'd had her sister. Now even she was gone.

They faced each other. Only inches separated their bodies. "Love is something I never thought much about...until I met you."

Ethan suddenly wanted more than anything to hold her. To pull her into his arms and stand there for the rest of his life and hold on to her.

The gentle call of a night owl was startlingly loud and they both seemed to swallow hard and turn at the same time.

"But how did you get to building a railroad?" she prompted, no longer afraid or angry—only curious.

He chuckled. "There was a train track right behind the building and nights I would listen to the trains pass and pretend to be on one headed for some faraway... This is silly. I'm sorry to—"

"No, it's not. It makes perfect sense. It's how I came to want this place so much." So his was a childhood dream like hers.

They walked on, the moonlight dancing between the leaves, the water making its melodious sound. The air was sweet and clean.

"Then what?" she asked.

"Oh, I left Pittsburgh, kicked around for a while...then there was the war."

"I thought you'd fought."

"Why?"

"The Navy Colt. It was standard issue, wasn't it?"

"Yeah. You know your weapons."

"A few."

She paused to sit on a rock. Ethan remained standing.

"Let me guess, that's where you and Billy met."

"That's right. How'd you know?"

"Your friend Billy was out here this afternoon. He's almost as good a talker as you are."

"Evidently, still not good enough."

She shook her head. "Not good enough."

They were quiet for a long minute, then she said, "You were telling me about the war."

"We managed to get through it without being hurt." He neglected to mention the fact that he was almost killed.

"I take that as your way of ending the discussion."

"Nothing in the past worth visiting, is all. Besides, we were talking about railroads."

"Unfortunately, we were."

He ignored the gibe. "When we got out, we were offered a job on the Union Pacific. I knew then that railroads were the future. I could have a future building them so I begged and borrowed money. Friends put their reputation on the line to get me investors. It was everything I wanted. My dream. My future."

"And all I ever dreamed about was a little house all my own with a porch to sit on in the evenings and a white picket fence and a place—"

"To plant your rosebush?"

He brushed the hair back from her cheek and felt the wetness on the backs of his knuckles. He knew she was crying still.

"There's nothing I can do about this, Molly. The railroad is close, but not so close that I can stop it where it is. It has to come through that pass. Your ranch sits at the mouth of that pass. God help me, if I could figure another way around this, I would."

He heard her intake of breath, heard the muffled sob. He pulled her into his embrace, holding her. Her arms went around his waist.

"I'm sorry, Molly. Please, please know how sorry I am."

She cried because she couldn't do anything else, because it was late and she was tired. Tired of fighting, of being alone, of being afraid.

"It's my home," she said between sobs. "Can you understand?"

"Oh, God, Molly, of course I understand." And he did. Because he'd never had a home of his own he understood what it meant to take hers.

It tore at his gut and at his heart and before he knew what he was doing, he simply dipped his head and kissed her.

Somewhere in the recesses of her mind she knew this was a mistake. There was Jack who'd been gone too long. Jack without a word. Jack, whom she knew deep down was dead.

Molly knew she should stop Ethan and yet she was so tired and it felt so good to be in his arms, to feel his strength holding her as though he would hold the world back for just this little while.

Her hands glided around his waist, then upward, the coarse cotton of his shirt rough against her fingers as they traced the hard muscles of his back.

The sensation of his lips on hers was warm and strong and blessedly welcome. His mouth was inviting, enticing, stirring feelings in her she'd never known before. His hand slipped up to cradle the back of her neck, his fingers pulling at the fine hairs there. She knew instinctively that he was searching for the pins that held her hair in place.

Releasing him, she answered his request by removing the four pins that dropped to the ground at their feet.

He lifted away from her then, as her hair fell heavy around her shoulders and down her back. His breathing was hard as he looked down into her upturned face, his fingers laced in her hair.

"Molly," he said, softly, gently, like a plea. "I want to make love to you." He brushed the hair back from her face again. "I want to love you until the world goes away, until there's no one and nothing but you and me."

Molly understood then, looking up into his handsome face, that she wanted him to make love to her. More importantly, she understood in that instant, in that single heartbeat, that she was in love with Ethan Wilder, that she'd never loved any man the way she loved him and that she doubted she ever would. It couldn't be wrong, this feeling. Surely the Lord wouldn't have sent her Ethan if it was wrong.

"Molly?" It was a question this time. "I've brought you pain and hurt and if you—"

She stopped him with the tips of two fingers on his lips.

His eyes searched her face and then a smile, slow and tentative, curved up the corners of his mouth, his beautiful mouth. His smile made her shiver in its understanding and its promise. His eyes were dark and soft and she thought there in the shadows of the night, she didn't care about land or ranches or railroads. She only cared that she was with Ethan, in his arms.

Lightly, so very lightly, his mouth brushed against hers again as though testing the answer to his question. Molly's eyes fluttered closed in anticipation of what was to come.

"Are you sure, Molly?" he asked a little breathlessly.

She didn't answer, didn't trust herself to form the words, so she lifted up on her toes and kissed him, her arms twining around his neck and up the back of his head catching the back of his hat. Absently, she grabbed the brim and flung the hat aside.

She thought she heard him chuckle. She chuckled, too. She was happy, she realized. Perhaps for the first time in so long, she was happy.

Ethan.

He hooked his hands under her arms and lifted her straight up off the ground until she was level with him. Then he took her mouth again, in a deep, slow, demanding kiss that left her feeling that she'd never breathe again and didn't need to. All she needed was Ethan Wilder.

Muscles along the tops of his shoulders tensed and trembled as he held her there, suspended above the ground. She was here, in his arms and all he knew was that he wanted her more than he'd ever wanted anything in his life.

"Molly, honey..."

"Yes," she breathed, her forearms resting on the tops of his shoulders. A lush smile punctuated her agreement.

And still he hesitated. He settled her to the ground. His hands cupped the sides of her face, his thumbs hooked under her chin. "Oh, Molly, I want you so."

She covered his hands with hers. Tears glistened in her eyes when she said, "And I want you, Ethan."

It was all he needed to hear.

This time when he covered her mouth with his, there was no holding back, no hesitation. His tongue traced her lips, teasing, demanding, igniting a fire in her she'd never expected. Her body flared to life, heat and longing the only feelings.

When his tongue plunged inside her mouth that fire turned into a raging inferno. His arms crushed her to him and she went willingly, eagerly, anxious for all that he offered. Her hands splayed out over his broad back, feeling the muscles pulled tight there, reveling in his power.

In and out, in and out, his tongue created a rhythm that her body seemed to recognize even if she didn't. Her heartbeat seemed to mimic the tempo like some ancient tune and within moments her whole body, muscles, flexed and moved to the tune, like the waves against the shore.

She trembled, nerves raw and aching and yet the rhythm continued, the tune growing stronger. She clung to him, her fingers curling to claw at his back through the fabric of his shirt.

Yes, her mind kept chanting. *Yes. Yes!*

Ethan kissed her cheeks and chin and the thin flesh under her jaw. His hands roamed her body from shoulder to hips and back again. Every part of his body was raw and alive with wanting her. Like some caged animal, he moved, flexed, ached with the longing that was quickly consuming him.

He wanted her. He wanted her naked. He wanted them both naked and now.

Deftly, he cast her shawl aside then reached for the front of her blouse. His fingers fumbled with the tiny buttons and eventually she had to help him, pulling the fabric free of her skirt, but she hesitated, suddenly feeling shy.

He saw the look of uncertainty in her eyes.

"Let me," he whispered, kissing her lightly while he slid the fabric from her shoulders so that she hardly realized her blouse was gone until she felt the cool night breeze on her bare shoulders.

Her eyes fluttered open and when she looked into his down-turned face, so close, he was smiling at her. He kissed her lightly again, quickly, and then worked the buttons on his own shirt.

He was about to shrug out of it when she bravely said, "Let me."

He did.

Gazes locked, he forced himself to stand very still while she put both of her hands, palms flat, on the center of his chest. His heart pounded like a fierce war drum and she must have felt it because she looked up at him.

Never saying a word, she slid his shirt open with the edges of her hands, her palms gliding lightly, sensually over his chest, brushing the fine black hair that curved over his nipples. He thought he felt her hands tremble. His eyes slammed shut against the suddenly pounding desire her touch stirred in him.

Slowly, she let her hands move upward toward his shoulders, testing, exploring until her fingers curled over the tops of his shoulders and she carried the shirt down and off his arms leaving him bare chested.

He was beautiful, she thought. His body was hardened by work, and tan—as though he'd done that work without a shirt. Without thinking, she retraced the path her hands had taken moments ago, this time letting her gaze follow the path, memorizing every valley and plane, every muscle and bone.

When he could stand it no longer, he took her shoulders in a hard grip. "Woman, do you know what you do to me?"

Hands still on his chest, she said, "Tell me."

Her words were provocative as hell and she knew it. What's more, he knew it.

"Tell you? Hell," he said, reaching for the ties that held her camisole closed over her breasts, "I'm going to show you." He pulled the ties free one after another. Then repeating her act he placed both hands, palms flat on the center of her chest, just below her throat. Then slowly, oh, very slowly, he let his hands glide down and out, pushing the fabric aside with the edges of his hands while the palms brushed lightly across the sensitive skin at the tops of her breasts.

Molly shivered then groaned in response.

"Ethan." She dragged in an unsteady breath. "Ethan."

"Yes," he breathed, leaning in close and letting his tongue trace a path down the side of her neck. He slipped the camisole free of her shoulders and the fine white fabric fluttered silently to the ground.

Ethan's hands curved around the knobs of her shoulders then glided lightly down her arms, while he laved and kissed and nipped at the sensitive spot behind her left ear.

Her hands sought him, needing something to cling to, needing him.

He blazed a path of fiery kisses down along the tops of her shoulders, then lower, moving steadily toward the firm mounds of her breasts now exposed to him. Slowly, slowly, licking, then kissing, occasionally simply breathing on the moist spot he'd created, he teased her, heightening the longing in her, the same longing he felt himself.

He kissed the valley between her breasts.

"You are so beautiful, Molly," he whispered, his lips moving on her flesh sending gooseflesh of delight skimming over her skin. "So beautiful."

Lower. A fraction more. Until his mouth found her nipple, already a hardened nub. He would make it harder, he thought as his mouth closed over the rosy peak.

Instantly, she flinched, pushing at his arms, which held her tightly around the waist.

"Ethan, what are you…"

He sucked at the nipple, letting his tongue lave at the tender flesh, brushing back and forth, back and forth, until she stopped pushing at his arms and instead, arched back, her hands thrusting into his hair as though to hold his head there.

"Oh, yes," Molly moaned, as waves of pure, illicit pleasure washed through her. "More, Ethan. Please more."

He was happy to oblige. He took the nipple between his teeth, lightly grazing the peak, pulling, sucking, feeling her tremble, feeling her flex and move against him.

He moved back, his body aching for the release he knew he'd find in the sweet body of Molly Murphy.

Wordlessly, he lifted his head, kissed her once hard and fast on the lips, then scooped her up and carried her the few yards to a spot he'd seen earlier when he'd been fishing with Katie.

In the shelter of the rocks, he laid her down on the mossy earth, sprawling on his side so that he partially covered her body with his.

Lightly, reverently, he stroked her, caressed her, kissed her again and again and again until she pulled him down to her, holding her there while she kissed him or he kissed her...he wasn't entirely sure, didn't care.

He undid the button on her skirt and pushed it down as far as her hips but there were petticoats and he silently cursed whoever had said women needed to wear so damned many clothes.

Molly found the tie on the petticoats and pulled the cord. Together, they got her out of the skirt and petticoats until she was wearing nothing more than her pantalets and stockings. Black stockings.

Ethan rolled onto her, letting his knee slide between her legs, then push hard at the core of her.

Molly was already moving, and with his leg there, she moved against it, the denim coarse and rough even through the fabric of her pantalets.

She reached for his belt and found the buckle for his gun belt instead.

Ethan sat up and quickly shed his clothes. Molly propped up on her elbows to watch and when he turned back the hard evidence of his arousal was there, and she thought he was magnificent.

She held out her arms to him and he went to her, sprawling partially on top of her, his bare leg back between hers again, while his naked body covered most of her. His hands played magic on her throbbing flesh, touching her in all the right places, making her nerves sing with delight and passion. Oh, yes, passion.

She began to move, to flex, while muscles in her belly lifted and pushed her hips against him. Her heart pounded wildly in her chest, and her fingers clawed at the moss that cushioned her.

"Ethan, I want…"

"I know what you want, sweet Molly. I want it, too."

Then he did something she'd never thought about, never imagined. His fingers found the opening in her pantalets and slipped inside to touch her, there, in that place that no one had ever touched her. Not like this.

Vaguely, she thought to protest, but his fingers, two fingers, glided knowingly over her womanhood.

"You're wet," he said, as though to confirm what she already knew.

"It hurts," she answered, moving against his touch.

He hesitated. "Hurts how?"

She moved against his touch. "Aches when you stop."

"Ah," he murmured. "And does this—" he slid his fingers over her again, deeper this time, more fully "—does this stop the ache?"

"Yes," she told him arching up, seeking his touch, "it feels so good. Do it again."

He did.

He stroked her, feeling her buck with each touch, feeling her arch and move and tremble, thinking she was like no woman he'd ever known. Her head flayed back and forth and, digging her heels in, she refused to let him stop. He didn't want to stop. He knew almost before she did, that she was peaking. Then he leaned down and took her nipple in his mouth. At the same instant he plunged those two fingers inside her.

"Ethan, yes!" she screamed and he covered her mouth with his to muffle her scream of delight.

He kissed her hard and stroked her harder and she worked against his fingers until suddenly she arched and lifted and grabbed his face in her hands.

He felt her convulse around his fingers, felt her shudder, heard the wild groan of ecstasy as she reached her peak, let the rush flow over and out of her, slick and thick and wet around his fingers.

She settled to the ground again and slowly opened her eyes. He was there, filling her line of vision.

Wonder was reflected in her eyes, in the flush of her cheeks, in the rawness of her bottom lip that she had bitten in the final explosion of pleasure.

He rubbed at the single droplet of blood there on her lip and she kissed his thumb. "Oh, I never knew it could be like that...that a woman could feel anything like..."

Ethan licked the blood, her blood from his thumb. "Oh, honey, then you've never been loved the way a woman should be loved."

She knew that was true.

Like a wanton, she pulled the string on her pantalets and shimmied out of them, leaving them under her like a small blanket.

Ethan watched, smiling in pure pleasure as she revealed herself to him completely. His hand caressed her lightly, from hip to breasts to belly to thigh. At each flash point, she moaned with delight and reached to stop his hand and hold it there, reveling in the touch.

Then she reached for him, covering his chest with the flats of her hands, rubbing hard as she let them slide upward to his shoulders and then around his neck. With a woman's unique ability, she pulled him to her.

"Then show me again how a woman should be loved."

Ethan drew his fingers over her sweet womanhood once more, feeling the slickness, the invitation as her body moved to greet his touch. Molly gasped and it excited him all the more watching her, knowing that now this time he would have her completely.

"There's so much I want to show you, to share with you," he said, his voice raspy with emotion.

Her arms slipped around his shoulders and she pulled him to her, wanting him, all of him, wanting this time together. His knee pressed between her legs and she opened them. She felt him poised at her entrance and every nerve in her body, every fiber of her being seemed focused on the hot, throbbing demand that pulsed between her legs. Her pulse raced, her breathing came in short shallow gasps as her body, eager for the pleasure she knew awaited, strained toward him.

"Please," she entreated.

"Yes, sweet Molly. Yes."

It was his last coherent thought before need, demanding and insistent, consumed him. He eased into her waiting body, slowly, wanting to feel each delicious inch as she enfolded him in her sheath. She was tight, the way a woman is who has been a long time without a lover, and he was glad.

As he lay buried deep inside her, he stilled, rising up on one elbow to look down into her passion-flushed face. Her blue eyes glistened and he kissed her cheeks lightly, tenderly. And then he began to move in her.

He took his time, wanting to please her again, wanting to bring her to lush completion again and desperately wanting to be inside her when she reached that point again.

Slowly, he withdrew, then slid in with a lover's care, letting her warmth wrap around him, so hot and slick it nearly drove him mad with desire.

She was all he'd imagined, every erotic fantasy he'd ever had and more, so much more.

Molly reveled in him, in having him inside her. It was right. She loved him and this was right. She was sure of it—as sure as she was of her next breath.

With Ethan it was as though she finally understood what love could be like between a man and a woman, what so many sought and so few found.

He whispered to her as he moved, words of promise and of explicit invitation, words that inflamed and excited her beyond all thought or reason.

He stroked and fondled, kissed and teased, as she could do no more than cling to him and be carried along on the wave. His rhythm was slow and steady, like a heartbeat, never faltering, never ceasing, never relenting. With each stroke, the demand that thrummed in her increased again and then again until she was in a pleasure-driven agony so powerful she thought perhaps she would die before she found the release she so frantically wanted.

So she met him stroke for stroke, urgent and wild.

Her nails dug into his back like claws of some fierce cat. "Ethan, please help me. I want it," she pronounced through clenched teeth. She arched and writhed under him, feeling his body slick with perspiration sliding against hers, his chest pressed hard against her aching breasts, his hips grinding against hers.

Release. Relief. Were the only thoughts and they no more than flashes like lightning in her brain.

It was there. She knew it, felt it like a violent storm moving fast to overtake her. She raced to meet it. Unafraid.

Ethan increased the pace; with each thrust he pushed harder, faster, deeper.

"Yes," she groaned. "Yes! More! Again!"

Suddenly she felt her body arch and dissolve in a liquid rush between her legs as she convulsed again and again around his hardened shaft. Pleasure. Pure and blinding. Carnal and licentious. Bliss.

Breathing hard, Ethan poured himself into her warmth, exalting in the release she had given him. The world and all its troubles disappeared, simply melted away to nothing, like snow in July. Never in his entire life had he felt this good, this complete, this glorious.

In a heartbeat he knew he'd found what had always been missing in his life. Molly Murphy.

He rolled over onto his back and pulled her into the curve of his shoulder, holding her close, feeling her hair pooling on his chest like silken fire.

He wanted her for his own.

He wanted her for now and more.

Forever.

He held her, reveling in the feel of her naked flesh against his. He didn't speak because there were no words to describe the bliss he felt.

He toyed with her hair while, with his other hand, he caressed her arm from shoulder to elbow and back again. Her skin was soft, smooth, and then he felt her tremble.

"Are you cold?" he asked.

Molly didn't answer, just sat up and reached for her clothes. The night was dark and there was a sudden chill in the air that she hadn't noticed before.

"Molly?"

"I've made a terrible mistake." She stood and began to get dressed.

He sat up beside her.

Molly kept getting dressed. All the while the truth of what she'd done kept going around and around in her head. She'd made love with the one man she could never have, should never want. Ethan wanted her land. He'd made that perfectly clear and still she'd...she'd... Shame flooded her. She had vows to honor, a commitment, even if her husband was less than the man she'd hoped for...less than Ethan.

"It was not a mistake," Ethan said. "I love you."

Molly was stunned by his statement. "No," she said, backing away. "You can't." It was wrong, all wrong, and yet for some fleeting moment his words, being here with him, felt so incredibly right she had to fight the urge to relent.

"I do mean it." He stood and started getting dressed.

Shaking her head in denial, Molly pulled on her skirt, then stockings then shoes. When she looked at him again he was fully clothed, just fastening the buckle on his gun belt.

He was there, close in front of her. "Molly," his tone was hushed, "I do love you. I think I've always loved you."

"No. No!" She shook her head adamantly, refusing to accept what he was saying. They could not be in love. They could not be together.

"Stop saying that."

"You love me, too."

"No, I don't."

"Look at me and tell me you don't love me," he ordered.

She couldn't. Head down she said, "Don't you understand? I *can't* love you."

He pulled her into his embrace, the clothes she held a small pillow between them. Ethan rested his cheek on the top of her head. The sweet fragrance of rose shampoo wafted up to his nostrils. He held her close. "Don't worry. It'll be all right. We'll live in Cheyenne. We'll—"

She pushed free of him. "What are you talking about?"

"Cheyenne. As soon as we're married, we'll—"

"I *am* married," she muttered in a cold and stark realization…and yet, was she? Could she have made love with one man if she thought she was married to another?

"Not for long. You'll help me get your husband

to sell the land. Then you'll get a divorce and we'll get married.'' He said it so simply, so easily. It made perfect sense to him.

It didn't make perfect sense to Molly. ''Sell the land! Sell the damned land! That's all you think about, isn't it?'' Her gaze met his directly. ''You'd do anything to get this land, wouldn't you?''

It took a few moments for her words, her meaning to sink in.

''No! Are you crazy? Do you think that I... That we just...''

''Sell the land, you said.''

''Of course. I want you with me and we can't stay here. It'll take a little work, a little maneuvering. I'll call in a few favors and see if I can hurry things along. In the meantime, you'll live in my house and—''

''For how long?''

''What do you mean, how long?''

''I'll live in your house and what, be your mistress?''

''Certainly not.''

''That's what it sounds like to me!''

''What are you talking about? I'm telling you that I love you, that I want to marry you as soon as—''

''As soon as I help you get this damned land.'' She saw it all clearly now.

''Woman, have you lost your mind?''

''No! I think I've just found it.'' With that, she stormed away, the hurt and realization almost too much to bear. Tears threatened and she fought them back, refusing to give in to them or him, never to him.

Ethan watched her go and watched his world crumble as she did.

Chapter Fourteen

The moon was still visible in the sky as the first light shone on the horizon. Blackness gave way to gray and then to pink, and finally morning shoved the night aside.

Molly wished she could shove her feelings aside as firmly. She couldn't. She was seated on the bench at the back of the house looking out over her garden. The early light caught the new green leaves of the beans where they started their climb up the row of poles she'd set out. Next to them were the cabbages, tiny now but in a couple of months they'd be large and fat. There were rows of squash and corn, only a couple of feet high now but soon...

Her garden. She'd worked so hard putting it in. She could remember every miserable day, trying to break the sunbaked earth with a shovel. A wry smile and a derisive chuckle punctuated her thoughts. The first time she'd hit the ground with the tip of that shovel the thing had actually bounced as though she'd hit granite. She'd thought she had. She'd hauled water and more water, softening the ground for days, dug with pick and shovel and hauled more water until she'd gotten a half a foot of ground turned over. Then fertilizer. The chickens and horses had provided that.

Her garden.

She leaned back against the cabin, the rough bark of the cottonwood logs poking her through her dress.

Her cabin.

Her home.

She'd worked so hard to make a home here, her first. Katie's first.

They had roots. They had a purpose. They had a place.

Oh, granted it wasn't much of a place, but it was hers and she was defying logic when she said she didn't want to give it up.

She sighed.

Her eyes drifted closed and instantly she saw him, them, as they'd been only a few hours ago. It had been heaven being in his arms. No man had ever touched her the way that Ethan had. No man had ever made her feel the things that Ethan had.

Almost from the first, she'd been attracted to him. She'd fought it, struggled against it. She knew he was the enemy, her enemy and yet, she also knew that, Lord help her, she was in love with Ethan Wilder.

It was late afternoon when Molly heard the horse lope into the yard. For an instant she thought perhaps it was Ethan, that perhaps he'd come back and... And what?

Wiping her hand on the towel, she turned just as the door to the cabin opened. A man's silhouette filled the doorway and then he said, ''Well, Molly. What? No welcome for your husband?''

Jack Murphy walked into the room. In what seemed like one motion, he kicked the door closed with his booted foot and tossed his hat then saddle-bags on the table.

Molly stood there staring at him. He'd never been all that tall but he was a lot thinner. His brown hair was matted and hung to his shoulders and his beard was streaked with gray. His red shirt was faded and nearly as threadbare as his denim trousers. It didn't take a genius to figure that Jack hadn't found that mother lode.

''You're dead...?'' she blurted out before she could stop herself.

Her husband was home. She should be glad. She wasn't. Thoughts of Ethan and their lovemaking fluttered like frightened butterflies in her stomach.

''Not hardly,'' he told her as he dropped down in a chair. ''What's the matter? Ain't you glad to see me?''

''You can hardly expect me to be glad when you've been gone six months leaving me and Katie here to—''

''Who?'' His brows drew down.

''Katie.'' Good God, the man didn't even remember the child. She wasn't his but you'd think he'd at least remember her name.

He nodded. "Oh, yeah." Arms on the edge of the table, he glanced around. "Where is she anyways?"

"Out playing with some new kittens."

"New kittens, huh? Sounds real nice." He rubbed his stomach. "I'm starving, honey. Can you feed a hungry man?"

Feed him? That was it? No questions about how she'd been, how she had managed while he was off chasing dreams? Yet he was her husband, a thought that made a knot in her stomach.

Too bad you didn't remember that pledge last night.

She stoked the fire in the wood-burning stove then dragged the kettle of soup to the front burner. As she stood there stirring the thick brown liquid to keep it from burning, she admitted she wasn't glad to see Jack Murphy at all. More than that, she wasn't sorry about making love to Ethan Wilder. Now, for the first time in her life, she understood what making love was supposed to be like, giving, sharing, pleasing. Not the crude, harsh encounters she'd had with Jack. His body crushing her into the bed while he penetrated her quickly and was as quickly finished before rolling over on his way to sleep.

Steam rattled the lid of the soup kettle and snapped her back to the present. Covertly, she glanced back over her shoulder to take another long look at Jack, at her husband. Muscles clenched in her stomach at the thought of sharing a bed with him again, and yet she knew she would have no choice.

Jack looked tired. His head down, he said, "That soup ready yet?"

"Yes. Don't get your tail in a knot."

"I'm not. I'm just asking is all. It's been a while since I had a decent meal."

She supposed that was right but it was also his fault. She took a bowl from the cupboard, ladled up a hearty helping and carried it over to him.

"So," she said, putting the dish down in front of him. "Did you find that gold you were so sure about?" She knew the answer even as she asked the question, but she took pleasure in the asking. A sort of "I told you so."

Jack was busy shoveling in the soup. But her question evidently touched a sore spot.

His expression was hard when he looked up at her standing there next to him.

"No." His voice was whiny and mocking. "I didn't find the gold." He dragged the back of his hand across his mouth. "But I'm close. Real close. I was starting to see a little color up in a canyon and I'm the only one what knows about it, so as soon as I get another grubstake..." He shoveled in another couple of spoonfuls of soup. "This is good." He grabbed her around the hips and pulled her close to him so that her hip was against his shoulder. "You feel good, too," he added in a tone that made Molly shudder. She twisted free. Frowning, he watched her take a seat at the opposite end of the table.

"There's no gold out there, Jack. You're wasting your time. We could use you here."

"There is!" he shouted defiantly. "I'm close, I tell you. A couple of more months, maybe weeks and—"

"You can't mean to go back out there again?"

"Of course I do. Whatcha think?"

"Where is it?" She braced her hands on the table top.

"What?"

"This 'little color' you found."

"I spent it on supplies."

"I see," she muttered, and she did. She remembered all the times her father had come in from a day of mining, excited over a few glinting flakes of gold, barely enough to see let alone make the months, the years of deprivation and eventually her mother's life worth the cost. Anger welled in her, not just at Jack, but at what this craziness had cost her.

Jack kept eating as though he hadn't seen good food in twenty years. He probably hadn't, at least for the time he'd been gone. Gold camps, especially new ones, were notoriously wet and cold in winter and hot in summer and there always seemed to be some disease like cholera or fevers. They were miserable places which was why she'd insisted on taking Katie out of there.

"More?" she said, already walking to the stove.

"Don't mind if I do," Jack agreed, with the first smile she'd seen from him.

This time she carried the pot to the table and let him help himself. Two more bowlsful and he finally seemed satisfied. Lounging back in the chair, he rubbed his belly and let out a big belch that in times past hadn't bothered her. Now, well, it seemed crude. "You always was a good cook, Molly," he said, his smile broadening.

It was the first kind thing he'd said since he'd walked in.

Jack continued, "Among other things." That smile of his had turned to a sort of leer that left no question what he was hinting about. Molly busied herself with putting the soup away and cleaning up the dish and spoon. She had no intention of tumbling into bed with Jack, not now. Eventually she would have to, she knew, but not now.

"Where'd you say the kid was?"

"She's outside but she'll be back any minute," Molly lied, having no idea when Katie would come barreling in the door.

"Well, we could always put the lock on," Jack said.

"No, Jack, we couldn't." Molly remained at the sink.

Jack's smile faded. "Look, Molly, a man gets lonely and—"

"And nothing. You've been gone six months. You never once wrote to say if you were living or dead. More than that, you never once cared if I—we—were living or dead. Did you?"

"Sure I did," Jack countered.

"Oh sure, you rode out of here and never looked back. All you cared about was finding that damned gold. Did you care about your responsibilities here? Did you wonder how we managed to put food on the table? Did you send any of that precious gold you say you found home to us?'' Suddenly, she cared nothing about Jack or his feelings—as he cared nothing for hers.

Jack's expression turned dark. ''Now look, Molly, I won't have you lecturing me like some school-marm.'' He surged to his feet, his chair scraping back as he did. ''I went off to find that gold for us.''

''For yourself, you mean. I never asked you to go. I asked you to stay, to help us make a go of this place.''

Jack raked his hands back through his greasy hair. ''I ain't no damned rancher. I only went along with taking this place cause it were winter coming on and I knew you wanted it, and like I said, a man gets lonely.''

A shiver of revulsion scampered over Molly's skin. She felt unclean. So there, it was said, what she'd known all along, but never wanted to admit. Now, looking at Jack, she realized it was a foolish dream of her own, as foolish as Jack's quest for the mother lode.

''Jack, I want to stay here. I want to be a rancher, a rancher's wife. I want to raise Katie here.''

''Well, fine. Who's stopping you?''

''I can't do this alone. There's too much to be done. The barn's got to be finished before winter. We need to dig an irrigation ditch from the creek to the vegetable patch in the back. You can see day-light through the log walls, and come winter—''

''Hell, woman, I ain't home ten minutes and you

got me working like some field hand. I ain't no field hand!''

"Not a field hand. A rancher. A farmer. Call it whatever you want."

"I call it stupid. This is stupid when there's gold out there just waiting for me to find it. Then I'll buy us a big house with servants and we can all live a life of ease."

"It's never going to happen, Jack."

"It is. I'm gonna do it." He thumbed his chest.

Molly shook her head in dismay. "You have about as much chance of striking it rich as there is of cows suddenly sprouting wings and becoming birds."

Jack glared at her hard. He even took a step in her direction and for a moment she thought perhaps he meant to hit her, he looked that angry. He didn't, though. Instead, he said, "How much money you got left?"

"What?"

He headed for the bureau and the porcelain dish where he knew she kept her stash. He had the drawer opened and was dumping her meager savings out into his hand by the time she closed on him.

"Hey!" she shouted. "Give me that!" She made a grab for the money but he turned and elbowed her aside.

"That's mine! You can't take—"

"Oh, yeah," he growled, shoving the money in his trouser pocket.

Molly blocked his path. "Look, Jack, you can go on back out there and hunt for gold if that's what you want but you aren't taking my money. That's all I've got to see me and Katie through.''

He tried to go around her and she spread her arms wide as though she could stop him, a hundred-pound woman against a work-hardened man. He shoved her aside as if he barely noticed her.

''I'm going into town!'' he announced as he grabbed up his hat and saddlebags and headed for the door. ''I'm going someplace where a man can get a drink in peace.''

With that he slammed out the door.

Molly was hot on his heels. She was primed and ready for a fight. Too many days of being alone and afraid. Her Irish was up.

The sunlight glinted in her eyes and she had to blink hard a few times, shading her eyes with her hand. Jack was already mounted on his horse and reining over.

''Oh, no you don't, Jack Murphy!'' She ran the few steps to grab at his horse's rein. ''You give me back that money!''

The horse reared, front hooves pawing the air. Molly had to duck to keep from getting kicked. Out of the corner of her eye, she saw Katie barreling full out in her direction.

As the horse settled to the ground, Jack said, ''Woman, you better watch yourself if you know what's good for you!''

''Mama! Mama! What's wrong?'' Katie was shouting as she slammed into Molly's side. Instinctively, Molly grabbed the child up and that was all the time Jack needed to make his getaway.

Teeth clenched, Molly watched him go. If he thought he was getting away that easy, he had another thought coming. That money was hers and she needed it…more than she needed Jack Murphy, she realized suddenly. Hell, she cared more about the money than she did her husband.

The dust was still settling when Molly, with Katie perched on her hip, marched for the corral. "We're going into town," she told the child, letting her slide to the ground.

She hitched the team in record time and whipped the horses all the way, the wagon rumbling and bouncing so that at times there were only three or even two wheels on the ground.

Still, Jack was ahead of her and she didn't catch up with him until she stormed into the El Dorado Saloon. All talking stopped and all heads turned at once in her direction. Some looked simply because she was a woman in a saloon but others, she knew, scowled because she was the troublemaker, the one and only impediment to their getting their all important railroad. Molly hated that railroad and she hated Ethan Wilder, and right now she was about to take all that hatred out on Jack Murphy.

Molly spotted Jack hunched over the table near the far wall. He was alone, pouring drinks for himself from a nearly full bottle. A bottle he'd paid for with her money.

Her rage doubled.

"Katie," she said firmly to the child as she shoved her back outside through the double glass doors. "You wait right here for me. Don't move. I have business to take care of."

She stormed through the doors like Grant taking Richmond, and men actually scrambled to get out of her way.

"Jack!" she shouted as she came up to his table. "Give me the money!" She held out her hand.

Jack looked slowly up in her direction. One hand was wrapped tightly around an empty shot glass and the other around the neck of the whiskey bottle. His expression was dark, his mouth drawn in a tight line.

"Get outta here woman, if you know what's good for you," Jack snarled. With that he straightened in his chair more and fixed his icy stare on Molly.

But Molly wasn't having any of it. She wasn't intimidated and she was too damned angry to be scared. "The money, Jack!" she demanded again. "It's mine, and I'm not going to let you have it to drink with or to go running after some pipe dream again."

"Woman, if you don't—"

Molly grabbed the whiskey bottle away from him before he could stop her and she hurled it across the room. The glass smashed against the painted wall making a wet brown stain as it dribbled to the floor.

Jack came half out of his seat. "Why you—"

"Excuse me," a male voice said close by and both Molly and Jack turned at once. "Name's Ed Bartel. I couldn't help but overhear what you were saying. You are Murphy right? You own the ranch down by the creek?"

"Yeah, that's me. What's it to you?" Jack snarled.

"Well," Bartel said. "It sounded as though you might be in need of some money and I'd like to buy your—"

"No!" Molly shouted. "He doesn't want to sell."

"Buy my what?" Jack's expression changed from one of anger to one of smugness. "Let the man talk."

"No," Molly tugged on Jack's sleeve like a mother trying to get an errant child to obey. "Let's go. We can talk about this outside."

Jack jerked free of Molly's grasp and stepped away, his concentration now focused on Bartel. "You wanna buy my ranch?"

"Yes," Bartel said.

"No!" Molly interrupted, but neither man appeared to be listening.

"So," Jack asked, "how much?"

"Oh, how does a thousand sound?"

"Dollars?" Jack repeated clearly stunned.

"Cash," Bartel said. "We can walk across to the bank and get it right now. All you have to do is sign a bill of sale."

Molly felt her heart sink. "Jack, we have to talk. You can keep my money, only don't—"

"Done!" Jack announced before Molly could finish. The men shook hands. "If you'll just sign this..." He produced a quick deed and someone quickly appeared with pen and ink. In what seemed only a moment, a few words were scrawled on the paper, Jack signed and the deed was done. The railroad now owned the land.

Bartel turned to everyone present and said, "Boys, drinks are on me!"

As the men surged to the bar shouting orders, Jack and Bartel started away. Molly's rage could not be contained. She rushed after Jack, grabbing him by the arm she spun him around. "I hope you're happy!" She spared those gathered a hard look. "I hope you all feel good about what you've done today. You put a woman and child out of their home." Some men looked sheepish, others seemed to laugh as though it meant nothing to them. Why should it, she realized. She was nothing to them, nothing to anyone.

"I'll never forgive you for this, Jack. You hear me? Never!"

"I don't care what you do," Jack replied. "I've had enough of you and what you want to last me a lifetime. Why hell, if I'd wanted to be nagged and railed at I could've stayed with my other wife."

Molly went very still as the words soaked into her brain. "Other wife? What other wife?"

"Why Mabel, back in California. She took to demanding I take up pig farming." He glanced knowingly around at the other men. "Can you believe it?"

Molly asked, "Are you telling me that when you married me you were already married?"

"Sure."

"Why, you son of a bitch!" Molly was not a violent person but this was more than she could stand. She balled up her fist and hit Jack Murphy. Hard. Right in the face. She heard the sound of bone crunching and the force of the impact sent pain ricocheting up her arm.

"Ouch!" he yelled as he grabbed at his lip that was already squirting blood.

Before he could do more, Molly turned on her heel and strode for the doors. Tears slipped down her cheeks and her hand ached but she wasn't about to let this man see her fall apart.

Just as she reached the door, in walked Ethan and another man.

Oh, great. This was all she needed.

"Let me pass," she ordered. But he didn't obey.

Ethan grabbed her by the shoulders. "Molly, what are you doing here? Did something happen?"

"I'll say something happened," Bartel said with a grin. Holding a piece of paper in his hand he hurried over to them. "This here is Jack Murphy and he's just sold us the ranch."

Ethan knew instantly what this meant. Molly had lost her home and he, Ethan, was the cause.

"Ethan," Billy said, shouldering through the doorway into the saloon. "This is great news." He took the paper and scanned it.

"We were just on our way to the bank," Bartel said. "Care to join us?"

Ethan still held Molly by the shoulders. She looked up at him then, tears glistening in her eyes. Her voice was thick with emotion when she said, "You win." With that she twisted free of him and, taking Katie's hand, she headed for the wagon.

Ethan just stood there. Billy was practically doing a jig he was so happy—as was everyone in the place. Except Ethan. But he'd had no choice. He had to take the land. He knew that; nonetheless the cost was high. Higher than he'd ever thought it would be, and he wondered what it would take to have her forgive him. If ever.

But Billy was dragging Ethan into the saloon even as Molly climbed up onto the wagon seat, Katie nestled beside her.

Shaking loose of Billy, Ethan started for the door. He couldn't let it end like this. He couldn't. But she was driving away as he reached the doors and he stood there and watched her go, thinking that some part of himself was going with her. He loved her. Married or not, he loved her and there wasn't a damned thing he could do about it.

Ethan declined to go when Bartel and Murphy went to the bank.

Billy studied Ethan. "What's the matter with you?"

"Nothing," Ethan snapped, seating himself at a nearby table. "Everything is just great."

Billy's expression turned serious. He glanced toward the now empty doorway then back to Ethan as though coming to some understanding. Billy dragged out a chair. Without asking, the barman brought them a bottle and two glasses.

The men ignored it.

"Ethan, is it the woman?"

Ethan's head came up sharply. "Be real careful, Billy."

Billy hesitated a moment then sank back in his chair. His voice was sincere when he said, ''I didn't know. I'm sorry.''

''Yeah, me too.'' Ethan helped himself to a drink. ''Can't you—''

''What? You want me to give her back the land?''

''We can't. You know that.''

''Yeah, I know that.'' He took another drink, tossing the liquid back in one swallow. He toyed with the glass.

Around them the men, local businessmen and a couple of ranchers were talking, laughing, celebrating. He was only half listening.

''…good thing Murphy showed up when…''

''…that wife of his has some nerve coming in…''

''…ain't his wife…''

There was a general laugh.

''Yeah,'' the barman spoke up. ''Who'd a thought Miss High and Mighty weren't nothing more 'en Murphy's secondhand woman.''

There was another round of laughter. What the devil were they talking about? He waved the barman over.

''What's going on?'' he asked cautiously.

The barman grinned. ''Turns out Murphy already had hisself a wife when he hitched up with the second Mrs. Murphy. Ain't that a laugh?''

Ethan came slowly to his feet. ''Let me get this straight. You're saying that Murphy and Molly— Mrs. Murphy—aren't married?''

''Yup.'' The barman glanced over his shoulder to the men lining the bar. ''That's right, ain't it boys?''

"Yup," they all seemed to say in unison.

"How do you know?" Ethan pressed.

"Murphy said so hisself. Said if he'd wanted to work like a field hand he coulda stayed with his other wife and raised pigs!" The barman doubled over in laughter. "Can you imagine..." He was laughing too hard to finish.

Ethan stared at the man. Could this be right? Molly wasn't married to Jack Murphy. Molly wasn't married at all?

Billy touched his arm and brought him back from his musings. "Ethan?"

"Yeah?" Ethan looked down at Billy.

"What are you thinking?"

Ethan sank back down in the chair and the barman went back to tending his customers.

"She's not married," Ethan mumbled. Then he looked Billy directly in the face. "No land and now no husband. Everything gone and it's all my fault."

Oh, God, Molly, I'm so sorry.

"I wouldn't say it was your fault," Billy countered. "Murphy's responsible for lying to her and for selling the land, though thank God he did."

Ethan nodded. "I know. We have to have the land for the track and yet I can't just leave it like this." *I can't let her go on hating me,* he thought to say but didn't.

"What are you going to do?"

"I don't know...."

Billy and Ethan walked outside together.

The day was bright and clear and Ethan had to blink a couple of times against the sudden sunlight.

Ethan moved around Billy and undid the reins of his horse from the hitching rail. "We're going to make that loan deadline."

Ethan swung up in the saddle.

Billy mounted his horse, mumbling a few choice curses under his breath.

"What's come over you, Ethan?" he demanded, adjusting the reins through his fingers.

"It's a good day." With that he rode off leaving Billy scratching his head in wonder.

Gone. Everything she'd worked so hard for was gone. Just like that. With a stroke of a pen her whole life was a shambles and there wasn't a thing she could do about it.

She strolled over to touch the yellow calico curtains, remembering the day she'd made them. Instinctively, her fingers straightened the creases in the fabric. Slowly she went to inspect the stove. It had taken her nearly a week to get it cleaned. Her knuckles and hands were red for two more weeks after from the lye soap. Standing there she could look out the window and see the garden, her garden. She'd never see the beans come in now, or the cabbages.

Tears welled in her eyes. "It's not fair!" she pronounced, her right hand curling into a fist that she pounded on the counter with.

"What's not fair, Mama?" a small voice said, and Molly turned. She had been so angry, so sad, she'd all but forgotten about the child.

Bending down, Molly swiped the tears from her eyes and forced a smile, shaky as it was. She took

Katie by the hand. "Honey, we are going to have to move."

Katie's expression drew down in hard concentration. "You mean leave here?"

Molly nodded. Her throat was clogged with tears and she didn't trust herself to speak.

"But why?"

Molly took a minute to clear her throat. "Well, Jack sold the land to the railroad so they'll be building here and we'll have to find someplace else to live."

Katie looked grim. "Where?"

"I don't know, honey." With no money she didn't know how, but she was determined to find a way.

"Is Jack coming with us?"

"Absolutely not!" Molly practically shouted.

"Good. Can we take Mr. Ethan? I like him much better."

At the mention of Ethan's name Molly's heart did a funny double sort of beat. She wanted to hate him for this and yet, deep down, she knew that she didn't. She understood now what this railroad meant to him, how much of himself was invested in it and she admired him for his work.

"Can I take my dolly and my kittens?"

Molly sighed with relief. "Sure. We'll take everything we can fit in the wagon."

But the more she thought about it—about the desperation of their situation, about what Jack had done to her, about losing her only home—it all became too much for her. Those tears wouldn't be held back and she sank down on Katie's bed and cried, great racking sobs.

Katie rushed to her side. Her little hand brushing Molly's hair back from her face. "Don't cry, Mama." Tears welled in her own eyes and slid down her cheeks. "Tell me where it hurts and I'll rub it for you," she said the way Molly always did for Katie.

Stop this! she told herself. *Stop this right now!* Molly sniffed and sat up and wiped her face with her skirt hem, then she hugged Katie. It was her and Katie against the world. Pretty much the way it had always been, she thought, except for a brief few days when...

"Hello in the house," an all too familiar male voice called out.

"Mr. Ethan!" Katie shouted and ran for the door.

Molly swiped her eyes. No way was she going to let him see her like this. She made a halfhearted attempt to shove her hair back in the bun she'd worn earlier today. Slowly, taking deep breaths as she moved, she went to the door.

He was there, standing beside his horse. He looked handsome and tall like he had that first day. "Hello, Molly," he said softly, so softly it sent a wave of gooseflesh skipping over her skin.

"Mr. Wilder," she said, pleased her voice sounded so calm. "Have you come to make sure I'm moving out? It'll take a couple of days to get packed. I'm sure you can wait that long."

Ethan dropped the horse's reins and walked over to her. "I'm sorry."

Of all the things she'd expected him to say, this wasn't it.

"I'm sorry about your house and I'm sorry to hear that Murphy...that you and Murphy aren't... weren't..."

"So you know that, too."

He touched her shoulder lightly, his strong hand curving over the top. Lord, it felt so good. No. She wouldn't allow it—him—to do this to her again. She stepped free of him.

"I'll be packed and gone by Friday," she said, taking Katie's hand.

Katie spoke up. "Are you coming with us, Mr. Ethan? He can come, can't he Mama?"

"No. Ethan can't come," Molly decreed.

A smile teased the corners of Ethan's mouth. "Actually, I was hoping you'd come with me."

"Not likely," Molly responded.

"Well, see, it's like this. I have a problem—"

"*You* have a problem!"

"Yup. See there's this woman, this redheaded woman who I realized a while back that I'd fallen in love with."

"What?" Her voice was a whisper.

He nodded in confirmation. "Yes, it surprised the hell outta me too, especially since there were... complications."

Molly stood very still. Was he saying that he loved her? After all she'd done, the way she'd treated him?

"So I've come out here today to ask this woman a question. It's kind of an important question and I was wondering if, being a woman and all, you'd tell me if it was a good idea…asking this question.''

"It's hard to say without knowing what the question is, but I'd say that the best approach to any problem is to face it square on.''

He seemed to consider this for a moment and then took two steps closing the distance between them until he was so close she had to crane her neck to look up into his down-turned face.

He touched her shoulders lightly and said, "I love you, Molly. Marry me.''

"I—I—''

"Oh, I forgot one thing.'' He pulled a piece of paper from his shirt pocket and handed it to her.

Molly unfolded the paper and realized it was the bill of sale that Jack had signed for the ranch.

"What's this?'' she mumbled.

"Just what it looks like.''

"But you need—''

"The only thing I need is you. Let me worry about the rest.''

Molly stared at the paper for a long time and realized what an incredible gesture he was making, realized that he was quite serious. That's when she knew.

Looking up at him, she slowly handed the paper back. "This belongs to you—''

"But—''

"And so do I.''

"Okay, let me make sure I've got this straight. You're saying it's all right to take the land.''

"Yes,'' Molly confirmed.

"And the marriage proposal?"

"Yes to that, too."

"Why, Molly?"

"Because I need you more than I need a piece of land. I want a husband who'll love me and Katie, who'll take care of us. That's what a family is all about. Not where you live. I know that now."

He pulled her into his embrace. "I do love you, Molly. And Katie. We'll make a home somewhere together, the three of us."

"It's fine, Ethan, just never leave us."

"Are you gonna stay with us, Mr. Ethan?" Katie asked hopefully.

"Looks like it, short stuff," he answered, grinning and picking her up in one arm. Then he hooked his other arm around Molly's shoulder and promised, "I'll never leave you."

Then he took her mouth in a long, heated kiss and when he lifted his head he said, "You think they've got a justice of the peace in town? I'm anxious to be a married man."

* * * * *

Take a romp through
Merrie Olde England
with four adventurous tales
from Harlequin Historicals.

In July 2000 look for

MALCOLM'S HONOR
by **Jillian Hart**
(England, 1280s)

LADY OF LYONSBRIDGE
by **Ana Seymour**
(England, 1190s)

In August 2000 look for

THE SEA WITCH
by **Ruth Langan**
(England, 1600s)

PRINCE OF HEARTS
by **Katy Cooper**
(England, 1520s)

Harlequin Historicals
The way the past *should* have been!

HARLEQUIN®
Makes any time special ™

HARLEQUIN®
SUPERROMANCE®

You are now entering

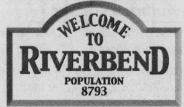

WELCOME TO RIVERBEND
POPULATION
8793

Riverbend…the kind of place where everyone knows your name—and your business. Riverbend…home of the River Rats—a group of small-town sons and daughters who've been friends since high school.

The Rats are all grown up now. Living their lives and learning that some days are good and some days aren't—and that you can get through anything as long as you have your friends.

Starting in July 2000, Harlequin Superromance brings you Riverbend—six books about the River Rats and the Midwest town they live in.

BIRTHRIGHT by **Judith Arnold** (July 2000)
THAT SUMMER THING by **Pamela Bauer** (August 2000)
HOMECOMING by **Laura Abbot** (September 2000)
LAST-MINUTE MARRIAGE by **Marisa Carroll** (October 2000)
A CHRISTMAS LEGACY by **Kathryn Shay** (November 2000)

Available wherever Harlequin books are sold.

HARLEQUIN®
Makes any time special ™

Visit us at www.eHarlequin.com

HSRIVER

Return to the charm of the Regency era with

GEORGETTE HEYER,

creator of the modern Regency genre.

Enjoy six romantic collector's editions with forewords
by some of today's bestselling romance authors,

**Nora Roberts, Mary Jo Putney,
Jo Beverley, Mary Balogh,
Theresa Medeiros and Kasey Michaels.**

Frederica
On sale February 2000
The Nonesuch
On sale March 2000
The Convenient Marriage
On sale April 2000
Cousin Kate
On sale May 2000
The Talisman Ring
On sale June 2000
The Corinthian
On sale July 2000

Available at your favorite retail outlet.